the Sisters and the novels of Linda Winstead Jones

The Star Witch

"Bewitching . . . a fabulous climactic romantic fantasy . . .
filled with fascinating twists, beguiling."
—*Midwest Book Review*

"A fantastic denouement . . . For an action-packed and
thrilling romance, *The Star Witch* is just what the doctor
ordered." —*Romance Reviews Today*

The Moon Witch

"I can hardly wait to find out how she will [entwine] all the
threads she has created! . . . This series is just too good to
miss." —*The Romance Reader*

"An enjoyable romantic fantasy that grips the audience . . .
Action-packed." —*The Best Reviews*

"A unique and imaginative realm . . . Prepare to be swept
away!" —*Rendezvous*

"[W]ill enthrall . . . Lushly imaginative."
—*Publishers Weekly*

continued . . .

The Sun Witch

"Entertaining and imaginative, with a wonderful blend of worlds and technology and magic. The characters are different and engrossing, the villain is fascinating."
—*New York Times* bestselling author Linda Howard

"Charming . . . Winsome . . . The perfect choice when you want a lighthearted and fun, yet sensual romance . . . with all the magic of a fairy tale."
—*Bookbug on the Web*

"Fabulous . . . The story is spectacular and this author is unforgettable."
—*Road to Romance*

"Let the fireworks begin! This whimsical, entrancing tale will satisfy the romance fan demanding something unusual and wonderful. With a skillful blend of the fanciful and the mundane, author Linda Winstead Jones weaves a marvelous tale of love and happy-ever-after, with a twist. Remarkable in imagination."
—*Word Weaving*

"Amazing adventures unfold . . . marvelously captivating, sensuous, fast-paced."
—*Booklist* (starred review)

"Hot."
—*Affaire de Coeur*

Titles by Linda Winstead Jones

THE SUN WITCH
THE MOON WITCH
THE STAR WITCH

PRINCE OF MAGIC
PRINCE OF FIRE
PRINCE OF SWORDS
(Available May 2007)

Prince of Fire

LINDA WINSTEAD JONES

BERKLEY SENSATION BOOKS, NEW YORK

THE BERKLEY PUBLISHING GROUP
Published by the Penguin Group
Penguin Group (USA) Inc.
375 Hudson Street, New York, New York 10014, USA
Penguin Group (Canada), 90 Eglinton Avenue East, Suite 700, Toronto, Ontario M4P 2Y3, Canada
(a division of Pearson Penguin Canada Inc.)
Penguin Books Ltd., 80 Strand, London WC2R 0RL, England
Penguin Group Ireland, 25 St. Stephen's Green, Dublin 2, Ireland (a division of Penguin Books Ltd.)
Penguin Group (Australia), 250 Camberwell Road, Camberwell, Victoria 3124, Australia
(a division of Pearson Australia Group Pty. Ltd.)
Penguin Books India Pvt. Ltd., 11 Community Centre, Panchsheel Park, New Delhi—110 017, India
Penguin Group (NZ), 67 Apollo Drive, Mairangi Bay, Auckland 1311, New Zealand
(a division of Pearson New Zealand Ltd.)
Penguin Books (South Africa) (Pty.) Ltd., 24 Sturdee Avenue, Rosebank, Johannesburg 2196,
South Africa

Penguin Books Ltd., Registered Offices: 80 Strand, London WC2R 0RL, England

This is a work of fiction. Names, characters, places, and incidents either are the product of the author's imagination or are used fictitiously, and any resemblance to actual persons, living or dead, business establishments, events, or locales is entirely coincidental. The publisher does not have any control over and does not assume any responsibility for author or third-party websites or their content.

PRINCE OF FIRE

A Berkley Sensation Book / published by arrangement with the author

PRINTING HISTORY
Berkley Sensation mass-market edition / April 2007

Copyright © 2007 by Linda Winstead Jones.
Excerpt from *Prince of Swords* copyright © 2007 by Linda Winstead Jones.
Cover art by Danny O'Leary.
Cover design by Lesley Worrell.
Handlettering by Iskra Johnson.
Interior text design by Stacy Irwin.

ISBN: 978-0-425-21481-7

BERKLEY SENSATION®
Berkley Sensation Books are published by The Berkley Publishing Group,
a division of Penguin Group (USA) Inc.,
375 Hudson Street, New York, New York 10014.
BERKLEY SENSATION is a registered trademark of Penguin Group (USA) Inc.
The "B" design is a trademark belonging to Penguin Group (USA) Inc.

PRINTED IN THE UNITED STATES OF AMERICA

10 9 8 7 6 5 4 3 2 1

For Linda Howard and Beverly Barton,
two remarkable and talented women
who have become sisters of my heart.

❖ The Prophesy of the Firstborn ❖

A darkness creeps beneath Columbyana and the lands beyond. This darkness grows stronger each and every day, infecting those who have an affinity for evil. As it grows stronger, it will also begin to affect those who are of weak mind, and eventually it will grow so strong no one among us will be able to defeat it. If this darkness is allowed to grow to this point, the world is doomed to eternal shadows, where evil will reign.

*

Only the firstborn children of three fine women *[later translated as Fyne]* have the power to stop the darkness and restore the world to light. These firstborn will be the warriors who lead the fight. Our fate rests in their hands, and in the hands of the armies they will call to them.

*

Of the three fine *[Fyne]* warriors who are called to this battle, one will find and wield the crystal dagger. One will betray love in the name of victory. And one, the eldest, will die at the hands of a monster who will hurtle a weary soul into the Land of the Dead.

*

Many monsters will rise from among us in this unholy war, soulless monsters such as the world has never seen. Heroes will be born and heroes will die. Death and darkness will threaten all those who choose to fight for the light.

Scribbled in the lefthand margin, in an almost illegible hand:

Beware Serrazone,

and beside it,

He who walks through fire may show the way.

Scribbled in the righthand margin:

Those who are called must choose
between love and death,
between heart and intellect,
between victory of the sword and victory of the soul.

The remainder of the prophesy is illegible scribbling and indecipherable sketches. A scraggly tree; a bird with wings too large; a flower; a heart; a dagger *[The crystal dagger, perhaps?]*. Do they have meaning or are they simply a dying old man's insignificant doodles?

I

SHAKING, TREMBLING TO HER BONES, KEELIA LIFTED her head and studied her own hands—pale hands which were pressed against a chilly gray stone floor. Tangled strands of red hair fell past one cheek and pooled against the rough stone. A hint of panic welled up inside her, but she did not reveal that panic in any outward way, other than the tremble which she could not control.

Her mind raced, but her body remained very still. Without moving from the spot where she found herself, Keelia gathered her composure. No matter what had happened, she would show no fear. No weakness. The gentle shaking of her body ceased as she quieted her mind and took control, searching for the memory of how she had come to be here.

She remembered standing over Giulia's bed studying an array of several overly ornate gowns in the style her little sister preferred. Her mind had not been on the simple task at hand. Ariana was coming, and there would be a celebration of sorts, even though Keelia's psychic powers had warned her that there were not many celebratory times in the near future for the Anwyn or the humans in the lands below the Mountains of the North. An unspeakable evil was coming. No, that evil was already *here*.

She and Giulia had been studying the gowns, and Keelia's mind had been drifting, and then . . . and then, someone had grabbed her. Someone had actually dared to *grab* her, and then he'd done something to her throat and everything had gone black. Until now. She turned her head and studied the cave in which she had awakened. It was no ordinary cave but was a prison, a cell with bars built into a slender natural doorway. A narrow cot had been placed against one cave wall, but she had not awakened there. Whoever had brought her here had simply dumped her onto the floor. A chamber pot was discretely stored beneath the cot, and a crude wooden table sat near the rear wall. This was not a temporary facility, but one in which a prisoner might expect to remain for a long while.

An unwanted lump formed in Keelia's throat. How much time had passed since she'd been taken? Hours or days? Who had taken her? Who would dare? She was rarely confronted with mysteries of any kind, but at the moment she grasped no answers to her questions.

"Ah, the Queen awakes," a deep voice rumbled from the shadows beyond her prison.

Flaming torches lit the segment of the cave beyond the bars, but not well enough. Not nearly well enough. Keelia narrowed her eyes and attempted to focus, and finally caught sight of the man who spoke. He lingered just beyond the circle of illumination cast by the nearest torch so that all she saw was a shape, a distant and unclear silhouette. The shape was male, like the arrogant voice, but she could sense little else.

Her powers of telepathy were usually quite sharp. Though they were far from all-encompassing, those abilities were strong and reliable. At least, they had been until recently. What had once been crystal clear was now muddy. Indistinct. Dreams continued to come even when the visions did not, but she occasionally misinterpreted even them, until she found herself questioning everything that came to her. Something was interfering with her gifts. Her mother believed that if Keelia would search diligently for her mate and settle down, she would know a calm that had thus far eluded her and the visions would become clear once again. Keelia suspected there was something darker at work here, perhaps the very evil she sometimes dreamed of.

It was true that in the past few months she had not been able to interpret the meanings of her visions well, as she should, but even when her powers were not at their best she could still reach into a person—any person—and know something of their thoughts. Were they scared? Angry? Well-meaning? Frustrated? It was a finely honed instinct she had relied upon all her life, and she needed it now.

Keelia reached for this man who had dared to kidnap her, and received nothing in return. Not hatred, fear, or self-satisfaction at a job well done. Not arrogance or anger. It was as if he were a complete blank. She had sensed nothing of him as he'd snuck upon her either, which was alarming.

Accustomed to being able to understand the people around her, Keelia was more afraid of the emptiness than of her imprisonment in this cell. It was as if someone had taken away her very sight or her hearing or her sense of touch. Without her gifts, she was not herself, and she felt horribly lost.

"Who are you?" she asked sharply, refusing to show fear to her abductor. "What do you want? Are you a coward who always hides in the shadows?" Maybe if he moved closer, she'd be able to read something of his thoughts. Maybe if she could see his face, she could reach deeper and understand his intentions.

She did not fear death. If this man had wanted her dead, he could've killed her there in Giulia's room.

"One question at a time, My Red Queen," the man said, stepping forward so that the flickering flame of the torch illuminated his face.

Keelia's heart reacted fiercely to the sight of that face, skipping a beat and racing and thudding so hard she was afraid he would hear it. This was not possible. He was supposed to be nothing more than a dream, a figment of her imagination, a fantasy she called upon when her fertile time came and demanded that she find physical satisfaction. This man, this face she knew so well, he was of her own making, her own imagination. He was not real.

She closed her eyes tightly, wondering if she was caught in some kind of nightmare. No, the stone beneath her was real, the pounding of her heart, real, her inability to see into her captor . . . real. She opened her eyes, wondering if perhaps she had made a mistake. Maybe her abductor favored the man of her dreams only in some small way, and in her panic she had imagined that he was her dream lover come to life.

Her eyes flickered over him, from head to toe. No, it

was not her imagination, not at all. The man who had kidnapped her had long dark blond hair oddly streaked with auburn. That distinctive ginger streak she had caressed in her dreams originated at his temple and shot back to eventually blend with the thick waves of the more ordinary blond. He was much taller than she, but a bit shorter than most Anwyn males, which had always suited her in her fantasies since, like her mother and sister, she was petite in size, and did not care for being completely dwarfed by the men in her life.

Her kidnapper wore plain brown trousers which fit loosely over long legs and were tucked into soft boots, and a worn leather belt which held a scabbard and dagger. He wore nothing else but a wide silver bracelet which graced his right wrist.

Keelia had been waiting for a long time for her mate to come to her. All Anwyn mated for life, and while the males had to move beyond The City to find their destined mates among human females, as Queen, she should have known for the past ten years or so who her mate would be. She was the powerful Red Queen who had been promised to her people, a Queen who—according to prophesy—would be like no other. She'd been trained from birth to rule, and her mother had gladly abdicated when she and the priestesses judged it was time. Juliet, now the revered Queen Mother, had had the duties of Queen thrust upon her. Keelia had been well prepared. At the age of fifteen she'd taken the throne with no doubts about her ability to lead, without even a hint of uncertainty. She'd not expected her King to immediately appear before her, but neither had she expected to be made to wait so long. She was twenty-five years of age, and still, her mate's identity remained a mystery to her. There were few mysteries in her life, and she had often wondered if this loneliness was the price she had to pay for her other abilities. Perhaps she would never have a true mate and know the love that came with such a union.

Her mother had always told her how she had been unable to read her mate's mind when they'd first met. The love that Juliet and Ryn shared had always seemed ideal to Keelia, and it was what she wanted most of all. More than being Queen, more than possessing remarkable powers like no other . . . she wanted what her parents had found. Was the fact that she was unable to read this man's mind a sign that he was her mate? Were the dreams and fantasies of him unrecognized visions of what was to be? She held her breath. Had she been dreaming about her mate all along? It was tradition for Anwyn males to abduct their mates, and while this scenario was extreme . . . perhaps he was the one. Perhaps her mate was a rogue who lived beyond The City walls, and he had finally come for her.

He wrapped his fingers around the bars that imprisoned her, and the bracelet he wore made a clinking sound as he settled his hands there. By the light of the torch, Keelia finally got a clear look at his face. The mouth was full and wide and wicked. In her dreams that mouth smiled often, but it did not smile now. The nose was perfect in shape, and the cheekbones were high and prominent. The eyes were slightly slanted and mysterious.

It was as she studied those eyes that Keelia put aside her wish that he might be the one she had waited for and she suffered her first real rush of fear. In her dreams, those eyes were as golden as her own. All Anwyn were graced with golden eyes, some deep amber and others brightly gold, with most colored somewhere in between.

Her captor's eyes were green. Not just any shade of green, but a deep and lively shade reminiscent of emeralds.

Her dream lover was a Caradon, and he was not a happy creature.

Keelia had always refused to accept that the ancient prophesy that the Red Queen would take a Caradon lover and thereby bring peace to her people might be true. It had been told so many times, for so many years, it had obviously been twisted and misinterpreted. Her mate would be Anwyn, not a contemptible Caradon!

The Caradon kidnapper gripped the bars tightly with large hands. Hands that had grabbed her, hands that had found a pressure point on her throat that had disabled her.

In her dreams, her lover whispered only sweet things in her ear as he used those hands for happier purposes, but in reality he scowled and asked hoarsely, "What have you done to my people?"

JORYN GRIPPED THE BARS SO TIGHTLY, HIS KNUCKLES went white. The woman who lay on the floor, draped in soft gold fabric and tumbling flame red hair, looked innocent and harmless and even tempting. He knew she was not innocent or harmless, and he could not afford to be tempted.

"What do you mean?" she asked, her voice even, her strange gold eyes unflinching. "Explain yourself."

For the past ten years, he had heard tales of the powers

of the Anwyn Queen, and when the Grandmother—the wizened old witch who had lived longer than any other Caradon—had come to him and informed him that the Red Queen was the one behind the horrid transformation of some of those among them, he had sworn to do all he could to stop her.

If he'd thought killing the Queen would end the dark magic, he would've done so already. Druson, another student of the Grandmother who had been present when she'd shared her knowledge, had suggested that Joryn kill the Anwyn Queen immediately. The Grandmother had strongly advised against such a dire measure. In fact, she had forbidden such action. The Queen must be forced to undo the dark magic she had used to curse his people. If he killed her, those who had been turned into mutant creatures that had no name would be doomed to remain in such a state.

"You know very well what I mean, My Queen. Undo what you have done, and maybe I won't kill you."

She huffed prettily, showing no fear as she rose up into a more rigid sitting position. Even with the floor as her throne, she appeared regal. Unshakable. "I am not *your* Queen, Caradon scoundrel, and I have done nothing which needs to be undone. I command that you release me immediately."

Joryn said nothing for a long moment. It was almost funny that the Red Queen believed she could command anything of him. He owed her no allegiance, no explanation, and she was in no position to hold any authority over him—or anyone else. But she did look pretty, sitting there issuing orders as if she actually expected his obedience.

The Anwyn Queen was beautiful, but he could not afford distractions.

He wanted more than her cooperation; he wanted answers. How was such bad magic possible, and why would she go to such lengths when most of the Caradon left the Anwyn in peace? Only a few outcasts felt compelled to annoy and on occasion attack the Anwyn beasts. Most were content to leave the wolf-people who shared these Mountains of the North alone.

In the beginning, only a few of his people had been infected. They had been cursed by this woman and wore talismans—stones hanging from thin leather cords—to mark them as bewitched. Not that anyone who saw them wouldn't know that they were no longer as they should be, but the talismans made it clear that whatever had happened was no mistake—no freak of nature. No, they had been purposely ruined.

Terrible as it was, that curse had been only the beginning. Those Caradon who had been turned into evil, monstrous things were now spreading their disease. Joryn had recently learned that a number of innocent Caradon who were bitten by the monsters had become like those who had lost their spirits to this witch, and on the rise of the next full moon after the attack they, too, were affected. Those who had been bitten began to change, as they always did beneath the full moon, but the transformation did not complete.

The infected ones were horribly caught between mountain cat and man. No longer human, but neither animal, they were twisted in mind and body. Some of them lost their minds entirely and ran into the mountains alone or threw themselves from cliff sides to their deaths. Others joined the rampage of the monsters who cared for nothing but violence and murder.

"As you do not care for being called Queen, perhaps

'witch' will suit you better." He clanked his bracelet against one metal bar that imprisoned her. "Do you wonder why you can't read my mind, witch?" He could tell by the flicker in her eyes that she did wonder, very much. "Your evil magic doesn't work on me because I am protected by the power of the ancient Caradon." The bracelet he wore had been fashioned by the Grandmother, and he had been warned not to take it off for any reason. Even when he shifted into a mountain cat, the bracelet would remain in place, and he would be protected from the Queen's probing magic.

"I am a witch," she confessed, "but I am not evil." Moving with a gentle grace, she unwound her body and stood.

Anwyn men were quite large, but apparently the females were small. The Queen was not much more than five feet tall, he would guess, and the other female who had been with her when he'd taken her was no bigger. Even her bones were small, as evidenced by the tiny structure of her wrists and the delicacy of her hands. She did not look at all powerful, but then he had been warned that she was well practiced in deceit and dark magic.

"If you are not evil, then why did you curse my people?" Joryn asked, his patience growing thin. "Only a creature with a dark soul would infect the innocent as you have."

A light of awareness came into her eyes, and she took a step toward him. "Oh, I understand."

She looked innocent enough, but he would not be fooled. "Of course you understand."

The Queen moved forward and stopped close to the bars of her cell, but not close enough to reach out and touch him. "The creatures you speak of have been changed, but that is not of my doing, I swear. Something terrible is happening, not only here in these mountains, but in the lands below. An evil is spreading to all corners of the land. I have dreamed of it. I have seen the growth of this evil in my visions, and the abnormality of your people is a part of that growing darkness."

Joryn didn't want to believe her, but he searched for deception in her face and saw none.

"Why should I believe you?"

The Queen was immediately incensed. "Because I do not lie!"

"Ah, a virtuous Anwyn. Of course you do not lie."

"Do not patronize me, Caradon."

"My name is Joryn, witch."

Her eyebrows lifted slightly. "I do not care what you call yourself. Your name is of no consequence. Release me this instant."

"No," he said calmly.

The Queen stamped her small foot and glared at him as if her stare alone would undo him. "I demand that you release me!"

He was unaffected by her anger. "You issue commands like a woman who is accustomed to having them obeyed."

Her lips thinned slightly.

"Does no one ever defy you, witch?"

"No one."

She looked at him oddly, almost as if she recognized him. He was certain their paths had never crossed, but he would admit—to himself, not her—that there was something familiar about this beautiful redheaded woman.

Maybe she had crept into his head with her magic, in spite of the protection of the bracelet. Maybe her powers were stronger than he, or the Grandmother, realized. At this moment he wished she were older, uglier, and lumbering. It would be easier to do what had to be done if that were the case. The Anwyn Queen was the kind of woman any male of any species might wish to call his own and protect.

He could not afford such fancies.

"Are you waiting for your mate to rescue you?" he asked. "Is that why you feel you're in a position to issue commands? I can assure you, no one will find us here."

Her eyes narrowed slightly. "An entire army is searching for me."

She did not mention her mate, and he found that strange. It was the weakness of the Anwyn, that they relied so completely on their mates. They were all but crippled by the connection, as if they were not whole without their other half. The Caradon had no such weakness. Joryn could not imagine being so dependent on another being that he could not function without her.

The Anwyn and the Caradon had been enemies forever. They shared one trait: they shifted with the rise of the full moon, three nights out of the month. The Anwyn transformed into wolves, the Caradon to mountain cats. Beyond that, they had nothing in common.

The Anwyn lived and ran together, congregating in their City and shunning all those who dared to be different. They mated for life, choosing one partner and pledging themselves to that one person for a lifetime. They adored their Queen and relied on their army to protect them. The Anwyn people very rarely birthed girl-children, but produced many large males who were forced to kidnap mates from among the lowland humans.

The females, like the Queen and her mother and her sister, were so unusual they were all but worshipped.

The Caradon ran free, beholden to no one and unfettered by cities or clans or marriage. There was no Queen, no King, no army, no unnecessary rules to bind them. They mated with whom they chose when they chose, and very few spent their entire lives with only one mate, though a few chose to do so. They also birthed many girls. Joryn's mother was Caradon by birth, a direct descendant of the Grandmother. His father had been a wandering human from Columbyana who'd caught her fancy for a few nights before she'd disappeared, taking his unborn son into the mountains with her.

Joryn enjoyed the freedom which was his birthright as a Caradon male. When his duty to his people and the Grandmother was done, he would return to the life he had enjoyed before the curse. He would study and increase his inborn magic, run wild beneath the full moon, and love with abandon.

Not that he was indiscriminate. Far from it. Joryn was a lover of beauty, particularly where women were concerned. Not many were as beautiful as his captive, not that he cared to touch her in any pleasurable way. She was, after all, Anwyn.

The Queen's expression softened, and she clasped her small hands at her waist, well beneath her small but very nicely shaped breasts. "There has been a terrible misunderstanding. Release me and I will return to The City on my own and tell no one of your mistake. You will not be harmed for your foolishness." She spoke to him as if he were a small child, or an imbecile.

"I'm not going to let you go," Joryn responded. "Ever."

Her mask of innocence dropped, golden eyes flashed with anger, and she rushed toward the bars, and him. Joryn stepped back as one small hand shot through the bars. There was not yet a full moon, but that arm . . . the arm only . . . shifted in a heartbeat to that of a russet wolf, complete with wicked claws that missed him by mere inches. Only that one arm shifted, and it was under her complete control.

He had heard that the Anwyn Queen had such powers, but he had not believed it was possible.

"You . . . you . . . *Caradon*!" she said as she swiped at him. "How dare you! You will release me, or I will have your head. Release me *now*, or I swear . . . I swear . . ."

"You swear what?" Joryn asked at a safe distance away from the bars.

Her eyes shone, but she did not shed a tear. "You will be sorry."

"Somehow I don't think so, *witch*."

Indignation rose within and around her, as if she infused her humble surroundings with her dignity. The limb she had tried to attack him with transformed into a delicate, female arm as quickly as it had become a clawed weapon. "You will address me as Majesty or Queen, you . . . you lowly Caradon kidnapper. I am your superior and you will address me as such."

"Yes, Your Wondrous Magnificence," he responded with an exaggerated bow, smiling at her before he turned and walked away. She continued to shout after him, using surprisingly vile language to describe him and his people. It was very unqueenlike behavior, in his opinion.

Joryn did not yet have what he needed from the Anwyn Queen, but he would in due time. Perhaps she was a powerful and fearsome sorceress, a queen accustomed to having her every desire fulfilled at the snap of her fingers, but she was also a female like all others. She was small and weak and afraid, and with the protective bracelet he wore to keep her from peeking into his mind, and the bars on her cell to keep her from touching him, she was powerless.

And best of all, she was his.

"DOES HE HAVE HER, GRANDMOTHER?" DRUSON asked, his voice too eager for Vala's liking.

"Yes, he does." Though some of her powers of divination had been dampened of late, Vala knew without doubt that Joryn had succeeded in capturing the Red Queen.

"Where has he taken her?"

Vala glared at the handsome young man who questioned her with such ferocity. Druson was one of several Caradon males who came to the Grandmother here in her home for magical instruction and teachings of the past. She was happy to assist those who had been born to magic or who were interested in collecting and sharing Caradon history, and she shared much of what she knew of the past and future of her people—though not all. Never all. It was not yet time.

Given the chance, Druson would gladly murder the Anwyn Queen simply for being who she was. He had little inborn magic, though he practiced diligently at simple magics and spells. Surely he understood that she could look at him and see his intentions. Some of them, in any case. She needed no magic to see his ambition.

"You do not need to know where Joryn has imprisoned the Queen. It is done, that is all you need to know."

Druson's hands clenched, but Vala felt no fear. The young Caradon would not do her harm. He did not dare. He was afraid of her and her magic, and he was very jealous of Joryn's talents.

"I wish only to help," he responded, almost pouting.

Vala reached out and patted his cheek. Druson had goodness in him, and one day he might be a good man . . . but only if he chose wisely in the weeks and months to come. She was not yet certain which path he would choose. Her wrinkled hand looked ancient against his smooth, young skin. "All is as it should be. Joryn has taken the first step in returning those who have been lost to us."

"When will he bring her here?"

"When the time is right. That is all I know." She should see more, but the truth of the monstrosities which had once been Caradon was lost to her. Much was lost to her. There was a dark magic at work in the world, a dark magic which hid that which she needed to know from her. With the Anwyn Queen at her side, perhaps she would be able to see more clearly. They could merge the powers of the Caradon and the Anwyn to battle against the evil that threatened them all.

Perhaps. If the darkness which had dampened her psychic ability had also touched the Anwyn Queen, then they were truly lost. Caradon, Anwyn, human . . . lost.

"I'm very tired," Vala said, dropping her hand and stepping away from her student. "You may come back tomorrow if you wish. Perhaps I will know more at that time."

The old woman who was reverently called Grandmother by the Caradon people passed her days in this small cabin which was so high in the mountains it was lost to human eyes. Her needs were simple, and that simplicity was reflected in her home. A long sparsely furnished parlor served for teaching and reading. Her small bedroom and narrow bed were sufficient for the few hours she slept each night. The kitchen was as large as the other two rooms joined together, and it was there that she cooked her meals and prepared her potions, when potions were required. Yes, everything she needed was here.

Druson departed, disappointed that she had not revealed more. Vala sat upon her favorite piece of furniture, an oddly shaped wooden chair which allowed her to rest her legs and lean back at a comfortable angle. Some restless nights she slept in this chair. Her needs were few these days, but she did enjoy her moments of silence, her moments of rare comfort.

Alone, at the end of a long day, she closed her eyes and thought of Joryn and his Queen. She reached for them, picturing Joryn in her mind and allowing the scene around him to expand and unfold until she saw him not as he had been, but as he now was.

Ah, they were both confused and angry, but that would pass soon enough and they would find their destiny in spite of their differences. If she had not thought that to be so, she would never have sent Joryn on his mission. The distance from her cabin to the prison her student had constructed was great, but for a moment no interfering evil kept her from glimpsing into the hearts of the two young people who held the fate of the entire world in their hands.

Certain that all was well with Joryn, Vala turned her

mind away from the cave where her student had imprisoned a Queen. She did not wish to peek too deeply into
their minds. There was so much undecided there, and
the whirling minds of young people exhausted her. The
girl was strong; the boy was determined. Together they
would save all the creatures of these blessed mountains,
or else they would destroy them all.

2

In her prison cave Keelia could not see the sun or the moon to determine the time of day, but she felt the passing of the sun and the rise of the moon in her blood, and like it or not, she needed her sleep. She did not wish to dream about her Caradon kidnapper, but she did.

In her dreams, the Caradon who had stolen her from her home was the lover she had fantasized about for years. He gave her the pleasure to which an Anwyn Queen was entitled, undressing her, smiling as he lowered his head to kiss her bare body everywhere. He whispered soft words to her, words she could not decipher. She did not care what he said to her. She only cared that he held her, touched her, promised her every pleasure she had ever desired. Her body hummed when he touched her, as if he brought her very blood to life, and while she slept, she did not even care that when she looked up into his eyes, they were green instead of gold.

In the dreams, she happily called him Joryn. The word rolled off her lips naturally, and she enjoyed whispering his name after years of not knowing.

As always, he made love to her in a sheltered green valley, with grass beneath their bodies and giant trees offering shade from the hot sun. There was such peace in this place of her own making, and here she felt free in a way she never did in real life. There was serenity and pleasure combined, in lying with her lover. There was unity and joy and harmony. As always, her lover aroused her with his hands and his mouth until she was shaking with need before he entered her body.

Not as always, she woke abruptly before finding release, trembling and needful and feeling horribly empty and alone.

Time passed slowly. It seemed as though she had been in this dreary cave for a long time, but by her reckoning she had been a prisoner for only four days. Four days, three nights, three dreams which left her shaking. The Caradon fed her once a day, slipping a roughly fashioned wooden plate piled high with dried meat, fresh fruit, and a tasty but tough bread through a small space near the ground. He also took her chamber pot through that space once a day, emptied it, and returned it. It was slightly mortifying to have him perform such a task, but preferable to the alternative.

He did not leave her in the dark, and while she would never tell him so, she was grateful that he replenished the flaming torches when it was necessary.

Her captor came to her at least twice a day to question her about the curse he claimed she had put on his people, and he never seemed to hear her when she told him—again and again—that she had done nothing to the pitiful creatures. Eventually, in utter frustration, she quit answering him at all, and he ended up standing on the other side of the bars staring at her with those terrible and beautiful green eyes.

Standing in her cell, Keelia felt the pull of the full moon even though she could not see the sky. Tonight Anwyn and Caradon would transform. She had the unique ability to be able to resist the change—as well as being able to transform at any time—but unless there was a reason to do so, she embraced the transformation and ran as a wolf under the full moon, as all Anwyn did. Here in this cell there would be no room to run, but perhaps if she shifted, she could pass the night without dreams of her kidnapper making love to her.

Her dreams were always different when she slept in wolf form. Under the full moon she dreamt of running unfettered in a shaded forest, or of leaping along mountain paths with the rays of the moon feeding her power. Sometimes she even dreamed of flying high above the mountains she called home. Those were always such dramatic and surprisingly peaceful dreams, when she soared as if she'd been born to the sky. Perhaps if she passed the night as a wolf, she would not awaken in the morning with her body trembling with need.

She refused to need *anything* from *any* Caradon.

Her kidnapper appeared not long before sunset. In her dreams he smiled often, but she had never seen that expression on his face in reality. He looked more somber than usual as he gripped the bars of her cell so tightly his knuckles went white.

"Tonight the Caradon who have been bitten by those you cursed will join the afflicted if you don't do something right now to save them. *Now,* Your Most Beautiful

Cruelness. Do you have no heart? What will it take to convince you that the curse must be lifted?" His green eyes narrowed. "What do you want in return for lifting the curse? My life? My fealty? What do you *want* from me?"

She had argued so many times that she had not cursed his people, to no avail, that she remained silent under his scrutiny. More than once she had rushed to the bars in an attempt to attack him with her claws, but he was fast and always moved beyond her reach too quickly. Today she remained still, her back close to the cool wall of the cave.

The Caradon grew angry, angrier than he had been before this moment. His jaw was tight, his mouth thinned, and his eyes . . . was it her imagination or were his green eyes now touched with flecks of glowing red? She cocked her head and took one step closer to the metal bars that separated them.

The man before her yanked his hands from the bars of her cell and held them out, palms up. Before her eyes, flickers of fiery flame began to dance on those palms. As each second passed, the flames grew brighter and more real, until her captor held a blazing ball of fire in each of his hands.

"Remove the curse, or I will burn you alive." He whispered, but she heard him quite clearly.

"I cannot remove a curse I did not cast," she insisted, her eyes on the flame that danced on one palm. She had not known, had not even suspected, that her kidnapper might wield such power. Her sister and each of her four brothers possessed some sort of inborn magic, but she had never seen anything quite like this. "I have never cursed anyone or anything."

"I don't believe you."

His eyes were more red than green now, and for the first time Keelia feared for her life. Joryn was no normal Caradon, but was a demon who had invaded her dreams and would murder her here deep in a mountain cave, where no one would ever find her body, and no one would ever know what had become of her. Her army, her devoted guard, should've found her by now, but no one had come to her rescue. A terrifying thought made her heart do strange things. What if they *had* come, and Joryn had attacked them with his fire? What if those who would save her were all dead?

For the first time, she felt truly lost and afraid.

Keelia dropped to her knees and lowered her head. In the past few days she had tried several times to reach out to her mother with the ability they shared. She had never felt as if the connection had been made, but now, with death only moments away, she tried again, calling out to her mother with all the power she possessed.

I love you all.

The danger I have been warning you about is real. Be ready when it comes.

Giulia is not ready to be Queen. Help her.

And then again, *I love you all.*

Not knowing if her mother had received the message or not, Keelia lifted her head and stared at her kidnapper. The flame in his hands had grown hotter and higher, but he apparently felt no pain. His anger and frustration had increased along with the flame, and she expected him to send that fire to her at any moment.

"I despise you and your people," she said in an even voice, "but I have never cursed them, or anyone else. That is not my way." Her dreams of pleasure must've been pure fantasy, because this creature before her possessed no laughter, no passion, and certainly no love. "If you are going to execute me . . . I'm ready." She closed her eyes and waited for the flames to consume her. *I love you all.*

CIRO SAT IN A NICELY PADDED, COMFORTABLE CHAIR which his soldiers transported in a small wagon, so that he would not be entirely without comforts on this journey. He searched the sky as his army, his soulless Own, set up camp for the night. He had promised them another village to raze, but there was no need to rush. There were many villages between tonight's camp and their final destination, and the destruction of all those villages would take place at the hands of his legion. In time.

Soon the moon would rise. On the mountain which was now days behind him, Anwyn and Caradon alike would transform, as would those he had called to him who were no longer the creatures they had once been. He had been tempted to summon some of the mutated creatures to him for his army, but he was marching to Arthes, and in the capital city the creatures would be too far away from the mountains to be affected by their magic. No, they had their work there in the mountains, and he had his in Arthes. Another would lead them; that was as it should be, the demon told him.

Ciro thought ahead to his return to Arthes. His father would be surprised to see him, he imagined. Surprised, and then dead. Once that was done, Ciro would be emperor. Taking the throne would not be the end of this journey. No, it would be the beginning. A wonderful, terrible beginning.

Diella sauntered over to him with her hips swaying. She was proud of her new body but still annoyed with him for the scar he'd left on her new face. The scratch he'd left with his teeth—before the body had become hers—had become infected, and the scar would only grow worse as days passed. He was already tired of the former empress's demands and her complaints, but she had a purpose to serve still, and he could not dispatch her just yet, much as he wished to do so.

"A few of the idiots who call themselves your Own have gone to fetch your supper from a nearby farmhouse."

"I know." Ciro knew everything that happened with his army. He knew their thoughts, their fears, their desires. The Isen Demon had taken his soul first, and then he had drawn in the souls of his Own. Those lost souls mingled with his and became something stronger than he had ever imagined possible. They became one with the Isen Demon, and Ciro's body housed the demon and all the power it possessed.

"Why can't they bring me a man as well?" Diella complained.

"You are surrounded by men."

"I am surrounded by drooling idiots who don't care much for bathing or cleaning their teeth," she retorted.

Diella's soul had been lost in Level Thirteen for many years, and now that she had a body to call her own, she was trying to sate more than forty years of need in a matter of days. Ciro was already tired of her attentions, and besides . . . he was saving his seed for his beloved Rayne. The Isen Demon had promised Ciro that he and the woman of pure soul would produce a remarkable son.

First he would take the throne, and then he would collect his beloved and they would make their special son. Some would call his son a monster, he knew, but

Ciro didn't worry about such. His child's powers would be remarkable. Dark, malevolent, and remarkable. The very idea made him almost giddy with anticipation.

He fondly remembered Rayne as he'd last seen her, chained to the wall of the basement of her father's house, begging to be released. If he took the drug Panwyr into his body, he could pretend Diella was Rayne, but he'd done so a few times, and while the physical release was real, it was not the same as having his beloved beneath him. What he felt under the influence of the drug was an illusion, a trick of his mind. No, he would prefer to save himself for his betrothed. He would wait for her. He would wait. She would make a fine empress, a fine mother to his child. Monster or not, she would love her child as a mother should.

Two of his men approached, dragging a reluctant young woman between them. The girl was pretty enough, in spite of the tears on her cheeks, but Ciro studied her soul, not her face or her body. Even from this distance he could see that it was tarnished. He was not yet strong enough to take a pure soul, but he had only recently progressed to the point where he could take a gray soul without the permission of that soul's owner. Soon no one, not even a man or woman with the purest soul, would be able to deny him, and when that happened, he would be unstoppable.

Ciro smiled, and the girl stopped struggling. Amazing what a disarming smile would do. He knew he was handsome, and that some females placed high values on his outward attributes. The girl stumbled at his smile, as her legs were much shorter than those of his soldiers who moved forward so quickly, but she no longer appeared quite so terrified.

"What is your name?" Ciro asked.

Diella huffed once and stalked away, searching the camp for someone else to annoy while Ciro attended to the business at hand.

The girl before him licked her lips. "My name is Ilda. I . . . I don't understand. These men killed my husband and my brother." She tried to yank away from the soldiers who held her fast. "Why? What do you . . ."

Ciro raised a silencing hand, and the girl ended her tirade abruptly. "I am Prince Ciro, Ilda, and I require your assistance." He could be done with the girl so quickly she would never know what had happened, but there was no joy in taking what he needed with such speed.

Ilda lifted a callused hand so that it rested between her small breasts. "You have need of me, Prince Ciro?"

"Yes. I'm afraid no one else will do."

She shook her head. "But why did these men kill my family? What purpose could that serve?"

Ciro's powers, the powers of the Isen Demon, grew stronger every day. He realized the emergence of a new power now, capturing the girl's eyes and holding them. He reached not for her soul, but for her weak mind. *I am your family now. You are not afraid. You trust me above all others. You will now walk forward and sit on my knee.*

Ilda walked toward him and sat as he had instructed. She weighed almost nothing, it seemed. She was tiny, and he had grown larger and stronger in the past few months. In truth, the girl was no more substantial than a bug he might step upon, or a fly he might swat away.

She reached out and shyly caressed a long strand of Ciro's fair blond hair. Her eyes were dreamy, soft and unfocused. If he touched her mind and suggested that she have sex with him here and now, in front of an entire army, she would not demur. But Ciro's lust for women had been replaced by a determination to have Rayne, who would soon be his wife, bear a son who would be like no other. No, it was not lust he felt as he held this girl in his arms. It was hunger. Deep, undeniable, hunger.

She stared into his eyes, rapt. Enthralled. Waiting.

Offer me your throat.

Ilda tilted her head to one side and brushed back a length of her own dirty-blond hair. Ciro saw the vein pulsing there, just beneath her pale skin. He lowered his head and kissed the flesh lightly, then trailed the tip of his tongue along the vein. He smelled the blood he needed, and felt the soul he craved dancing just out of reach.

Ilda placed a steadying hand on his shoulder and sighed, as if she desperately wanted what he was about to offer. It was interesting that he could reach into the girl's mind and make her his in all ways, but there was no challenge in taking a soul in this manner, there was no joy without the fear.

Ciro abruptly disconnected himself from the girl. Her body twitched, and the hand that had been resting on his shoulder began to push and slap ineffectually. "What are you doing to me? Let me go!" She tried to struggle, but could not get away. She was no match for him. No one was.

"Fight me, Ilda," Ciro commanded as he buried his face against her throat. "Fight this ugly death I offer you, if you can."

He felt her growing fear as she struggled, tasted it as he bit into the vein that had teased him. Blood and a tainted soul poured into Ciro, nourishing him. Ilda might look innocent enough to the average eye, but she was far from innocent. She'd stolen, lied, and cheated. Why did he worry about not being able to take pure souls when there were so few of them in the world?

As Ilda's blood and soul poured over his tongue, Ciro saw some of her past, felt many of her hopes and fears. She was a foolish girl, not terribly bright, who'd used her pretty face and convenient lies to get what she wanted. She'd never appreciated the simple pleasures of her life, but had constantly whined and complained and wished for that which was not hers.

She would cherish her simple life if she had the chance to take it now, but that chance was gone.

When Ilda's soul was entirely his, she stopped struggling. Ciro continued to feed, taking every drop of her blood into his body and luxuriating in the feeding. With every soul he took, he grew stronger. The Isen Demon grew stronger, and the demon worked—worked, saw, breathed, and lived—through him. With a new soul inside him, he felt invincible. There were those who would oppose him, he knew, but they were powerless to stop him.

As he finished feeding, Ciro thought of Rayne. After their child was born, if she did not please him, he would dispose of her just this way. He would be able to take a pure soul by that time, and if he was not, then he would see that her soul was tainted. He didn't know how that could be accomplished, but it could be done, he was sure. Nothing could stand in the way of what he wanted; not anymore, not ever again.

When Ciro was finished with the supper his soldiers had provided, he dropped the body at his feet. Two of his Own came to take it away, and he settled back with a sigh of contentment. Soon the Isen Demon would snatch away the soul for itself, but as he and the demon grew more connected, that emptiness did not come so quickly, nor last so long. There was very little of the man Ciro had been left in this body, and soon, very soon, even that would be gone, and all that remained would be demon.

The demon spoke to him. At the moment, they were both satisfied and hopeful. It was odd that a demon could hold such hope, but Ciro felt it as surely as his own. The prince was not the demon's only general in this war. There were others who would gladly trade their souls for the power the Isen Demon promised. All was proceeding well. There were still obstacles, but at the moment those obstacles seemed insignificant.

Ariana and her wizard and her army might try to stop them, but at the moment they felt entirely unstoppable.

THE CHANGE WAS COMING. JULIET COULD FEEL THE call of the moon in her blood. In her very soul. She so loved these nights when she embraced the wild wolfen side of her nature and ran unfettered, with Ryn at her side. They had been traveling, living the life of a pair of rogues for many weeks now. She missed her children, and it was almost time to go home, but she did so love this time alone with her husband. It reminded her of their first days together.

No one was about but Ryn, as she began to undress so as not to ruin yet another gown. There wasn't much to her frock, since the days were growing warm and she had no tolerance for the heat, but still, she liked this garment and did not want it to be ripped as she transformed.

Here high in the mountains, far from everyone and everything, she had very few visions. In truth, her visions had been few and far between for months, no matter where she was. Perhaps it was simply a part of growing older, and she should be grateful. In an odd sort of way she missed the gift she had so often dismissed as unwanted.

As she contemplated her changing powers, a voice—Keelia's voice—rang clearly in her head. *I love you all.*

Juliet reached out and grasped Ryn's arm. It was already too late. Her husband was changing, and so was she. Before the form of wolf consumed her, she whispered hoarsely, in a voice that was not entirely her own, "Keelia is in trouble."

ONE FLICK OF HIS WRIST, AND THE RED QUEEN would be dead. She wasn't going to reverse the harm she had done. She wasn't even going to admit to her actions. So why should he keep her alive?

She was brave, and Joryn admired that bravery even though he should not, could not, admire anything about the Anwyn witch. For a long moment her eyes remained closed and then she opened them slowly. Her eyes met his, and she did not even tremble, much less beg for mercy. No, this was a woman who never begged for anything, he imagined. She commanded. She ruled. She greeted death with her chin held high and her eyes dry of tears. There was no pleading, no begging for mercy.

One flick of his wrist . . .

And he could not do it. He could not kill this maddening, evil woman. Only an evil woman could've done what she'd done, and yet he did not feel malevolence from her. He did not possess psychic powers as she did, and yet he did have inherent instincts. Should he trust the Grandmother, who told him this woman was responsible for the ruination of his people, or his instinct, which told him that she was not washed in the darkness he sought? The Grandmother had told him not to harm the Queen, but if she refused to cooperate, what else was he to do?

Though he could not see the moon, Joryn felt the change in his blood. It was coming quickly. In moments he would be mountain cat, not man, and his gift of fire would be dormant until morning. This was his last chance—at least for tonight—to be rid of the woman who had cursed his people.

The fire on Joryn's palms died suddenly, and he dropped his hands. He looked for signs of the moon-induced transformation on his prisoner, but saw none. Since she could change her form at will, as he had already discovered, could she also remain in her womanly shape beneath a full moon?

Without a word of explanation for his captive, Joryn stepped away from the cell and into the shadows, where he quickly undressed, setting his trousers, boots, and dagger aside moments before his bones began to shift. He usually embraced the transformation, but not tonight. Tonight more Caradon, all of those who'd been bitten since the last full moon, would find themselves infected by a dark evil the Anwyn Queen had made.

KEELIA DIDN'T MOVE FOR A LONG WHILE. IN TRUTH, she could not. She'd tried very hard not to show fear, but to be faced so closely with death had shaken her to her very core. Why hadn't her captor killed her? She knew the moon had called him. Had it interrupted his plans for her? Would he simply toss that magical fire her way in the morning?

A low growl . . . no, it was more of a deep *purr* . . . caught her attention, and her eyes were drawn to the shadows of the cave beyond the bars of her cell. A large cat, dark blond with one russet ear and a streak of red from that ear down one side, walked into the light of the torch overhead. Even if she did not recognize that streak of red, she could not mistake those eyes. From facing her captor, from the dreams, she *knew* those green eyes.

Caradon. Beast. Enemy. Lover.

The silver bracelet he always wore also remained, only now it girded one furry limb. It had grown smaller, in order to fit the animal without being loose, which meant there was magic in that bracelet. Was that why she couldn't see into her captor? Of course. He'd said he was protected by the magic of the ancient Caradon, and it made sense that the magic had been channeled into the silver of the bracelet. No wonder she hadn't felt him sneaking up behind her; no wonder she did not see his intentions. The bracelet protected him.

"What is it going to take to convince you that I didn't curse anyone?" she asked. She felt the wildness calling to her, and cell or no cell, she would change tonight. Moving slowly, Keelia removed her gold gown, taking her time in unfastening the clasps at her shoulders, letting the dress fall and then stepping out of it.

The cat before her cocked his head to one side, as if studying her naked body. Keelia didn't care that he looked, that in the morning her captor would remember what he'd seen. Many of her guards had seen her prepare for the change by shedding her clothes, and she'd set aside any modesty she might possess long ago. Excessive modesty was a human trait, and made little sense to her.

Thanks to her powers, the transformation which was painful for some and quite slow for others was effortless and quick for Keelia. In the blinking of an eye, she changed from Queen to wolf.

In animal form, she slowly crossed her cell to face the Caradon. The bars remained between them, between cat and wolf, between male and female. There was an increased power in Keelia's body, a power that ran through every limb, every muscle. As she longed to escape from this small prison, a new thought occurred to her.

She sauntered to the far side of the cell and turned about slowly. From there, she studied the cat who had dared to imprison her. She wanted to run, to jump, to *fly*, and she did.

Keelia pounced across the cell with all her might, slamming into the barred cell door. The metal rattled against stone as bits of mortar loosened. Unfortunately she did not make much of an impact as the cell was sturdily built. Returning to the opposite side of the cell, she attempted to loosen the bars once again, running, springing into the air, crashing into the metal bars.

She attempted to break down the bars several times, while the Caradon watched. Was that a smile on his furry face? Was he amused by her efforts? Imagining that he was amused only made Keelia try harder. Again, and again.

Exhausted, she finally lay down on the floor to rest. She'd cut herself in several places, crashing into the bars as she had, but none of her injuries were serious. The mountain cat moved closer to the bars, studied her for a moment, and then turned to run.

Her captor would have the joy of running beneath the moon tonight, but she would not. She would feel the pull of the moon while caught here in this small cell that did not allow her even a glimpse of the sky.

Throughout the night she attempted to loosen the bars of her cell by rushing into them with all her might. If she were larger, perhaps it would work, but she was not only petite in her human form, but was a smallish wolf as well. Yes, she was significantly stronger in wolf form, but not strong enough to break out of her prison. Bloodied and sore from her continued efforts, she lay down before the cell bars to rest, and a deep sleep claimed her.

She was wolf tonight, but she had the dreams of a woman.

JORYN STAYED CLOSE TO THE CAVE THROUGH THE night, though he indulged in the power of his feline form and ran with great speed along steep trails for a long while before stopping to sleep beneath the full moon. Usually he did not dream on the nights of the transformation, but tonight as the moonbeams washed over him, he dreamed quite vividly.

He dreamed not of killing the Anwyn Queen, but of holding her. Kissing her. Fucking her. She was passionate in his dreams. Demanding, passionate, and wild. She was a fierce and insatiable lover who laughed and screamed and whispered gentle words in his ear. He did not know what she said, but those words filled him with something unexpected and important. Whatever it was she whispered in his ear, the message was *important*.

And still, he did not care about her words. He cared only for her bold touch, her soft skin, the way she cried out, the way it felt to sink into her warm, welcoming body.

Joryn awoke before sunrise, remembering that he'd left his prisoner attempting to escape. He hurried back toward the cave, and arrived just as the transformation to his human form took place. He ran into the cave, made his way down the snaking stone corridor, and caught sight of the cold torch outside the cell. With a flick of his fingers, the torch flamed to life, illuminating the natural corridor and the cell.

His prisoner lay in the center of the cell, her pale skin bare and bruised, cut in many places from her attempts at escape. Joryn checked the bars and found some of them slightly loosened. The prison remained sturdy, but if the Queen continued to use her strength against the bars, eventually one or more would give way.

He had promised the Grandmother that if he could not get the Queen to end the curse, then he would transport his prisoner to that cabin high in Caradon Territory, where the ancient witch had taught him so well. His gift required much instruction and supervision, and for years that cabin had been almost like home to him . . . if he cared to call any place home. It was clear that Queen Keelia wasn't going to undo anything, but they could not travel until after the next two nights of the full moon had passed. He could not take the chance that she would slip away from him while he was in his animal form and she had the power to take her human shape. What other unexpected powers might she possess? No, before they traveled away from this place, he had to know that he could call upon his gift for fire if it was needed.

The Queen moaned once, and lifted her head from

the floor of her prison. Her long red hair was wild and tangled, and covered one cheek so that he could not see her face well enough. Not that his eyes were drawn to her face at the moment. In her gold gown she was beautiful, with curves aplenty and a regal grace. Naked, she was exquisite. Did her skin glow, or was that a trick of the firelight?

Joryn didn't pretend that he wasn't admiring her when she stood. Might as well not pretend, since all he wore was his enchanted bracelet, and his reaction to her state of undress was evident. Her eyes were drawn down his body, and the only reaction was a slight lift of her eyebrows . . . and a tightening of small nipples.

The Queen used both hands to push her tangled hair away from her face. She did not try to hide her nakedness. The animal was a part of her, as it was of him, and she did not possess the reserve that so many ordinary women had been cursed with. She allowed him to look upon her, and as he watched, her cuts and bruises began to heal, slowly but surely.

She asked, her voice even, "Are you going to kill me now?"

"No."

She didn't seem surprised. Did she ever? "That's quite an interesting gift you possess." She licked her lips, and if he hadn't already been hard, that would've done it. "Fire."

She didn't know everything, and he wasn't about to tell her. He might question whether or not she was evil, he might dream about her—he might even want her body beneath and around his. But that didn't mean he was foolish enough to trust her.

His prisoner had moved closer to the bars than was

safe, considering her abilities and his exposed state. If Queen Keelia—ruler of the Anwyn and gifted seer—killed him, she'd never get out of her prison. She was smart enough to know that. Still, he took a step away from the bars.

Joryn's eyes were drawn down the Queen's fine body, which he admired openly until he came to a small mole positioned against fair skin just beneath her navel and slightly to the left. In his dream, she'd had just such a mole. He knew because he'd kissed that mark on an otherwise flawless body and she'd laughed. He remembered the laugh, the taste of her skin, the quiver of her flesh, as if it were all real.

He reached for the bracelet which was supposed to protect his mind from hers. Obviously the Grandmother's protective magic was flawed. The Queen couldn't read his mind, but apparently she could reach into his dreams.

And she was trying to seduce him into releasing her.

IT WAS ALL TOO EVIDENT TO KEELIA THAT SUMMER
was approaching. There wasn't much of a breeze in her
prison cave, though on occasion she caught a whiff of
fresh air. She missed her cool baths, her fans, and the
welcomed brush of fresh night air against her flesh.

The cell was slightly more tolerable when she was
unclothed. Since she wasn't shy about her body, she
began to pass the days in that state. Her captor seemed
alternately amused and annoyed, but she did not care.

When her army found her, she would insist that they
take her to the nearest body of water before returning to
The City. She did not wish her subjects to see her in such
a sad condition, sweating and overheated and flushed. For
a while she had wondered if her kidnapper had killed
those who were searching for her, with his remarkable
gift for fire, but a few moments of quiet meditation had
ended that worry. Her army, her devoted guard, were alive

and well, but they were far away from this prison. She'd tried to reach out to them, as she had her mother, but as she had no mental connection with the soldiers, she was quite sure nothing had happened. She didn't see anything of her own future with certainty, but she did have hope that her guard would find her. Eventually. In a place like this one, hope was necessary.

Joryn appeared with her meal for the day, slipping it quickly through the portal made for that purpose. There was no more fresh fruit, apparently. The bread would be hard, and the meat was dried and tough. Even though she was hungry, Keelia did not rush to collect her meal. From her position on the stone floor, which was harder but also cooler than the cot, she rose up slightly.

She did not want to suffer this physical attraction to the man who had kidnapped her, but her body seemed to have a mind of its own where Joryn was concerned. She clenched in deep places which were normally dormant, and her nipples hardened. It was the dreams, she knew. Her body had the mistaken notion that this Caradon captor was already her lover, and it wanted more. It wanted touch. Intimate, hot touch.

All her life, she had dismissed the prophesy which said the Red Queen would take a Caradon lover and thereby bring peace to her people. The Anwyn had been at peace for many, many years. The Caradon were nothing more than nuisances. Why would such an extreme sacrifice be called for to end what was no more than an annoyance?

But now there was a new evil rising, and there was evidence of that evil everywhere. Her psychic abilities had been dampened; the Caradon monstrosities attacked even their own; her vivid visions of violence among the humans in the land below were all too real. Still, how could lying with a Caradon bring peace? How could making this man her lover stop an evil that seemed to her to be unstoppable?

There was only one logical explanation.

Joryn studied her without attempting to hide his appreciation. Arms crossed over a finely muscled chest, feet firmly planted, hair loose and thick. And clean. Keelia closed her eyes and took a deep breath. "You have been in the water."

"Yes. It is a warm day, Your Most Royal Splendor."

He had latched on to her insistence that he address her as her station required, and on occasion had quite a lot of fun with it. Not when he was at his angriest, but when he only wanted to annoy her. She did not wish to argue with him, not now. She was tempted to order him to take her to the same water he had enjoyed . . . but in the past, issuing orders to her kidnapper had accomplished nothing. Perhaps she should try asking instead. In her sweetest and most demure voice, she began, "I don't suppose I could convince you to take me . . ."

He began to shake his head long before she could finish her question.

Keelia sat up slowly, and still she didn't move toward her food. Hiding her frustration at his refusal, she tried again. "I have a proposition for you."

"I'm sure you do," Joryn answered, a touch of humor in his voice. He gripped one bar of her cell with one large hand. A very nicely shaped hand, she could not help but notice. "I know what you've been doing, so . . ."

Keelia blinked a couple of times. "I haven't been doing anything. In fact, I believe I have been an ideal prisoner for the past few days."

"Do you think I don't realize that you've invaded my dreams?" her captor asked. "Do you think I don't realize that you're trying to seduce me in a way that only a powerful witch could?"

Keelia swallowed hard. He'd been having dreams about her? Dreams like hers? It wasn't possible that her mate was a Caradon. It was unheard of. And still, the dreams were a part of the connection, a part of the realization of one's mate's identity. "I have done no such thing," she said calmly. "I receive information psychically, but I do not influence the minds of others." Unless she had been able to reach her mother . . . "I don't affect their dreams and thoughts. It would be terribly rude. Communication is possible, in rare and special circumstances, but if you believe I'm capable of . . . of mind control, you're mistaken. Perhaps you have experienced perfectly ordinary dreams and you're confused."

"They're not ordinary, I assure you." His eyes drifted down. "That mole on your belly. I saw it in my dream before I saw it on you. Besides, the dreams are very . . . real."

"Yes, they are," Keelia sighed.

"So, that is your proposition, I suppose? Come on in, Joryn, and I'll show you the pleasures you have dreamt of." There was more than a touch of sarcasm in his voice, and perhaps a little pain. "Come into my prison cell, Joryn, and make me scream your name. Come to me, Joryn, and in the name of pleasure let's forget that we are enemies."

Keelia rose to her feet, moving slowly. "Actually, I was going to say something entirely different. Release me, Joryn. There is evil coming to these Mountains of

the North, and I believe Anwyn and Caradon are destined to fight it together."

"RIDICULOUS," JORYN RESPONDED AS HE SHOOK OFF
the Queen's proposition. "Do you think I'm a fool who
will believe anything that comes out of a beautiful
woman's mouth?"

Keelia tilted her head to one side. Silken red hair
drifted over pale, perfect, bare skin. Yes, this was definitely seduction of the most blatant sort. "You think I'm
beautiful?"

He threw his hands up in frustration. "Yes, but that
has nothing to do with the fact that you're the enemy.
Anwyn and Caradon will never work together. There
will *never* be peace between your people and mine."

"Do you know of the ancient Anwyn prophesy of the
Red Queen?" she asked, and amazingly, her face flushed
as if she were embarrassed. Naked, passionate in his
dreams, and now embarrassed about some old portent.

"No. I am not familiar with Anwyn lore."

Keelia took a step toward the bars, and Joryn moved
quickly back. Innocent as she looked at the moment, he
could not forget that her soft, delicate hands could become deadly weapons in the blink of an eye.

"It is said that the Red Queen will bring peace to
the Anwyn people by taking a Caradon into her bed,
by taking a Caradon lover."

"Nice try, Your Naked Magnificence. So, we fuck,
and suddenly all is well with the world?"

She did not even blink hard at his response. "Perhaps
you should call me Keelia."

He enjoyed mocking her station; it helped him to maintain a necessary distance between them. And still . . . "Fine, Keelia. Are you telling me that sex will save the world? Not just sex, but you and me—"

She interrupted before he could get more graphic. "I think the prophesy is unclear, as prophesies often are. They are often delivered as riddles, and then they are told and retold until the original meaning is twisted, or perhaps even lost entirely. I believe that Anwyn and Caradon must join together. Sex is simply a metaphor for the union of two very different species, and that union is meant to come in my time. It's the only possible explanation, I see that now. The evil which has transformed some of your people into monsters is spreading not only here on the mountain, but in the lands below. Humans, like my cousin Ariana, are fighting that evil as we waste time here in this prison you constructed because you do not yet understand what's happening. Our determination to defeat that evil must be more devout than our hatred of one another."

It would certainly take a great evil to transform so many of the Caradon people into monsters set on violence, and he still did not sense great evil from this woman. That didn't mean she was telling the truth.

"So, according to your prophesy, we become lovers and the rest falls into place? Seems a little bit too simple to me."

Keelia wrapped her fingers around the bars of her cell. She gripped those bars tightly. "I have dreamed about you, too. I have been dreaming about you for years. Years, Joryn." For the first time, tears shone in her eyes. "But I do not want you. I want what my parents have found, what every Anwyn is entitled to. I want a mate who will remain beside me for life. A male who is in essence the other half of me. I want loyalty and fidelity and love. As Queen, I am obligated to produce children. Since my mate has not come, it has been expected that I will take lovers until he shows himself to me. But I have not taken a lover. When my fertile time comes and my body demands release, I put myself into a trancelike state and find that release in a rich and almost real fantasy, but I have never—"

"You're a virgin?" He didn't mean to sound horrified, but he did.

"Yes," Keelia answered softly. "Do not be led astray by the words I have spoken about the prophesy. I do not want you. I want to be touched only by the Anwyn who is meant to be my mate. I want a forever love, and that is something with which the Caradon are not well acquainted. The fact that we are not meant to be lovers doesn't mean we aren't destined to work together, to fight against the evil that threatens your people and mine. I think that perhaps the identity of my mate has been hidden to me until I accomplish this important goal."

So, maybe she wasn't trying to seduce him, after all.

Joryn turned his back on the Queen. He could not look at her face and be logical. He could not maintain his determination in the face of her nakedness. He did not know the truth, and there was only one way to find out.

Nighttime was best for his excursions into the in-between land where lost spirits roamed, but since tonight he would be mountain cat, and he did not wish to wait until tomorrow night, this afternoon would have to suffice. The Grandmother had warned him not to utilize this part of his gift unless he was in her presence. She did not think he was ready to go on alone, and there were many dangers involved in crossing between worlds. Without the Grandmother's ancient magic to pull him back if something went wrong, there were many risks involved.

Not only did he have no control over exactly where he would land when he crossed over, but he knew there was no guarantee that he would make it back into this world, not without the Grandmother's assistance. If he stayed too long, he might be trapped in that in-between world. Forever.

If it was true that a new evil was threatening the world and his people, then it was a risk he had to take.

In the open, rocky area just beyond the cave's entrance, Joryn adopted a rigid pose, hands lifted, palms up. Fire grew on the palms of his hands, growing hotter and higher with every passing heartbeat. The power, the hot energy that fed the flame, came from a place at the center of his soul. His magic resided there, sleeping until called upon. Resting until awakened.

When there was sufficient power in his hands, he directed the fiery energy onto the ground. The two balls of fire immediately swirled together and flames leapt high, twining and growing and swirling. They grew together until they were one, and then the doorway was formed. To another's eye, the wall of flame would look simply like a brilliant fire. To Joryn, it was a gateway to another world, one he leapt through without fear.

He landed on the other side in a cool green meadow where spirits caught between life and the afterlife awaited him. They were dead, but for some reason they had not moved to their final reward—or punishment. Those who were caught here had something undone in the world they had left behind, or else the Angel of Death had not yet decided where they belonged.

Usually there were one or two spirits waiting, spirits who were willing to speak with him for the few moments he was allowed to stay in the world in-between, but today there were many. Too many. Joryn searched the crowded meadow. Hundreds of spirits faced him, solemn and on edge.

Though the land in-between was not paradise, it was a peaceful place for those who waited. There was usually little solemnity here, and he had never felt this sort of tightly coiled energy before, not even from the most restless of spirits.

One male spirit, dressed in a brilliant white robe and carrying a large gray feather which had some meaning Joryn did not understand, stepped forward. "I have been chosen to speak," he said. "There is no time to tell you all you will need to know, but hear me well. The Red Queen speaks the truth. She did not curse your people. You share a common enemy, and you must trust her."

"She is Anwyn," Joryn said simply. The very idea of trusting an Anwyn was foreign to him, almost unthinkable.

"She is *good*, and so are you. Everything else must be put aside, until the Isen Demon is defeated."

"Isen Demon," Joryn repeated.

The gray feather trembled. "It is an eater of souls that will destroy the world you live in, and when that is done, it will move here, where no evil was meant to tread."

"Eater of—"

"Yes! He is on a path of utter destruction, and if he makes his way to this place, the walls between your world and this one will fall. The walls will crumble, and nothing will ever again be as it should be. You and the Queen must unite your people. Together."

Joryn shook his head. "Impossible."

"You'd best hope, as we do, that it is not. Now go," The spirit gave Joryn a shove. "You cannot come here again, not until the evil has been stopped. The dark energy the demon creates in your world disrupts the doorways, and it is not safe for you to use them again."

"But if I need guidance … ."

"The Red Queen will guide you. Listen to her."

Joryn was horrified by that prospect, but he had no time to argue. The spirit gave him another, more forceful shove, and he fell backward toward the narrowing doorway. Before he could fall through to the place where he would begin this journey, something caught his arm. Something strong. Whatever stopped him had been in this land a long time—longer than was usual. Otherwise such strength would not be possible. A male spirit's taut, pale face hovered above Joryn's for a moment. Time seemed to stop.

"Find my sons. They are rightful heirs." His expression softened. "Find Liane. Tell her I'm waiting." The hold on Joryn's arm was suddenly gone, and he fell backward through the fiery doorway. He landed on the ground with a thud, just as the moon began to rise. With his gaze on that moon and his mind reeling with questions, his bones began to shift.

THE LAST NIGHT OF THE FULL MOON PASSED WITH more alarming and vivid dreams. Keelia began to wish for the horrid and violent nightmares which had been disturbing her sleep for the past few months. Those nightmares left her shaken and uncertain, but she was able to dismiss them because the subjects of those dreams didn't arrive in person soon after—or before—she awoke.

This morning she woke to find the subject of last night's dream staring at her. Staring as he always had, and yet—differently. He seemed more skeptical than angry. More uncertain than she had seen him to this point.

He held a key in one hand.

As he rammed the key into the lock in her prison door, he began to issue orders. "Dress yourself, Your Red Supremeness. We're going for a long walk." His head snapped up before he unlocked the door, and those green eyes warned her. "Unsheathe your claws to threaten me and I will burn you, I swear it. Can we call a truce, you and I?"

Keelia nodded as she jumped to her feet and reached for the gown which had been neatly folded and placed on her cot. "Yes, a truce most definitely will be necessary to accomplish that which must be done. And please, I did ask you to call me Keelia." Your Red Supremeness simply would not do.

"What happened to the edict that I should address you in a manner to which a Queen is entitled?"

"I was angry," she explained. "You had kidnapped me, so I believe I am entitled to a moment of annoyance."

"A moment," Joryn repeated.

"Or two," Keelia said softly. She could not lose her temper and ruin this new treaty with the Caradon. If she was right, then the reason she had not yet found her mate was because she had this duty to accomplish first. Unite the Anwyn and the Caradon, save the world, and then she would be free to discover who her Anwyn mate was meant to be.

The door opened with a squeak, and Keelia could almost taste freedom. She'd been in this prison seven days, and she longed to see the sun and the moon, to breathe fresh air and bathe in cool water.

"Put on your clothes," Joryn ordered.

He backed away from the doorway, and Keelia stepped into the stone-walled corridor, the filmy gold dress draped over her arm. "I wish to . . ." she began sharply, and then she took a deep breath. She had to remember that this man did not respond well to commands. In order to get what she wanted, she needed to be more genial. "Would it be at all possible for me to bathe first? You said there was water nearby, and I am in desperate need of a bath." This time of year the water would still be cold, and she was in need of that chill as well. Not only to ease the Anwyn warmth that always ran through her veins, but to ease the heat her captor aroused.

Joryn sighed as if she were causing trouble with her simple and very pleasant request, but he reluctantly agreed before leading her down a snaking corridor toward the sunlight that grew stronger with every step she took.

Outside the cave, Keelia stopped and took a deep breath of fresh air. Only then did she take the time to survey her surroundings. No wonder her army had not found her! She was much farther from The City, much deeper into Caradon Territory, than she had imagined.

"You carried me all this way," she said.

"You are very small, and I am very strong."

"Still, I remember nothing of the journey."

Joryn smiled, and Keelia's heart reacted with a flutter. Just as in her dream, there was a deep dimple in one smooth cheek.

"You did something to my neck." She touched the place on her throat where she remembered that initial pinch as he'd approached her—*surprised* her—from behind.

"And I will do so again if you give me any trouble," he warned.

"I have never given anyone a moment's trouble," Keelia responded.

Joryn did more than smile at that. He laughed out loud. "You are selfish, haughty, spoiled, demanding, and when offended, you strike out with deadly claws at the end of a delicate and seemingly innocent arm. Not a moment's trouble?" He leaned toward her, reaching out to pat her cheek . . . not the one on her face. "My Arrogant and Beautiful Highness, I doubt that very much."

THEY WERE MANY DAYS FROM THE GRANDMOTHER'S hut, even if all went well. The trip might take weeks if he ran into resistance along the way.

So far, the Queen did not seem to be considering resistance or flight. In fact, she seemed oddly set on this unlikely union. Caradon and Anwyn, fighting together. He had never even considered the possibility, but if she was right—and according to the spirits he had spoken to, she was—then a temporary union would be necessary.

They'd had only one real argument since beginning this journey. The Queen wanted to return to her palace in The City in order to gather her soldiers and plan the coming war and the coming truce with the Caradon. He insisted that they go to the Grandmother's hut first as he had promised the old woman he would do. He would be an absolute fool to walk into the Anwyn City alone, no matter how oddly genial his captive had become in the past few days.

In the end he had won the argument. The Queen had given in. Not easily, but she had acquiesced. Maybe the psychic in her realized that he was right in this.

Joryn remained slightly behind his captive as they moved along a rocky portion of the trail. At least she was clothed once again, after having herself a quick swim in the cold mountain lake. Human females often covered themselves completely from head to toe, no matter what the weather, but the Anwyn Queen did not. The gold gown draped almost clingingly over her body, her arms and a goodly portion of her chest were bare, and he could swear the fabric moved in an unnatural way, as if it were an actual part of her body.

He had simply been too long without a woman; that was the only logical explanation for his wandering thoughts as he watched the Queen hurry along the path as he had directed her. It had taken him many days to build the prison, to formulate the plan, to call upon the Grandmother's magic in order to sneak into and out of the Anwyn City unseen. Many, many days, days in which he had neglected the necessary pleasures of the flesh in order to complete his mission.

In the days ahead he could lie with his captive if he desired. The Queen might say that she was waiting for her mate to arrive, but she was drawn to him in a way he could see and smell and almost taste. It would not take much in the way of seduction to get her to open herself to him, to unite Anwyn and Caradon in a entirely different way than she had planned.

But he would not. The Queen was also a witch, and he was already too near to being enchanted by her. In his dreams she whispered something of great consequence in his ear. Perhaps those words were part of a spell meant to keep him bound to her, a curse that would take away his blessed freedom and tie him to the Anwyn Queen.

No, that would never do.

It was essential that he keep his focus on the matters which had taken him to capture the Queen, not the way her body moved.

He touched the bracelet at his wrist, silently thanking the Grandmother for her gift. At least with this enchanted silver in place, the seer Queen couldn't see into his mind. It wouldn't do for her to know that she was in his thoughts so often. Besides, it was best that she use her talents to lead them to the answers they sought.

Joryn increased his step and was soon striding beside the Queen. "Tell me what you know of the mutated creatures which were once Caradon."

She glanced over and up at him, and again he was taken aback by the delicacy of her features, the fragility of her appearance. He had to remind himself that she was anything but fragile.

"There is a demon," she began.

"Yes," he said impatiently, not wanting to waste time on repeated information. "The Isen Demon."

"He steals the souls of those who are dark, of those who are touched with evil."

"Are you telling me that the Caradon who were affected were all evil?" he snapped. "That must be easy for you to believe, but I find it unlikely."

"If you constantly interrupt me, then this conversation will not be done until the next full moon!"

"Cease your rambling and get to the matter at hand."

His captive, the beautiful Red Queen, stopped walking and placed her hands on her hips in a pose of pure impatience and disgust. The thin gold gown hugged her breasts and her hips. "Rambling and explaining are two different things, you infuriating, kidnapping, mocking Caradon scoundrel. Just because I have agreed that we have a task to accomplish, that doesn't mean I will tolerate your continuing disrespect. I am no longer your prisoner. I am now your *partner*. No, I am your *superior*, and you will treat me as such. I have attempted to be amiable, but my efforts apparently mean nothing to you."

She took a deep breath, and her face flushed in anger.

Joryn sighed. So much for his promises to himself. Like it or not, he would lie with her before this was done. He was drawn to the Queen in such a way that he could no longer deny the blaze that danced between them. He was male, she was female, and before this journey was over, they would share that which they both so obviously needed.

With that in mind, he decided that perhaps it would be best if he did not annoy her overmuch. Women could be quite spiteful when it suited them. Still, he could not allow her to take control of the situation. "Partner, I can tolerate. Superior, I cannot."

Her eyes narrowed slightly. "Unlikely as it seems, I can be your partner, but you must treat me as such. I am no longer your prisoner, Joryn."

"I apologize for my angry words. I am simply frustrated, Keelia."

She nodded, and he could tell by the expression on

her face that he had been forgiven. "Very well, then." She continued walking down the path, and he remained beside her.

"Some things which should be clear to me are not," she said, "but I have been getting quick and sporadic visions as we move deeper into Caradon Territory. Flashes of truth. Pictures from a mind not my own. The Isen Demon has allied with a vile Caradon wizard who has been practicing dark magic for many years."

"Caradon do not practice dark magic."

Keelia snapped her head around. "This one did, and does. I know it is difficult to face, but you do not know every member of your species. This one has been hiding for years, building his skills and . . . and murdering Anwyn and Caradon alike." She shuddered in obvious distaste.

He wanted to believe that his people were inherently good, but he knew there were some who had chosen a wilder, darker path. "I suppose for now I have no choice but to take your word on the matter."

"That will do," the Queen said gently before continuing. "At the demon's instruction, this Caradon wizard made and cursed a number of talismans. He placed these talismans around the necks of Caradon, males and females, who were neither dark nor light, but somewhere in between. They possessed gray souls until the stones of the talismans touched their flesh. When that happened, the demon took their souls, and they . . ." She shuddered, as if she saw and felt all that had happened. "They transformed into soulless creatures trapped between human and cat. They move at the silent instruction of the wizard who made them, and the wizard is under the control of the demon."

"Their numbers are increasing."

"Yes. The evil that infected them has become a disease, spread through their bite. Their saliva enters the blood, and in that way the curse is spread." She looked up at him, and her already pale face went snow white. "It can be spread to Anwyn as well as Caradon. If we don't find this wizard and stop him, the Mountains of the North will be overrun with soulless creatures from your people and mine, and nothing will ever be right again."

SITTING CROSS-LEGGED ON THE STONE FLOOR OF HIS cave home high in Caradon Territory, eyes closed to shut out the distractions of the things around him, the wizard Maccus smiled. He could feel the Red Queen coming closer, as if there were an invisible tug between them. His blood seemed to burn as it rushed through his veins; it seemed to dance in anticipation.

The power he had been promised by the Isen Demon was so near he could taste it on the tip of his tongue.

Knowing she was moving near, as he had always known she would, he ended his meditation and leapt to his feet. He had made a fine home, here in these connected caves. All the comforts any man might want were here. They were his. Soon they would be hers, too. He walked to the table where he often worked, and lifted the medallion which was resting there. It was a circle of silver adorned with a protruding gem. He had infused that stone with his power, with his enchantment, every day since the first full moon of winter. With an anxious finger, he caressed the stone. It was meant for the Red Queen. It would make her his in all ways.

Maccus wore a similar medallion against his own chest. It was through that metal and stone that the Isen Demon infused him with an incredible power that had seemed unimaginable just a few years ago.

There were times when the wizard was certain that the demon was actually inside him, but those feelings never lasted long. They did connect on occasion, when the demon had commands to issue, but Maccus's soul remained his own, at least for now. He had a feeling that would not be true much longer.

The power he had always craved was finally his, and the cost did not seem too high, not to Maccus. What he had accomplished was remarkable, but when the Red Queen arrived, he would be elevated to a status higher than he had ever imagined possible.

Again, his blood danced, and the stone in the medallion which hung from his neck sparkled, green and black and bottomless.

4

THERE HADN'T BEEN A SINGLE DAY IN HER LIFE THAT Keelia hadn't felt different. As an Anwyn, as a psychic, as a woman . . . always different. It would make sense that she'd become accustomed to those things which set her apart from others and embrace the fact that she was unique, but in truth the reality that she was not like others grew more painful with every passing year. She spent most of her life in human form, and yet she was not entirely human. Her Anwyn blood set her apart, so that even though she might appear to be of the same species as her many lowland cousins, she was in fact quite dissimilar. While it was true that there were lowland humans as well as Anwyn among her ancestors, both of her parents had Anwyn blood. That was unusual, or had been before her mother's arrival in The City had changed everything. It was expected that she and Giulia would continue the tradition and produce more children who could be called pure Anwyn, but that could not happen until her mate presented himself. Her Anwyn mate.

She longed for a touch of normalcy in her life.

Taking a Caradon as her mate, as the prophesy had mistakenly said she would, would only set her farther apart from the others. No, her supposition that the destined union was a purely political one made more sense than the idea that she might spend a lifetime with this creature who had kidnapped her. Even if she did experience sensations she had never felt before when she looked at him, even if the dreams did tell her that there would be more than a political alliance between them, she could and would be the mistress of her own fate. She was in control and could choose not to follow the natural—or unnatural—instincts.

Traveling with Joryn proceeded more smoothly than she had imagined it would on this, the first day of their journey. He had some dried food and hard bread in a small rucksack he carried over one shoulder, and carried fresh water in a wineskin, for those days when they might not find good drinking water along the way. The dagger at his waist would likely provide fresher meat at some point in the journey, if he did not hunt with balls of fire. For today they existed on the provisions he carried.

If he'd expected her to behave like a frail female who needed constant attention and care while traveling on foot, then she'd surprised him. She had energy and strength, and did not mind calling upon all she had in order to accomplish her objectives.

And she did try to be well mannered.

Keelia lifted her bound hands gently. "This is not necessary," she said in an emotionless voice. "I want to stop the darkness that has invaded these mountains we call home as much as you do."

"Why?" The fire Joryn had started with a flick of his fingers illuminated his face in the dark of night. The line of his jaw was tight, tense. Like Anwyn males, he grew no hair on his face or chest, so that jaw was smooth, as always. His lips were thinned, his eyes hooded. "Your people have not been affected."

"Not yet," she whispered.

She saw that they would be if the unnatural Caradon creatures were not stopped in time. The disease which distorted their bodies and stole their souls would spread if they didn't find the wizard responsible and . . . and . . . Keelia closed her eyes. She could see the wizard, working in a cave much like the one Joryn had made her prison. His face was unclear, and she wasn't sure if the darkness she saw around him was caused by his evil or his coloring. Did he have black hair, or was that his energy she saw? All she could see well were his hands, strong, male hands, neither young nor ancient, which cupped a green stone that glowed on his palm. She caught only a brief glimpse of that stone, but she immediately realized its importance.

If they destroyed that stone, the spell would be reversed.

Long, strong fingers closed over that stone in her vision, as if the wizard realized the enchantment was threatened and sought to protect it.

"What do you see?" Joryn asked.

"I see the Caradon wizard who set this misfortune into motion," Keelia answered without opening her eyes.

Joryn did not want to believe that one of his own

could be responsible for the curse which had sent him
to her, but he did. For some reason, he did believe her.

"A name, a face, a place . . ." he said sharply.

"Not yet," Keelia whispered. "In time perhaps I will
see more, but not tonight."

"I thought you were an extraordinary seer," he
snapped. "I thought nothing was secret from the fabulous
Red Anwyn Queen."

The vision was gone, over in a flash, and Keelia
opened her eyes. "Once that was true. Almost true, at
least. It isn't meant for anyone to see all. I can't even
imagine how crippling that would be. There was a time,
not so long ago, that if I reached for knowledge, I could
find it, unless it pertained strictly to my personal life."
She pursed her lips. It was every psychic's downfall that
his or her own future was difficult or impossible to see.
If she knew all, then she would've seen her mate years
ago. If she knew all, then she would've known that this
Caradon would kidnap her. If she knew *all*, then perhaps
she could know whether or not she would ever find
a mate.

Of course, Keelia's father had the ability to block his
wife's talents when he so chose. Former Queen Juliet
said no one else had ever been able to keep their thoughts
from her the way her husband did.

"What happened?" Joryn asked sharply. "Why have
your abilities changed?"

"I believe the same evil that affected your Caradon
wizard dampened my inborn skill. Months ago I began
to have trouble interpreting visions, and there were . . .
are . . . blank spots in the knowledge that I reach for. It
takes a powerful magic to interfere with energy in that

way." Her mother thought it very possible that the impaired visions were her body's protest against not taking a lover, a price she had to pay for failing to fulfill her duty to create Anwyn princes or princesses, but Keelia had never believed that theory. Yes, she was distracted by the increasingly demanding fertile times, but that wouldn't affect her magical abilities. Would it?

She lifted her hands again, and silently asked Joryn to release her. After all, she had been cooperative since the moment she'd realized that they must work together in order to defeat the powerful dark magic that threatened to ruin everything she held dear.

He shook his head.

Keelia sighed. If she released herself, displaying her superior power, what would he do? Bind her more securely? Cease trusting her at all? Releasing herself from iron bars had not been possible, but her current bonds were nothing more than a rough length of rope.

Of course, Joryn could always render her unconscious, as he had when he'd taken her. Somehow she didn't like that idea. She was meant to be here, meant to stop the evil that threatened her home. She could not do that while senseless, which meant she'd best not surprise her captor . . . her partner. "I'm simply being polite. I could rid myself of these bonds quite easily on my own, but I'm trying to honor our supposed truce."

"*Supposed* truce?"

"If it were a true truce, you would not feel the need to restrain me."

"I need to sleep," he said, as if that were explanation enough.

"So do I, and this rope is very uncomfortable. It's chafing my skin."

"Already?" Joryn stood with grace and crossed their small camp to drop down beside Keelia.

She found herself holding her breath as he moved the rough rope aside and examined her skin, which was somewhat reddened. By morning her wrists would be raw if he insisted that she wear the bonds all night, but at the moment her thoughts were more focused on the way his fingertips brushed against her skin. The transformation from woman to wolf came with a kind of lightning that coursed through her body, and his touch elicited the same sort of sensation. Lightning. Fire.

But to lie with a Caradon would make her forever different.

"How do I know you won't run in the night, or slash my throat with your claws while I sleep?" Joryn asked.

Keelia stared at his strong sun-kissed hand against her pale arm. That simple sight reminded her of many dreams, of fantasies she had retreated to when her Queen's fertile time demanded release. Thank goodness it was not time for that heat to be upon her, because if she was caught in that frenzy and he was here, she would not be able to contain herself.

And her firstborn child would be half-Caradon, and forever different.

It was not her fertile time, however, so a half-breed child was not a concern. She did not think of their differences at this moment, but of what they could share if they chose to do so. Not as lifelong mates, but as temporary lovers. If he could ease the quivering need inside her, if he could offer her delight and pleasure in a difficult time, shouldn't she allow it to happen?

As the unwanted lightning coursed through her body, she dismissed all her reservations and wondered what it would be like to take Joryn as a lover. Not during her fertile time, but now, or tomorrow, or in the days to come, just so she would know if reality was better than fantasy. No one but the two of them would ever have to know, and when their duty was done, they would part forever, and she would be free to discover the Anwyn male she was meant to spend her life with.

Had the priestesses not told her time and again that it was not only her right but her duty to celebrate all aspects of the body? Hadn't her mother offered the supposition that if she took a lover, her powers would be restored in their entirety? Logically Keelia knew she was grasping for any excuse to allow her mind to accept what her body already knew . . . and she didn't care. Not when Joryn was so close.

"I promise you I will not harm you, nor will I escape. I am as dedicated as you to finding the wizard and destroying the stone he called upon to begin this blight."

"Stone?" Joryn asked.

Keelia sighed. She had not yet told him all about the vision. "A green glowing stone. The wizard we seek works in a cave, and he protects the stone because he knows if it is destroyed, the curse will be ended, and the demon will destroy him in retribution."

Joryn nodded. "We will need something more specific than a cave as our destination. There are many caves in these mountains. Perhaps together you and the Grandmother will be able to discover more."

"I will find him," Keelia said confidently. Joryn said the Grandmother had answers they would need, but she wasn't sure about involving the old woman in their truce. She had put her faith in Joryn, but to ally herself with an endless number of Caradon . . . she could not quite grasp the possibility. "Trust me." She leaned slightly closer to him, and the backs of her fingers caressed his arm. "Trust me."

He hesitated only a moment, and then he retrieved the dagger from his belt. The dagger had a simple but pretty handle, she noticed as he used the blade to slice the rope he had earlier used to bind her hands. It wasn't fancy, but there was a simple scroll pattern in the cross-guard. The blade was well tended, sharp and without nicks in the steel.

Keelia stretched her freed arms and rubbed her wrists as Joryn backed away from her. The bracelet he wore kept her from peeking into his mind, but she saw one comforting truth in his green eyes.

He wasn't entirely happy about the fact, but Joryn *did* trust her.

IT WAS LIKELY THE ONLY TIME THE PAMPERED QUEEN had slept on the ground was after she'd run beneath the moon as a wolf. Did she indulge in that pleasure, even though she could contain the animal when it called? Judging by the way she settled very comfortably on the ground with no pillow, no bedding of any kind, he had to believe yes, she had done this before. When her hands were free, she very quickly fell into a deep slumber.

Joryn's eyes were drawn to the redness of her wrists. Her skin was so delicate, it hadn't taken any time at all for the rough ropes to begin to rub her flesh raw. A wave of unexpected and unwanted guilt washed through him, even though he knew she would heal quickly. He'd wanted only to contain her, not harm her. Could he sleep at all with Keelia so close and so free? What if she changed her mind in the night and fled? Or worse, killed him in his sleep?

The Red Queen will guide you, the spirit had told him. *She is good.* The spirits he spoke to on the other side of this life had no reason to lie, and he had to admit that his instincts were in line with what he had learned in the land in-between. She was not washed in dark energy. In the beginning he had thought her talented at hiding her evil, but now . . .

She confused him in many ways. He wanted her, but he was afraid she would bewitch him with her body. Queen Keelia was a talented seer; she could shift her body at will and maintain her womanly shape beneath a full moon. She freely admitted to being a witch, so what other gifts might she possess? Might she possess the power to entrap a man—of any species—if she so desired?

There were moments when he felt as if he were halfway there, almost enchanted, almost trapped. He should not have been moved by the sight of her raw wrists, but the very idea of hurting her had touched him and he'd been horrified at the thought of her pain.

He had never felt a moment's protectiveness toward a female before, especially one who had not lain beneath him with her legs wrapped around his hips and her throat bare and offered in the ultimate indication of trust.

Keelia was a virgin, and he had never before mated with a female who was not skilled in the art of making love. She was a Queen, and he was a student of magic who wanted nothing more than his freedom and the safety of his people. Nothing good would come of a union that went beyond joining forces to fight the war against an evil that had the power to destroy his people, and hers.

Well, *something* good would come of their union, but long term . . . Joryn snorted. He had never thought of long term where any woman was concerned, not before tonight.

Maybe he was already enchanted, and he simply didn't know it. Something was definitely not right. All the more reason to keep his distance.

As if she knew he was watching, even though the fire he'd created had died and there was nothing but a slightly-less-than-full moon to illuminate her, Keelia sat up, and in one smooth motion drew her gown over her head and tossed it aside before lying down once again and quickly returning to sleep. She turned onto her side, so he was presented with a nicely shaped moonlit back, the delectable curve of a pale and womanly hip, a perfectly rounded and firm ass, and attractive legs. He knew why she'd removed the gold gown, and for once did not even consider that there might be an attempted enchantment in her disrobing. Her blood ran warm, as his did, and with the night air against her skin she was more comfortable. Cooler.

Joryn was suddenly quite sure that he would not sleep at all tonight.

THE FIRST WARRIOR OF THE PROPHESY OF THE FIRST-born, a woman who can truthfully call herself a healer, a witch, and a soldier, Ariana Fyne makes her way down the Mountains of the North, traveling toward a reunion with an army. Her army. Even though she has found love and great hope with a man she calls husband, all is

not as she had hoped it would be at this time. Ariana felt
as if the days were passing by too quickly, as if time itself had been altered and she didn't have enough of it on
her side. So far nothing was going as planned. Keelia
had not been found, and instead of a large Anwyn army
led by her cousins, true Princes of the Anwyn, she was
returning to Merin and the others with a small contin-
gent of Anwyn soldiers—all that The City could spare
with their Queen missing.

Sian was beside her, a fact which outweighed all else
and eased her heart. When she worried, she had only to
look at him and feel calmed. This enchanter who had
once proclaimed that he would not fight in this war was
now one of its most important soldiers.

She would've preferred to march all night, but everyone in the party needed rest. Even her.

Even though she rested comfortably in Sian's arms,
sleep was impossible. Realizing that she was tense and
nowhere near sleep, he gently tipped her face back so he
could look into her eyes. "Don't worry so much," he
whispered, so as not to wake the sleeping Anwyn soldiers. Other soldiers kept watch, but most of them slept.

"How can I not worry? Ciro is closer to Arthes,
which means his father, the ailing Emperor Arik, is in
grave danger. My little sister Sibyl is in the palace. Good
heavens, Sian, I asked for her help before I realized
what we were up against, and now she's . . ." Ariana
pushed down a rush of guilt and tried to concentrate on
the larger picture, the picture of war.

"An untold number of souls have surely been taken
or destroyed by the demon while we wasted days waiting for Keelia to be found. Every soul the demon takes
increases its strength, so that is not an unreasonable

concern. And what of Taran? I sent the young sentinel on a mission of great importance, and we have no way of knowing if his journey to the Southern Province is proceeding safely or not."

"You're babbling, love," Sian said in a calm voice.

"I am not." Perhaps she was speaking rapidly, but that didn't mean she was babbling. "Oh, and what about my brother? Duran probably knows by now that I tricked him to get him away from the palace before I left so he wouldn't feel obligated to join the march and throw himself between me and every danger. Someone had to collect Lyr, that's true, but if Duran isn't livid then he will be when we come face to face again and he realizes what happened. No one knows what's become of Keelia, and according to the prophesy she is necessary in this war. *Necessary*, Sian. If Ciro wins . . ."

Sian stopped her with a gentle finger against her lips. "Stop. All that is true, but you cannot dwell on that which you cannot change. Think instead of what you can do in the days to come. You can and will snatch back souls from the demon when we have access to his wounded soldiers, his blasted Own. In doing so, you will weaken Ciro and the Isen Demon. You can and will take these fine Anwyn soldiers to Merin, who has surely doubled his army's size since last we saw him. We know what we're fighting now, and in future battles we will be more prepared. You can and will make Arik well again with your enhanced healing powers. Sibyl will not be harmed. We will make her safety a priority." He sighed. "We can and will find a priest so that we can be properly married. Properly, legally, quickly, righteously . . ."

Ariana laughed gently, and with that laugh she found herself drifting toward the sleep she needed. "You're right, of course, husband. I can still call you husband, even though we're not yet wed properly, legally, and all the rest, can't I?"

"Of course. You, my love, can call me anything you'd like."

Sleep called, it felt closer, but she was not yet ready to fall into that much-needed slumber. "What comes of the prophesy your grandfather penned if Keelia isn't found?" Her heart hitched at the thought of her cousin in the hands of an enemy from Ciro's wretched army.

"If the Prophesy of the Firstborn is correct, and so far it has been, she's well and will play her part."

"So, will she be the one to betray love in the name of victory or will she wield the crystal dagger?" Ariana herself had already visited the Land of the Dead, fulfilling that part of the prophesy. Of course, Sian's grandfather had not predicted that she'd *return* from the Land of the Dead, but she had. What else did they not know?

Sian pushed a length of wildly curling hair away from her face. "I wish I could tell you."

Ariana yawned. "Maybe the dagger, though in a way it makes more sense for Lyr to fulfill that part. I love my cousin, I truly do, but Keelia can be cold. Not cold, precisely, but distant. Detached. I think her gift has created an isolation she's never found her way past. One has to know love in order to betray it, and I don't think she has ever given away much of her heart. Maybe she never will. I don't know. Maybe that coldness means she's well suited to betrayal. This is all speculation, so . . . why am I torturing myself with these questions?"

She settled herself more comfortably in her husband's arms. He was insistent that they marry as soon as possible, but in her heart, she and Sian were married and had been since he'd bound them together with the twine that encircled her throat, and his, in what she'd come to call their wedding chokers.

As she drifted toward sleep, her enchanter husband created an illusion for her benefit. Instead of a thin rough blanket over the rock of this mountain as their bed, there was a soft mattress and fine sheets. Instead of an almost full moon, there were candles galore to illuminate their world. They were covered by the softest of blankets. It wasn't real, but for the moment it felt real enough.

"Sleep well, love," Sian whispered as sleep claimed her.

He tried to hide his worry from her, but she heard the apprehension in his voice.

KEELIA AWOKE SLOWLY, STRETCHING HER LIMBS AND fighting wakefulness. No, no, she wasn't ready to wake up. The dream she'd been enjoying was too good to leave behind. In the dream Joryn had been atop her, and the sensations they created were beyond anything she had imagined.

She sighed, and tried to move, and found herself stuck. No, not stuck. *Pinned.* To the ground.

She suffered a moment's panic before she realized how she was pinned. Joryn, apparently still afraid she would run away while he slept, had decided to spend the night with one arm and one heavy leg draped across her body.

The position might not bother her so much if she hadn't been dreaming about him so vividly.

It was very nice, the sensation of his body against hers. She was naked; he wore only those annoying trousers.

His chest and his arms were bare, and they rested against her own bare flesh. His skin was warm, but she found she didn't mind the added warmth. Like the touching, it was nice. It made her feel intimately connected to Joryn, even though he was a Caradon and most definitely not the mate she had waited for.

Having him so close, on the heels of a decidedly passionate dream, made her wonder why she'd waited all these years for her mate to arrive. It wasn't required that she wait for anything or anyone. As Queen, she had numerous privileges others did not. She could order any Anwyn male to fulfill her every desire, and he would have no choice but to obey her. In fact, he would be honored. Privileged. As Queen, she was given everything she wanted, and right now she wanted this Caradon. Her mind and body had been at war for many days, and it appeared that her body had won this particular battle.

She might be a virgin, but it wasn't as if she didn't know what to do. Not only had she suffered the endless instructions on sexual behavior and practices from the priestesses who wished for the palace to be filled with princes and princesses as soon as possible, but she'd experienced sexual relations in her dreams and in those visions which were more real than dreams. Now she wanted the experience to be entirely, utterly, real. Her mate, when he came—if he came—would understand that she was obligated to seek out the pleasure her body demanded.

And her body did demand. Inside, where she wanted Joryn to be, she clenched. There was a new and deep tremble, and an ache . . . a true and deep ache reminiscent of her most ardent heat, though the time was not right for that demand.

No, she would not conceive a child today, but she could and would experience the release she had only dreamed of.

Joryn's eyes opened slowly, as if he instinctively knew she'd awakened. The sharp color of those eyes still startled her, but of late they'd been green in her dreams, so it was not entirely a shock to see them so close and so intensely emerald.

Not wanting to make any missteps in this, her first sexual encounter, Keelia did her best to recall the lessons of the priestesses, lessons she had all but ignored until now. As Queen, she was not only entitled to pleasure, but obligated to follow the commands of her body. As Queen, she embodied the urges of the animal and the needs of a woman. Sex was right and natural and good, and with Joryn's body against hers, Keelia could not recall why she had waited so long for a mate who might never come.

She caught his gaze and held it. As he wore the blasted bracelet, she could not see into his mind, but in truth she didn't need to. There was passion in his eyes, and she could almost find release simply by staring into those eyes and imagining what would happen next.

His hand rested on her bare hip. It stroked there, very gently. Would he be a gentle lover or a frenzied one? Would he arouse her before the act began, or simply roll atop her and enter quickly? In her dreams, in her visions, he had done both, and both were pleasurable. Both were amazing.

While he gave her a sleepy smile, her Caradon cupped one breast in his large hand and teased the sensitive nipple with his thumb. She reeled, catching her breath and instinctively rising so that his hand cupped her breast more firmly. His fingers trailed across her flesh in a familiar way, roughened fingertips trailing across the sensitive flesh of her breasts until Keelia gasped with the pleasure of it and reached out to grab a handful of his long, tangled hair.

His hand descended slowly, raking across her belly and delving gently, very gently, between her legs to stroke her in a way that made her gasp again and lurch, her hips rising to meet the intimate caress of his hand. It was as if her body once again had a mind of its own, as if it knew exactly where and exactly how it needed to be touched. Ribbons of pleasure shot through her body, and her breath would not come correctly. It was lovely, it was exciting . . . but this wasn't what she wanted.

Keelia found her tongue, in spite of the coiled tension that wound through her entire body threatening to steal away all logical thought. "I command you to lie with me," she said, her voice shaking only slightly. Maybe he wouldn't hear that telling tremble. "I want you inside me. Now."

The fire in Joryn's eyes died suddenly. "What?" He ceased stroking her flesh, and he took his hand away.

"I have issued a Royal Directive, which is not subject to question," she said sharply. Why had he *stopped*? "I am in need of physical gratification, and you are the only male present." Her voice sounded much too breathless and needy. She did not want to need anything so desperately. "You do know what to do, don't you? You led me to believe that you were well acquainted with the methods of sexual gratification. Did you mislead me?"

She felt the distance more than saw it. Joryn drew away from her, but his leg remained in place, restraining her. "Am I mistaken, or did you just *order* me to have sex with you?"

Keelia blinked. "Did I do so incorrectly?" In her furor she had forgotten that Joryn didn't obey commands. In fact, he seemed quite put off by them. The priestesses had told her no man would dare to deny her when she issued such an order, but they had never met this maddening Caradon.

Joryn rolled away from her, and she felt suddenly bereft. Empty. Alone.

"No woman orders me to do anything, and where my pecker is concerned, I make my own rules and decisions, thank you very much."

"Your, uh, *pecker,* if that is what I believe it to be, though I have never heard that term before, seems to have made up its mind without you." Keelia rolled up into a sitting position. He was ready for her, she was ready for him, she had issued a decree . . . What was the problem? Why was he walking *away*? "You have pleasured women before, have you not?"

He faced her, not at all embarrassed that his cock was hard and its thrust made his trousers misshapen. "Yes," he snapped. "Many times."

"Do you not enjoy sexual relations?"

"Very much so."

She felt her face grow hot. A Queen should never blush, but she suspected that was the case. "And yet you do not want me."

"I am not one of your subjects, and I will not be ordered to your service. I am not Anwyn, Your Magnificently Naked Majesty."

"I see," she said gently. "I repulse you because I am Anwyn, is that correct? I will admit to having the same reservations about you in past days, but I have been able to overcome my prejudices and . . . and . . ."

"And order me to fuck you," he finished when she stumbled.

"I issued a perfectly acceptable decree. By law, you are obligated to obey."

Joryn gaped at her. "I am not Anwyn," he said once again. "What makes you think I am obligated to satisfy your every whim?"

Keelia pouted. "Not every whim." The moment was ruined, and she was no longer lost in that thrilling, lusty haze that had driven her to issue the command Joryn had ignored. "Just one."

He shook his head. "For someone who's supposed to be able to creep into anyone's head at will, you don't know much about males of any species."

Keelia jumped up and grabbed for her frock, pulling the gown over her head as she walked toward Joryn. "I don't understand. What difference does it make who initiates the sexual contact, as long as both parties are agreeable?" She sighed. "To be honest, I'm no longer sure why I asked."

"You never asked. If you had, we would *not* be talking right now." His eyes narrowed. "Try again, if you'd like. A little begging and—"

"I never beg!" Keelia snapped, mortified at the very idea. "Not for anything."

"I imagine all your life everything you ever wanted was given to you without question."

"Well . . . yes." And he made it sound like a bad thing.

Joryn turned away from her and began to laugh. To *laugh*. She followed him along the pathway that would lead deeper into Caradon Territory, toward the Grandmother he said would offer answers to all their questions.

At the moment, Keelia didn't care about the curse, the Grandmother, the evil they would try to destroy. Time for those worries would come soon enough. She was no longer lost in the passion that had compelled her to order Joryn to lie with her, but there was the principle to consider. He had denied her, and that would not do.

If only she could peek into his mind, just for a few minutes. Her eyes fell to the bracelet that protected him from her powers. One way or another, she was going to have to get that blasted thing off him.

5

HER MAJESTY'S EDICT HAD ENDED JORYN'S INDECI-
sion where she was concerned sexually. Maybe he did
want her, maybe he did dream of her, but that didn't
mean he would be *ordered* to lie with her. Since she was
a virgin, she likely wouldn't be any good as a sexual
partner anyway. He wasn't missing anything by denying
her what she wanted. In fact, the very idea of her needing something he could provide and not getting it gave
him great pleasure of a different sort.

So what did it matter that he was hurting as well?
What did it matter that he was denying himself as well
as her?

They'd marched many miles toward their destination, and made camp on rocky ground near a cliff side
that offered a magnificent view of the hills and valleys
below. It felt as if they were near the top of the world,
alone and safe and without dire responsibilities. Joryn

could look out on the seemingly peaceful scene and almost forget that there was evil at work.

He and the Queen had passed the day with very little conversation between them. They discussed food, drinkable water, when and where to rest . . . and nothing else. It was best that way, but now that they'd stopped for the night, the silence seemed to be a weighty thing that made the center of his spine itch.

He wasn't ready to tell her all that he could do, but since she was powerful in her own way, perhaps she could shed light on some of the mysteries he had faced when he'd last visited the world in-between.

"Do you know of someone named Liane?" he asked.

Keelia's head popped up sharply, and her golden eyes widened. If she tried to deny she knew the name, he would know she was lying. She said she did not lie, but how could he trust such a statement?

"Where did you hear that name?" she asked.

"So, you know it."

"Yes, from a long time ago. I haven't heard that name in many years. Why do you ask about her now?"

She might not lie, but he could. And did. "The Grandmother mentioned it to me before I left her to seek you out . . ."

"Before you left her to *kidnap* me," she corrected sharply.

"Call it what you wish."

"There's no need to deny what we both know to be . . ."

Joryn held up a silencing hand. Keelia's shoulders squared at his insolence, but she did quit speaking. "Truce, remember? Now, tell me what you know of this Liane."

Keelia claimed a place near the cliff's edge, where she could look out on the world Joryn had been studying. She sat, maintaining her queenly air and dignity, not for one moment appearing uncomfortable with nothing but rock as her throne. She wore no crown, and her clothing was dirty and torn. Her hair was slightly tangled, and there was a smudge of dirt on one cheek.

And she still looked very much a Queen.

"Once, when I was visiting with my cousins in the Southern Province of Columbyana, and my mothers and her sisters were having one of their long conversations about times past, my cousins and I overheard a discussion about a woman they called Liane." She looked up at him, and then patted the ground beside her. "Sit and rest. It has been a tiring day for both of us and this is a rather long story."

Joryn sat, so that he could relax and enjoy the view as she did. He was not so close that he could touch her, not without reaching out, and the mood was unexpectedly companionable. Truce, he reminded himself much as he had reminded her.

Keelia spoke for a long while about Emperor Sebestyen and his last empress, Liane, who was the sister of Keelia's Aunt Sophie's husband, Kane Varden. The basics of the story were well known, they were history, but since he was not well versed in Columbyanan history, she told him what he needed to know. Apparently Liane had been kidnapped by Sebestyen's soldiers at a young age and made a concubine, but in her years in Arthes she had risen in the palace hierarchy and finally married the emperor. She'd become his fifth empress, the fifth in a long line of ill-treated wives.

Joryn had never cared for any history but that of the

Caradon, but Keelia told him a tale of rebellion and war, of marriages and betrayal. She told him of a horrid place called Level Thirteen, a place which sounded like a fictional story meant to scare those who misbehave, rather than a true accounting. Still, she told it as true, and he believed her.

"As I said," Keelia continued, "one day a few of my cousins and I came upon my mother and her sisters talking. Since my mother was present and it's impossible to get anything past her for any length of time, we didn't hear much of what they said before being caught, of course," Keelia said, "but I remember hearing the name 'Liane.' Even then, as a child, my psychic abilities were finely tuned and I immediately knew what my cousins did not. I knew that Liane had survived, that she had not been killed as it was believed, and I also knew that she'd given birth to not one child but two. Twin sons. My mother and her sisters knew, too, and they had been protecting Liane and her sons for all those years. I understood that if word spread that they'd survived, they'd be hunted down and killed, so I never said a word about them to anyone."

"You protected them all these years, just as your mother and aunts did."

She shrugged as if it didn't matter, even though there was nobility in such protection. "The children were innocent, and I didn't want to see them harmed. Eventually, I just . . . forgot. I put Liane and her sons in the back of my mind. I hadn't thought about them for years, until you mentioned her name."

The spirit who had grabbed Joryn as he'd been leaving the otherworld . . . he must have been Emperor Sebestyen, and the heirs he spoke of were the children Keelia had protected with her silence. Were they important to the destruction of the evil he and Keelia were fighting together?

Perhaps, but for now he would keep what he knew to himself. He and the Anwyn Queen had reached a truce, yet it was anything but easy and solid. They would not reach the Grandmother's hut for many days, and until he knew more, he saw no reason to tell his partner everything he had learned.

"Think on them if you can," he said. "Perhaps the children you protected with your silence will play a part in this battle."

"Perhaps."

He heard the hesitancy in her voice, and he suspected uncertainty was not normal for the pampered Queen.

"What's wrong?"

She turned and looked at him, her eyes unflinching. "Nothing is as it should be. My gift has been tainted for months. Months, Joryn. I can no longer grasp everything I reach for, and sometimes when I do have a vision, it's wrong. Wrong or impossible to decipher. I am never wrong," she said indignantly.

"Everyone is wrong on occasion."

She looked away from him and sighed. "In making my own personal decisions, yes. I have been mistaken in making decisions for myself, and I suspect that will never end. That is a part of life, one I try to accept. But in reaching for knowledge of what tomorrow holds for another, I should not be wrong. So many of my visions have been unclear, or else I interpret them incorrectly, that I have begun to question everything."

He wondered if she was thinking of her interpretation of the prophesy which said the Red Queen would take a Caradon lover. She had deduced that was a metaphor, not a clear fact, but obviously she wasn't certain.

The sun set and darkness fell, and Joryn built a fire. Not for heat, which neither of them needed, but for light, until they slept. His keen sense of smell and hearing told him no one was near, and they would be undisturbed in the night. Keelia had the same fine senses, so she was not concerned about being attacked either. No, their concerns were of a different sort.

He was drawn to her, even though he had decided that their relationship would remain distant. If she'd asked for sex this morning instead of ordering it to be so, they would be lovers, but they were not, and perhaps it was best that they keep their interactions focused on stopping the Caradon wizard who had cursed his own people.

That didn't mean he couldn't admire her body and her scent, that he couldn't think about what it might be like to lie with her.

Maybe if she begged.

As if that was likely to happen. Keelia was a Queen who was accustomed to having everything she wanted given to her without question. He was a man who could not allow a woman to command anything of him, not even if he wanted the same thing she did.

They ate dried meat and fruit. In a matter of days he would have to start hunting for their sustenance, and that would slow their progress somewhat. The pack he carried wasn't heavy, but it would be impossible to carry enough rations for an indefinite journey. He had no idea what awaited beyond the Grandmother's hut, how long he and Keelia might be traveling companions. When they moved into the forests ahead, game would be easy to catch and cook. Perhaps he'd save the dried food for lean days, or days when they simply did not wish to stop. Neither of them ate much in spite of their arduous trek. Keelia took only a few bites, but she did drink a healthy portion of water. Water would be more important than food in the days to come.

When their brief meal was done, Joryn watched Keelia as she moved away from the edge of the cliff and removed her dress. He should have been accustomed to her nakedness by now, but he was not unaffected. His insides coiled at the sight of her body. His fingers curled and everything in him tightened. He knew what was expected of him, but it was not natural for a man and a woman to be partners in one way, to be constantly together, and yet deny themselves the natural partnership of male to female.

Instead of lying down to sleep, as he had expected she would, Keelia sat cross-legged on the ground and lifted her face to the night sky. Her hands rested on her knees, palms up, and she took a few very even, very deep breaths.

"What are you doing?" he asked, but she didn't respond. It was as if she was no longer aware of his presence.

KEELIA HAD NEVER ATTEMPTED TO PUT HERSELF IN this sort of trance when she was not in her fertile time, but since she had actually been considering ordering Joryn to have sex with her, and he was unlikely to obey, she decided to try. The trance was preferable to begging for what she needed, or being refused and denied in a disturbing way that was new to her. If this fantasy could satisfy her during the heat of her fertile days, it could certainly handle and dismiss the annoying sexual attraction she suffered.

He is not my mate, she reminded herself. *I am just beyond my time for taking a lover and I'm confused by the disruption of energy in the world.* It was that simple.

She breathed deeply, and very quickly isolated herself from all reality. The world she created, the green meadow where she had nothing to concern her but love and passion, was her reality for now. She inhaled a recent rain on the green grass, smelled and heard the water that ran nearby in a clean, clear brook. The sun was shining, and there was no evil in the world. Not in this perfect world of her own making.

Smiling, Joryn laid her back in the grass. He had rid himself of those annoying trousers and boots, and wore nothing but the silver bracelet. Nothing at all. At the moment she didn't care that she could not read his thoughts. His thoughts did not concern her.

He started where he had stopped so abruptly and rudely that very morning. A hand stroked her breast, teasing the nipple. Another hand stroked between her legs, arousing and promising. Keelia's back arched against her soft grass bed. She closed her eyes and enjoyed the sensations that shot through her, thanks to Joryn's touch.

It was rather like swimming in a pond slightly warmed by the sun. The sensation was similar to the wash of water against her skin, the pleasure of ripples against her flesh and even beneath her flesh. She thought it could be no more pleasurable, and then Joryn lowered his head to take a sensitive nipple into his mouth. She caught her hand in his hair, winding the long strands through her fingers and holding him there.

"Harder," she commanded, and he obeyed.

A moment later, "Softer." Again, he did as she asked.

She ran her hands down his body, testing the angles and muscles of his form, arousing him as he aroused her. He quivered beneath her touch, and then he rose up just enough to offer her his throat.

Keelia had craved the taste of Joryn's throat for so long that she all but attacked it. She kissed and licked and then bit . . . very gently, of course. Like her, he healed quickly, so even when she drew a small bit of blood, blood that now marked him as hers, no sign of her attentions remained on his skin.

This encounter was like so many others she had created in her mind, but it was also very different. She knew the true scent of Joryn now, as she knew the true touch of his hands on her body. It was more intense than she had imagined, more real and right.

Her heart and the very core of her body pounded and then screamed as she spiraled out of control.

Keelia caught Joryn's hair in her hands and forced him to look her in the eye. Green to gold, male to female, soul to soul. "I command you to join with me, Joryn."

As this was her world, he did not protest. Instead he smiled again, wickedly so, and stroked her thighs as he spread her legs wide and entered her body, just as she had commanded. He moved slowly at first, not entering her fully but teasing her. Bringing her to the brink of release and then backing away. Her hips moved with and against his, gently at first, and then more insistently. At her urging he moved faster and deeper, until she raised her hips up off the soft grassy bed and he buried himself deep.

Her release was like no other. Harder, fiercer. It came wave upon wave, until she had no choice but to scream, in pleasure and relief and joy. Her body lurched and trembled, and as her own orgasm faded, she felt Joryn's release.

And then he settled his head on her shoulder, and whispered something in her ear. Soft words. Sweet words. Words she could not quite understand. At the moment, she didn't care. The lightning they created had satisfied her yearnings, and she was satiated. Happy. Content.

She sighed and opened her eyes to reality to find Joryn watching her intently. "Are you all right?" he asked.

Keelia smiled widely. "Yes, I'm very fine, thank you. Very fine."

"What happened?" His expression was puzzled. "You didn't move for a long time, and then you . . . your body jerked a little bit." He swallowed hard, judging by the workings of his throat.

"Did it?"

"Yes."

"Hmmm." Keelia lay back and closed her eyes, quickly headed toward sleep.

"Are you ill?" he asked.

"Not at all."

"Then what . . ."

"Good night, Joryn."

He mumbled something beneath his breath. From the tone she suspected his words were not, "Sleep well."

* * *

HE HAD NEVER SEEN THE ANWYN QUEEN SO BLASTED happy. She'd slept soundly, and awakened with a smile on her face. Not once all morning had she ordered him to do anything at all. Once he was almost certain he heard her humming a cheerful tune.

It was decidedly odd.

By late morning they'd moved into a wooded portion of the mountain, taking a well-worn path that led them upward. The shade was nice, and he liked the scent of the forest. He had begun to sense and smell that more of his people had passed this way recently, perhaps on this very pathway. That was not unusual, as they were moving deeper into Caradon Territory very quickly. Five more days, at this rate, perhaps six, without running into trouble, and they would reach the Grandmother. And then what? He would have to rely on the Grandmother to tell him what came next.

He knew that Keelia sensed the Caradon presence as well, by the way she studied the paths and the woodland darkness with such care and wrinkled her nose on occasion. She smelled the native people of this land as he did, but to her it was not a familiar or pleasant scent.

And still, her odd cheerfulness lasted until they came upon the pitiful creature by the stream, where they'd stopped to drink and bathe.

Joryn immediately and instinctively placed himself between the creature and the Queen, drawing his knife and holding it ready. He wasn't sure what good, if any, the short blade would do against the mutant who looked as if its transformation from cat to man had been halted. There were tufts of hair and patches of skin, a misshapen snout, and almost human eyes near catlike ears. The body was stooped and malformed, but the muscles seemed sturdy enough. The arms were more human than animal, but the claws at the ends of those arms were sharp.

Fire was available at a flicking of his fingers, if the blade was not enough as a weapon, and Joryn was ready to call upon that fire. He lifted the hand which did not hold the dagger, ready to use his gift, but a gentle hand on his arm stilled him.

"Wait," Keelia whispered as she came to stand beside him. "I don't think he means us any harm."

He or *it*? To Joryn, the creature seemed much more like a thing than a Caradon or a man.

"Look at the eyes," Keelia said gently. "He is not one who has chosen evil. There is no talisman around his neck, and I do not detect anger, only . . . pain. Such horrible pain."

Keelia made a move as if she intended to approach the mutant, but Joryn stopped her with a firm hand. "Do not move closer. Any creature in great pain is capable of lashing out."

She obeyed his order, and stopped her approach. But she did not return to her place of safety behind him. She directed her words to the creature. "You were bitten," she said.

The creature tried to speak, but could only make a pitiful sound that was somewhere between man and animal. Finally it nodded once.

"I'm sorry. I'm so sorry." Keelia sounded truly sympathetic. Still, Joryn half expected the Queen to command the creature to complete its transformation and move on, but apparently she saved her directives for him.

The creature by the stream lifted its claws and pointed at Keelia. This time it struggled to make near-word sounds. "Thy. Ah. Mo."

Keelia took a step toward the creature, in spite of Joryn's warnings. "Please, again?"

"Thy. Ah. Mo." Each word was half-growl, half-word.

Joryn sniffed the air. Someone was coming.

Keelia lifted a hand to her forehead. "Think your words *here*. Direct them to me, if you can."

The green-eyed mutant nodded his head quickly, closed his eyes, and then said again as he concentrated, "*Thy. Ah. Mo.*"

Keelia spun around quickly, her eyes widening. "There are more."

Five mutants, much like the one they had found by the stream and yet distinctively different in their fury, burst from the woods and effectively surrounded Joryn and his Red Queen. It was the first time he had been so close to the monstrosities bent on violence, and for a moment his heart stopped. They were so unnatural, so horribly wrong.

There was no time for dwelling on the horror. Joryn drew Keelia close to him and surrounded them with a circle of fire. The flames, which quickly grew high and powerful, might scare the creatures away. Many wild creatures were afraid of fire, and these things might be no different. He still needed the Anwyn Queen to end this horror, and even if all else failed, he had to protect her.

The creatures moved closer, not at all intimidated by

the fire. One of them stuck a misshapen claw into the flame, and twisted its mouth in what had to be an attempt at a grin,

"We can fight them," Keelia said in a lowered voice.

"We?" They would eat her alive. They would tear her apart.

"We. Truce, remember? Anwyn and Caradon fighting together." She looked up at him. "It starts here."

The first beast leapt through the wall of fire, and Joryn placed himself between the creature and Keelia. A blast of fire blinded the creature for a moment, giving Joryn time to thrust his knife into the chest where a heart should be. The mutant fell.

Another had already entered the circle of flame, and Keelia faced it bravely. Her arms were transformed, her claws ready. The sight of those claws took the creature by surprise, long enough for Keelia to swipe out and open its throat. It fell to the ground without ever touching her.

She was not only strong; she was fast, much faster than he had imagined was possible. The hideous beasts were frightening in their deformity and their rage, but Keelia displayed no fear as she fought. The second beast she faced was prepared for her claws, so the fight was not as simple as the first. Joryn wanted to assist her, but he had his own attacker to battle. The creature was not afraid of fire, and it took several attempts to harm the tough monster.

That's what these things were, Joryn decided. Once Caradon or not, they were now monsters who needed to be destroyed if they could not be saved. He had put three down, Keelia had defeated two. As it seemed that the battle was done, her arms became a woman's soft, seemingly gentle arms once again, and she took a long, deep breath that spoke of relief. Joryn allowed the wall of fire to die.

The last thing he wanted or needed was this grudging admiration for the Anwyn Queen. But she fought well; she did not demur or wail in the face of danger, not even when that danger arrived in the form of decidedly unpleasant monstrosities. Perhaps she was accustomed to getting her own way, perhaps she did think she was entitled to command all that she desired, but she was not entirely spoiled and useless. Admiring her bravery and her willingness to fight made her even more attractive. Had he ever wanted a woman more?

They believed that the battle was over, that they were safe at last, and then the creature by the stream, the one which was apparently harmless, rushed toward them, screaming a ghastly, ear-splitting shriek.

Joryn turned and grabbed Keelia, trying to move her out of the creature's way as the beast hurled itself into the air and intercepted a sixth attacker who leapt from the woods.

The two beasts wrestled, rolling across the ground just a few feet away as they bit and slashed. Deformed claws lashed out, grappled, and drew blood. Teeth were bared and used with vehemence until the gentle creature fell still, his throat bleeding and his heart ripped out of his chest.

The monster that had appeared last, the one which had killed the gentler creature, immediately sprang toward Joryn. The thing was female, smaller than the others but just as deadly, as was evidenced by the dead mutant on the ground. Keelia's claws appeared and Joryn readied a ball of fire, which might at least slow the beast's progress. At the last moment the monster shifted course and came in low, burying her teeth in Joryn's leg just above his boot.

It happened quickly. Tearing through his trousers with sharp teeth had been no problem for the thing, and she chomped down with vigor and even joy. Joryn felt the venom enter his blood. It burned as it spread, moving into his veins too fast for him to think that he might be able to stop the infection.

For a moment he froze, realizing his fate was sealed, knowing that on the rise of the next full moon he would become like them. A monster. A thing which should not exist.

It was Keelia who grabbed the creature by the ears and yanked its ugly mouth away from his body. Her strength surprised the thing, and they took advantage of that disbelief. Before it had a chance to turn on the woman who had pulled it away from its prey, Joryn sliced his dagger blade across the monster's throat.

The female monster didn't die instantly, but instead dropped to the ground and twitched a few times before falling still.

Suddenly all was quiet in the once peaceful clearing. Joryn didn't move. Keelia stared down at his bleeding, infected leg, as motionless as he. Blood soaked his trousers and the top of his boot, making clear that he'd been well and deeply bitten.

"We can fix this, can't we?" she said, her words quick and low. "Your Grandmother, *the* Grandmother, she can fashion a spell or a potion or *something* that will stop—"

"No," he interrupted sharply. "If she could bring an end to this madness alone, she would not have sent me to fetch you."

"Kidnap," she corrected without her usual fervor. "You kidnapped me."

He hadn't thought the Anwyn Queen capable of shedding tears for a Caradon, but as she stared at his wound, tears dripped down her delicate, pale cheeks.

6

"It's not too bad," Keelia said, her voice quick and a touch too high-pitched. "Maybe you aren't infected. It's possible that the spreading of the disease only happens in some instances, not all. Maybe . . ."

"I can feel it," Joryn said as he sat down by the stream and rolled up his trouser leg to expose the break in his skin. Like her, he would heal quickly. Of course, it wasn't the external wound that concerned her, but the poison that was rushing through his bloodstream at this moment, dooming him to become, on the rise of the next full moon, like the repulsive creatures who had attacked.

Shaking, Keelia sat beside the wounded Caradon. It was the battle that affected her so deeply that tears welled up in her eyes and her entire body trembled. She had been trained in defense, of course, but she had never participated in an actual battle before today. *That* was the reason for her pounding heart and the heated rise of emotion, not Joryn's injury or the fact—no, the *possibility*—that he would turn into one of the cursed creatures in a few short weeks. He was Caradon, after all, and he'd kidnapped her. He was an insufferable enemy, an insolent man, and she could not suffer this pain on his account.

It was the dreams and visions which made her think of him more fondly than she should, and those fantasies were not real. If he became a monster, it was not her concern. True, their partnership would have to be severed if he became evil and twisted, but . . .

"I want you to kill me before I turn into one of those things," Joryn said, his voice calm and certain. "I will try to accomplish all that we must do before the next full moon, but if I don't . . ."

"I will not kill you," Keelia blurted, before she thought to curb her emotion. Like it or not, she did care. Whether the emotion was real or a product of fantasy didn't seem to make any difference. She *did* care. "What if you are not affected? We don't know everything about this curse, and if it's possible that you are not affected, then it would be foolish of me to kill you before your tasks have been completed." Best to make it sound as if she cared only for their mission, not for him personally.

"At least promise me that you'll kill me if I *do* turn into one of those things."

Keelia pursed her lips. She should not even hesitate, but her heart clenched. It was a connection created in her own mind, she knew, that made her feel more for this enemy than she should. As genuine as the visions seemed, those images of love were not real. They were fantasy. They were illusion.

Besides, she would not want to survive if she were cursed in such a way, so she understood his request. "All right," she said gently. "If you become like them and there is no other choice, I will take your life."

He looked down at her. "Swear it."

Again, she hesitated. Taking the lives of the attackers had given her no pause, not then or now, but where Joryn was concerned . . . she reminded herself of who and what he was, and nodded her head crisply. "I swear it."

He was visibly relieved.

"If you would remove that bracelet you wear," she said innocently, "perhaps I could see into your future and tell you whether or not you will be infected."

"That would be a useless exercise. I know I have been—"

"Oh, you don't *know* anything," she snapped. "This is a new and unheard-of corruption of the body and soul. How can we say with any certainty that everyone who's bitten will become like them?"

"The Grandmother said it was true."

"Did the Grandmother see that you would be bitten?"

"No," Joryn answered crisply.

"Then she is not without flaw in her divination."

Joryn twisted the wide bracelet on his wrist, but did not remove it. "Why was the first creature we encountered different from the others?" he asked. "He was not evil, he even assisted us in the fight and paid with his life, such as it was. Why was he not a member of the pack that ambushed us?"

Keelia glanced back at the bodies which littered the landscape, her eyes landing on the beast in question. If she were to be killed while she was a wolf, she would soon shift to her human form. The same was true of all Anwyn, and Caradon as well. These beasts did not shift; they remained twisted and unnatural in death as they had been in life. She took a deep breath and reached for the knowledge she needed. Some she already knew, just from the moments she had spent speaking to the creature, but she wanted—needed—more.

"The curse doesn't just twist their bodies, it takes their very souls. A darkness rises up from the ground . . ." She shuddered. What she sensed was very much like her dreams of the atrocities that were taking place among humans, in the lands below her mountain home. "It rises up and takes their souls. Some few, like the first beast we met here, fight for their souls. They cling to their spirits and deny the demon what he intends to steal and feed upon. It isn't easy, and the battle is constant, so they are in great pain and eventually they know they will lose. That's why they jump off cliffs or cut their own throats, or . . ."

"Or throw themselves into a battle which they know they cannot win."

"Yes," Keelia answered softly.

She did not like the worry that welled up inside her. Again she reminded herself that Joryn was Caradon, and that he had disabled her and snatched her from her home and mocked her and refused her and . . . and he was fighting for his people, in the same way she would fight for hers.

"Our plans must change," she said in a crisp and authoritative tone of voice. "Instead of wasting time going to see your witch for more information, we need to find the Caradon wizard who is behind this curse as soon as is possible. Once the stone I saw in my vision is destroyed, the curse will be ended. I'm not sure what will happen to those who have already been transformed. The ones who have been able to fight for their souls might return to their normal selves. Those who have lost their souls"—she shuddered at the very thought of such an unnatural tragedy—"I don't know what will happen to them. Their souls have been taken. Maybe they'll be returned when the curse is ended, but it's possible those souls are simply . . . gone." She turned her mind to what she *did* know. "If we can destroy that stone, I'm certain that you, and any others who've been bitten since the last full moon, won't suffer the change on the next full moon."

"What if the Grandmother can lead us to this wizard?" Joryn asked.

"What if she *can't*, and we waste precious days which we cannot afford to waste?" She looked again at the wide silver bracelet on his wrist. "I can't see everything, not from here, but if you would remove that enchanted bracelet and allow me to reach for what is meant for you in the days and weeks to come, then—"

"What if I don't want you peeking into my head?" he snapped.

"You would rather become like them than let me help you?" She did not look at the bodies behind her, but she jutted one finger in that direction. "That doesn't seem to be a very smart decision, and until now it never occurred to me that you were stupid. Stubborn, insubordinate, bad-mannered, and immoral, yes. But not stupid."

He didn't make a move, and Keelia finally lost her temper. "I demand that you remove that bracelet immediately." Her hand shot out and she clamped her fingers over the enchanted silver. She wanted to know if the man who had kidnapped her would change, like the monsters they had slain. She wanted to know if he would be in terrible pain, if he would fight for his soul until his last breath. She wanted to know if they would find the blasted Caradon wizard and undo his dark work before it was too late.

Joryn's hand clamped over hers. "You're very fast," he said.

"When I need to be."

Once again, his eyes caught and held hers, and she was reminded of her dreams. "You could've escaped any number of times, once you were out of your prison cell."

She swallowed hard. "I gave my word, and whether I like it or not, I do believe that you and I are meant to work together."

"Work," he whispered.

"Yes, work."

With some hesitation, he removed his hand from hers. "Take it, then. Take the bracelet, and tell me what you see."

With caution, Keelia worked the silver band up and off Joryn's thick, muscled wrist. For the first time, she was afraid of what she might see. What if she learned that he was her mate, the one she had waited for all her life? What if she saw that he was meant to become a monster like those they had battled, forever cursed?

What if she saw that her dreams and visions were meant to become real?

The end of the bracelet snagged on his arm, and then came free. Keelia waited for a rush of knowledge, but nothing happened. Of course, she continued to hold the enchanted piece that protected his mind. She dropped the bracelet to the ground, expecting something to come to her. Again, all was silent. Dark. So quiet.

In desperation, she reached out and grasped Joryn's wrist in her small hand, her fingers taking the place of the bracelet. Even though her gift had been dampened, she should feel something. A wave of emotion, a glimpse of the future, a vision of his past. Her fingers tightened and she closed her eyes.

Nothing.

JUDGING BY THE EXPRESSION ON HER FACE, THE NEWS wasn't good. Joryn began to think he'd be better off not knowing what the future held.

Keelia's grip on his wrist tightened until it was almost painful. For a little thing, she was surprisingly strong. She could've put up an impressive fight at any time along the way, but she hadn't. Was she truly honoring her part of the truce, as she'd said? The Anwyn were annoyingly straitlaced and law-abiding in many ways, so that was possible.

Finally she yanked her hand away as if she had been burned by his skin, and turned her attention to the stream before them. She apparently found the rush of water fascinating, the way she stared at the rivulets dancing over stone. Her jaw was tighter than usual, her lips slightly thinned.

"Well?" he prompted.

"I believe you are still tainted by the bracelet's protection. The magic apparently has a lingering affect."

"What does that mean? You're not seeing clearly?"

"I'm not seeing *anything*," she snapped.

"Oh." He leaned back, propping up on his elbows in a deceptively casual pose. "Does that happen often?"

"It actually never happens," she said. She screwed up her mouth in a way that told him she wasn't sharing everything. "As I told you, my gift has been affected in some way in months past, but I can always see something of a person when I attempt to do so." Again, she pursed her lips in evident frustration.

"But . . ." he drawled, prompting her to go on.

Her chin came up, and her spine stiffened. "When my mother and father first met, she couldn't see into him the way she did other people." She spoke without emotion, even though a muscle in her jaw twitched. "He was able to block her ability to see his thoughts. Mother said it was a part of their connection, a sign of their destiny to be mated. He had to give himself to her freely, body, soul, and mind. He could not be subjected to an intrusion against his will."

"I don't understand." What did her parents have to do with this?

"Neither do I, entirely. It's really not . . . possible."

"What's not possible?"

She sighed and turned to look at him, her eyes narrowing slightly. "Over the years my mother speculated that when my mate did show himself to me, I would not be able to read his thoughts, as I do others. She suggested that in that way I might know who my mate is, if I don't sense him in the normal way." She squirmed, a little. "I . . . I don't sense anything of you, and that does make me wonder . . ."

Joryn almost forgot about his wound, and his fate. "I'm not anyone's mate for life. The Caradon don't live that way."

"I know that," Keelia said sharply. "Do you think I want to consider the possibility that my mate is a *Caradon*? Prophesy or no prophesy, it is entirely unacceptable."

"Maybe we're worrying about nothing, and the problem is a lingering magic from the bracelet the Grandmother made for me."

"Maybe," she said, her voice slightly less strident. "When were you born?"

"What difference does it make?"

"Anwyn mates are born on the same day, or very close to it. They come into the world intended for one another. So, when were you born?"

"Early summer, twenty-five years ago."

She sighed. "Me, too."

Joryn leapt to his feet. "This is ridiculous. I'm not meant to be bound to any one woman, least of all an overbearing Anwyn *Queen* who is quite comfortable when it comes to issuing commands."

"Surely some of your people form lifelong bonds. They're not all vagabonds who spend their lives unconnected and wild and alone. Are they?"

She seemed horrified by the prospect of living life alone, when in truth it was all Joryn had ever wanted. What he perceived as freedom, she apparently saw as loneliness. What he wanted most, she feared.

"A few Caradon do choose lifelong bonds," he explained. "Some of them even marry, but what you're speaking of requires no choice at all. It's more barbaric than any custom of my people."

"To mate for life is not barbaric! It's beautiful and special and right."

Suddenly he understood why she was so upset. "You

have not yet found this thing that's beautiful and special and right, so when you can't see my thoughts, you mistakenly assume—"

"It's more than that." She ticked the reasons off on her slender fingers. "You kidnapped me. That is the Anwyn way, as I imagine you know. I dreamed of you long before we met, and you dreamed of me. Don't deny it, you already told me so. Remember the mole?"

Yes, he remembered vividly.

She continued with her reasoning. "We were born at the same time, or close to it, and I can't see anything of you or your future even without the enchanted bracelet on your wrist. All that together with the prophesy of the Red Queen and the Caradon makes it all quite clear, whether I like it or not."

He leaned down so his face was close to hers. "I am not mated to anyone, nor will I ever be."

Her lips pursed, and then trembled. "Fine," she said crisply. "You'll probably be dead in a few weeks anyway, so I don't know why I bothered to mention my suppositions. Maybe I am wrong. I hope I'm wrong, and when this calling is over, I can go home and discover my true mate, who will be Anwyn, not Caradon, and who will enjoy the idea of bedding me and becoming my King. I don't *want* it to be you," she insisted, "but I felt obligated to mention the possibility since there are so many oddities here."

"When the magic wears off, you'll be able to read my mind, and then we'll know that you're wrong."

"I certainly hope so."

She turned and walked to the bodies of the mutant Caradon. After hesitating for a long moment, she dropped down and touched one bloody, hairy claw. Her eyes drifted closed, and she took a long, deep breath.

"If we go to the Grandmother, we will be too late to stop the wizard before the next full moon. We cannot afford to go out of our way to ask for her guidance." Her eyes remained closed. "It's not just you we have to save, Joryn. Many more will be bitten between now and then. Many more will be afflicted if we don't find that stone and destroy it."

She saw all this through the dead beast, and yet she saw nothing at all from him. Odd, but obviously explained by the bracelet. "Where is he? Where is the wizard?"

Without standing, without opening her eyes, Keelia lifted one fine, delicate—and very strong—hand and pointed. East, not north, which was the direction they had been traveling in order to reach the Grandmother's hut.

"I told the Grandmother . . ."

Keelia shot up quickly, and with grace. "You would prefer death to disobeying an old witch who claims to see what's meant to be but did not see *this*?" She pointed to Joryn's wounded leg. "You would prefer to become a soulless monster than to change your plans and make an old woman *wait*?"

"I thought you said I might not be infected," he said calmly.

"Of course you're infected! I tried to convince you *and* myself that it might not be so, but what these monsters spread is vile and poisonous and it spares no one."

He had no powers like her own, but he instinctively knew what she spoke to be the truth. In this instance, at least. The part about him possibly being her mate was ludicrous. Even if he had dreamed about her; even if watching her tremble and twitch in her naked trance last night had made him hard and had almost sent him into her arms.

"The Grandmother can wait," he said. "We will search for this wizard you have seen."

She sighed, obviously relieved.

"But don't forget what you promised. You won't let me become like them."

"I won't," she said, her voice gentling.

As Joryn collected the bracelet Keelia had set aside and dropped it in his sack, he wondered if he could trust the promise of the Anwyn Queen. She said she did not lie, but in this case would she hold out hope until it was too late? If he lost his soul, became a twisted monster and retained his gift for fire, he would quickly do more damage than these beasts had done in the months of their rampage. If he opened a door to the world in-between and let the evil from this world in, chaos would follow. Quickly and decisively.

Would he have the strength to kill himself, if Keelia could not or would not? He looked at the dead monsters on the ground, and imagined himself in that state. That thought alone should be enough to give him the strength he needed.

IN THE COURTYARD OF THE HEADQUARTERS OF THE Circle of Bacwyr, the newly appointed Prince of Swords, Lyr Hern, trained for a battle that might never come. With the exception of a few minor clan rivalries, the country of Tryfyn had been at peace for many years. His father had told him many times—and told him still—that while peace was lovely it was no excuse for laziness. A defeat many years ago had cost the Circle their legendary strength, and such a misfortune could not be allowed to occur again. All the Circle warriors trained daily at swordplay and hand to hand combat, but none was more dutiful than Lyr.

The new sword was magnificent. Lightweight and amazingly sharp, it quickly became an extension of Lyr's arm as he exercised in the yard that had been designed for this purpose. The grip was plain, but the balance was perfection. He felt as if he could wield this particular sword with two fingers if it became necessary.

Straw-filled enemies surrounded Lyr, and he practiced making the cuts of a certain depth, or placing them on a particular spot in the lumpy body, and even carving designs in the cloth. There was an exhilaration in wielding such a fine weapon, and true joy washed through him.

The only thing that was capable of making him halt his practice session was his mother's shocked voice.

"What have you done to your hair?"

Lyr stopped and faced his mother, grinning as he lifted a hand to the newly shortened strands. When last he'd practiced with his second in command, the stocky, bald Segyn, the man had grasped his braid in one fist and—for a moment—gotten the upper hand. Later Segyn had laughed and proclaimed his baldness an asset in battle.

Lyr was not bald by any means, but he no longer had nearly enough dark hair to braid. "I cut it."

"You cut it off," she said as she strode forward. "All of it."

"Most," he said as he lowered his hand and the new sword. "Not all."

His mother, Isadora Fyne Hern, was a powerful witch called the Star of Bacwyr by those in the Circle. To them, she was a powerful leader and advisor. To Lyr and his two younger sisters, she was simply an overprotective mother. She tsked as she moved close.

"You had such lovely hair," she said with a sigh, running her fingers over the short strands as if she could not believe what she saw.

"It's not proper for the Prince of Swords to be petted by his mum in the practice yard. People are watching, I imagine." His sessions usually drew a crowd, whether he sparred with a live soldier or a straw-filled dummy. He didn't understand why anyone would care to watch him prepare for a battle that might never come, but he had been told he was entertaining to observe.

Even when he didn't call on his magic of shifting time.

His mother dropped her hand. "Your cousin Duran is here, and he has a sealed missive from the emperor of Columbyana. He refuses to give it to anyone but you." She seemed annoyed by that, and he imagined she had offered to deliver the message to her son herself and been refused.

"We should arrange a banquet for this evening," Lyr suggested. "We haven't seen Duran in a long time."

"The plans are already under way." She took his arm and led him from the practice yard. "Now, let's go see what that message is about, shall we?" They stepped into the building which now housed his family as well as many high-placed members of the Circle of Bacwyr. When Isadora Hern had come here as a bride, twenty-five years ago, the Circle had been primarily housed in a series of caves. That had not been acceptable to the bride, and she'd quickly gotten the construction of these headquarters under way. As they walked down a long, wide corridor, she tsked again.

"Your *hair*."

KEELIA WONDERED WHAT SHE WOULD'VE DONE IF JOryn had insisted that they continue on their path to the cabin of the Caradon witch he called Grandmother. She knew, as well as she knew anything, that there was no time to waste when it came to stopping this madness.

Fortunately he had seen the wisdom of her suggestion, and they traveled a different path away from the stream. They would stop less often for rest, sleeping in shifts and for short snatches of time. From here on out they had no choice but to trust one another. They were truly comrades. Partners. *Mates*?

He refused to believe that was possible, and she wanted to agree with him wholeheartedly. But there were too many facts which hinted otherwise.

What if, against all reason, the Caradon kidnapper truly was her mate? Not simply the lover the prophesy had named, but her actual lifelong mate. What if he was the one she'd been waiting for? If something didn't happen quickly, she would be forced to kill him before she knew with certainty. Was she meant to live her life alone, without that which she craved most?

They remained on a narrow wooded path throughout the afternoon and into the night, and she sensed no malevolent presence. No presence at all. There was no recent scent of Caradon on this trail, other than Joryn's, and his scent was different from the others. She had come to know it well. While the Caradon scent she had caught on the trail this morning had put her on edge, Joryn's seemed more pleasant. More . . . hers.

Last night's trance should've satisfied her for at least a few days, but at the moment she didn't feel at all satisfied. What if Joryn was her mate, and they only had these few days together?

It didn't matter. He had made it very clear that he didn't want her in that way . . . or in any other way. He had been truly horrified at her suggestion that they might be mates for life, even if his life was destined to last only until the next full moon. She would never forget the expression on his face when she'd voiced her concerns.

He wanted no bonds, no connection that went to the heart and soul. His freedom was important to him, and he was clearly horrified by the Anwyn traditions. Love, commitment, forever. Why did he think of those as unwelcome burdens instead of heavenly gifts?

Keelia knew she could play his game and beg him to make love to her, as he had suggested, and she could pretend that what she wanted went no deeper than the sexual connection to which he assigned so little importance. But that would be a lie of the worst sort, a lie of the heart.

She saw well enough in the dark, and when she looked back, her gaze dropped to Joryn's wounded leg to study it with genuine concern. He'd left that trouser leg rolled up, so she could see that the bite mark was already healing—at least on the outside. "Do you need to rest?"

"No. Not yet."

She wished she could see inside him to know if he was truly well or if he was hiding his pain in the name of making progress. Even though he no longer wore the silver bracelet, his thoughts were dark to her. He did still carry it in his pack. Was that enough to keep all knowledge of him from her?

"There's water up ahead," she said. "Not much further. Perhaps we should stop there for a while."

His eyebrows arched in surprise. "You've been this way . . . ?" He stopped abruptly. "No, you just know what's ahead, is that it?"

"I know some of what's ahead." Not all. Not anywhere close to all.

"When we come to water, we'll rest but not for long."

He was as anxious to find the Caradon wizard as she was.

As they trudged forward, she tried to imagine taking Joryn's life if they could not stop the curse in time. She would rather be dead than be turned into a monster so she understood his request, but still . . . could she take his life? Could she continue to dream about lying beneath him, about hearing him laugh, and then, if time ran out and they didn't destroy the stone, kill him? How would she accomplish the task? With her claws or his dagger or some other weapon which she did not yet possess? She tried to imagine . . . and could not.

They came upon a small pool of water, and not very far away from that pool was a flat, grassy area that would serve well enough as a place for them to rest. They would sleep one at a time from here on out. Monsters were out there, and even though they didn't smell or sense that the beasts were near, that didn't mean the things couldn't move near very quickly.

"You sleep first," Joryn said.

"I'm not all that tired, and you're injured," Keelia

argued. "Why don't you go ahead and rest while I keep watch?"

He looked at her oddly, and almost smiled. "You didn't issue a command that I sleep first. You sound almost reasonable, and very unqueenly."

She could take offense, but chose not to. "I'm trying to compromise. I'm trying to approach this venture as your partner, not your Queen."

"You're not *my* Queen."

"As I am very well aware." She had to admit, while the words had initially annoyed her, she did wish Joryn would call her "My Red Queen" just once more. "Are you trying to start an argument? You seem very irritable tonight."

"I was bitten, which gives me the right to be irritable."

"I suppose it does," she agreed.

He crossed the distance between them and placed a hand on her cheek. It was an easy hand, and the touch was gentle. That caress, simple as it was, reminded Keelia of her visions, and she wanted what she dreamed of to come true. She was tired of living in her head, of experiencing life and love in a pristine world of her own making, instead of in the real world where it came with complications and uncertainties. She had planned to visit that alternate world again tonight, to ease the pain of not having what she wanted, but suddenly that illusion of love seemed cold and lonely. She wanted more. She wanted all the complications that came with having a real and true lover.

"Truth be told," Joryn said, "I don't think I can sleep. Not for a while, at least. Would you mind if I took the first watch?"

"Not at all," she whispered. "Wake me when you're ready to rest. Don't let me sleep too long."

"I won't."

He dropped his hand, and she drew her gown over her head. As the once fine frock was all the clothing she possessed at the moment, she needed to preserve it as much as possible. Besides, the night air was warm enough. She was very well aware of Joryn's gaze on her body as she lowered herself to the ground, and she wished once again for a peek into his mind.

Joryn swore he would never take a mate, but did he long, deep down, for more than fleeting relationships that were doomed from the beginning? Did he ever, in the deepest part of his heart, long for that which he did not think he was meant to have?

No matter how diligently she tried to see into Joryn's mind, all remained inaccessible. Dark.

Complicated.

THE LIGHT RAIN THAT HAD BEEN FALLING HALF THE day hadn't slowed Ariana and Sian's travel, but it did mean they pitched a tent when it was time to make camp for the night. A few of the Anwyn soldiers pitched tents, too, but those who were on watch didn't seem to be bothered by the gentle shower.

Under the protective canvas of their shelter, Sian cast a circle of wizard's light. Ariana studied the Prophesy of the Firstborn by that light, searching for a clue she might've missed. The majority of the body of the document was clear to her, except for the phrase *One will find and wield the crystal dagger. One will betray love in the name of victory.* The more she thought on it, the more sure she was that Lyr was meant to wield the dagger. Not only was he Prince of Swords and therefore gifted with blades of all sorts, he was also staunchly noble. She could not see Lyr betraying anyone or anything.

The writings in the margins were even less precise than the body of the prophesy. The drawings were almost maddening, and in one margin there was written, *Those who are called must choose between love and death, between heart and intellect, between victory of the sword and victory of the soul.*

Ariana had chosen between life and death when she'd had to decide in an instant whether to return to Sian and the battle or rest easy in the Land of the Dead. Sian said he'd been offered a similar choice when she'd asked him to take her life if Diella rose up and claimed possession of her body.

What of the others? What of Lyr and Keelia? They had been called just as she had, though they didn't yet know of the prophesy Sian's grandfather had written on his deathbed. For Ariana, the decision had been an easy one. Sian proclaimed he'd faced no real choice at all, that he would not have killed her even if doing so would've saved the world. Realizing how detached Keelia could be, Ariana wondered if the choice of the soul, the choice of love, would come as easily for the Queen. And Lyr . . . Lyr was so young, and he was a soldier who would be naturally inclined to choose the sword.

Ariana had realized that the growth of love in this world made the demon weaker, that the might of that powerful energy sapped the Isen Demon's strength. Her cousins wouldn't understand that fact. Not yet. Not until she had the chance to speak to them, face-to-face.

"Your grandfather should've been more specific."

Sian wrapped a protective arm around her. "My grandfather wasn't *specific* when he was well, and he was quite ill when he penned this prophesy."

His arm was warm, his body close to hers was comforting in a time when comfort was treasured.

"I just wish I knew . . ."

Sian rolled up the paper she'd been studying and moved it out of her reach. Though she was tempted, she did not try to snatch it back.

"We are not meant to know," he said logically and with a maddening calmness. "Not yet."

The rain increased and pattered more loudly against the tent above their heads, making Ariana glad for the shelter. And for the privacy. "I could not do this without you," she said, dismissing her worry for a moment. Or two.

The wizard's light extinguished, Sian's lips met hers, and Ariana gladly put war, demons, and her cousins from her mind.

7

THE BITE ON JORYN'S LEG HEALED QUICKLY, AS WAS
usual, but he could almost feel the poison in his blood. It
did not weaken or sicken him, but still . . . he sensed the
wrongness of the venom.

As they traveled, Keelia chattered often, in a way she
had not in the time he'd known her. She spoke about her
family—parents, brothers, and a spoiled sister; aunts, un-
cles, endless cousins—telling tales from long ago as if he
knew them, or ever would. The concept of family was not
entirely wasted on him, but he did wonder at the wisdom
of maintaining such strong bonds over the years. He did
not tell her that he found her tales odd. His wound—and
the fact that she could not see with any certainty the result of it—had made her anxious, and the chatter apparently calmed her nerves. He would wager that the Anwyn
Queen was not often uncertain.

In the two days since the attack, Joryn had often

wished that he'd swallowed his pride and obeyed her early morning command for sexual gratification. Their coming together would've felt just as good as if he had commanded *her* to please *him*, he imagined. It would have been as pleasurable as if she had begged, as he'd angrily suggested. Being constantly close to her did nothing to ease his natural desire for her . . . though he tried to convince himself that he would've felt the same for any woman in this situation, even if she were not so beautiful or so brave.

There was no trail to speak of in this wooded terrain, but he could tell that others had walked this forest not so long ago. Unnatural disturbances marked the paths they had taken. A broken twig, a bush's branches moved aside, a scuffed place in the dirt or in fallen leaves. Keelia seemed not to see these disturbances, and yet she continued to move in a direction that possessed the markings of other travelers.

She marched before him, her path taking them down for a long ways, and then up and across the mountain in a manner that was not at all arduous. Still, the journey was beginning to tell on her. Her hair was tangled, and her gold gown had been snagged on brambles and branches in several places and was also ripped along the hem. She scratched her own skin often, but she seemed not to feel the pain, and like him, she healed quickly. There was determination in her stride and even in her chatter.

Without warning, she stopped. Caught by surprise, Joryn took one step too many and ran into her. When she stumbled at the collision, he steadied her with his hands on her bare arms. She did not shake him off as she once would've, but instead turned her head up to the bit of sky they could see through the treetops.

"A storm's coming. A big one." She sighed. "We don't have time for this delay, but I'm afraid we won't make much more progress today."

Joryn studied the blue skies with skepticism. "It doesn't look like rain, much less a storm."

"Well, it's coming nevertheless." She resumed her journey, but this time the path seemed to veer in another direction. "It won't do us any good to get stuck in mud behind a curtain of rain that obscures our vision."

"I didn't think you needed your eyes to lead you," Joryn said, half-joking, but in part serious.

"Well, I do. This way." She pointed upward, and turned to a more sharply inclined path.

A short while later, Joryn smelled rain on the chilled breeze that slapped their faces and made the leaves flutter vigorously. Not long after that, the clouds completely obscured the sun. And then, the raindrops began to fall.

At first, the thick growth overhead protected them, but soon the rain was falling faster and harder, and the ground beneath their feet grew slick. Their clothes were soaked and the hard rain made it difficult to see where their steps were falling on this dangerous terrain. Still, Keelia seemed to have a plan; she seemed to be heading in a particular direction.

On a slick slope, she stopped and lifted a hand to shield her eyes from the rain. She pointed again with that slender, pale arm that he knew to be dangerous. "There," she said, shouting to be heard above the wicked weather.

"I don't see . . ." Joryn began, but Keelia moved forward with a quickened step. She veered to the right, stepping onto more level ground. Again her pace increased, until she was almost running.

And then she veered sharply to the left, and disappeared.

Joryn stopped and spun around. The heavy rain, the thick growth, the wind in his eyes, they all dimmed his vision. Still, how could Keelia be gone? In a heartbeat, without warning . . . gone.

"Keelia!" he shouted, but it seemed the wind caught the name and carried it away too quickly. He thought of the misshapen creatures and how quickly they'd attacked by the stream. He should've sensed them, smelled them, but he hadn't. Not soon enough. What if they had the Anwyn Red Queen? What if they didn't stop at a bite, but tore out her throat, or her heart, or both? Perhaps it would be a better end than his own, but still . . . the pictures in his mind made him shudder.

What if they simply bit her as they had bitten him, and when the full moon next rose, she turned into a strong, brave, gifted monster?

A flash of white, the color of Keelia's skin, caught his eye and he spun toward it. From the low entrance to a cave, she waved at him.

She *waved*, as if he had not just imagined her ravaged by the mutant beasts.

He followed her direction to the cave, dipped down, and walked inside. There was little light here, so perhaps she would not see his scowl, or his worry. Not for the first time, he was very glad that she could not peek into his mind, as she did others.

The cave was larger than he had imagined it would be, judging by the entrance. Keelia was able to stand in an area the size of the Grandmother's meeting room, which was small but adequate for the witch and her students. The cave was certainly more than adequate for two weary travelers. Given the storm beyond the stone walls, it was quite comfortable. He never would've found it on his own.

The Queen peeled off her wet gown. "If you will build us a fire, our clothes and hair will dry faster."

Joryn directed his special energy to a spot near the entrance, and a small fire leapt to life. It provided not only heat to dry their clothes, but light. Light by which Keelia's skin glowed.

She was so incredibly beautiful. Not for the first time, he wondered why the Anwyn Queen couldn't be ancient and ugly, instead of a gorgeous woman who had picked up the annoying habit of suggesting that they were meant to be mates. For life.

"Your clothing will dry faster if you take it off," she said, gesturing with wagging, slender fingers to the trousers he wore.

"I'm fine."

"I can already tell that you're aroused, if that is why you hesitate." She cocked her head to one side. "You insist that you don't care for me in any way, you say it is ridiculous that we are meant to be mated, and yet your body responds to mine."

"My body responds to any naked woman," Joryn said, remembering the moment when he'd believed she'd been taken by the mutant Caradon. That feeling of panic had been unlike any other he had ever experienced, but he could not tell her that. Nor could he dwell on it.

Keelia placed her soaked gown a short distance away, draping it on an overhang that jutted out from the cave wall. The thin material would surely dry quickly. She moved closer to the fire, her limbs loose and relaxed, her skin pale and flawless. She shook her hair above the flames, allowing the radiating heat to dry the long, red strands.

Outside the cave, rain fell hard, and the wind howled. A crack of thunder shook the mountain. They'd found shelter from the storm just in time, thanks to Keelia's senses.

It occurred to Joryn too late that he might be better off battling a wicked storm than battling a determined Anwyn Queen.

THE RAIN CONTINUED LONG AFTER DARKNESS FELL. They made themselves comfortable, as much as was possible given the circumstances, and Joryn delved into his pack and took out some of the last of the dried meat. He passed a piece to Keelia and partook of a bit himself.

She tried not to let Joryn see that she was terrified. Terrified that he might be her mate; terrified that he was not. Terrified that they wouldn't reach the Caradon wizard in time; terrified that he would be saved and he still wouldn't want anything to do with her.

It wasn't like her to fear what tomorrow would bring, but at the moment it seemed she feared everything.

When they'd finished their meal, Joryn sat near the fire. He'd removed his boots, but almost dry trousers still hung on his stubborn body. His wounded leg, revealed beneath a rolled-up hem, looked almost normal. After a few moments of silence, Keelia scooted closer to him and reached out to lay her hand over the scar, hoping the closeness would bring her some knowledge. He twitched when she touched him, and then settled down without pushing her away or uttering a protest.

She still saw nothing.

Joryn reached again for his pack. Since they'd already eaten, and they'd drunk plenty of water, Keelia couldn't imagine what he wanted from his meager supplies. He reached into the pack and came out with the bracelet which had been enchanted by the Grandmother. Her heart sank a little. He was going to put it on again, to make sure she never saw his thoughts or touched his mind. She couldn't have even that much . . .

"Here." Surprisingly, he offered the wide silver bracelet to her.

After a moment of hesitation, she took it. She'd never studied the simply crafted jewelry closely before this moment, and she noted the faint scrollwork in the silver. Her fingers traced a particularly pretty section. "What am I supposed to do with this?"

"Wear it, as a sign of our accord," he said. "Allow the bracelet to remind you of the reasons we're here."

"It won't fit me." She turned the large piece over in her hands. The wide bracelet had been made for him, not her, and would fall off her arm if she dared to wear it.

"It will fit." Joryn took the bracelet from her, grasped her hand in his, and slid the bracelet onto her wrist. Immediately, the silver shifted. It shrank and curled and conformed to her smaller wrist, just as it had done when he'd shifted into his feline form.

The bracelet felt very much at home on her wrist. Did Joryn think it would continue to keep their minds separate? Or did he simply want to remind her of the seriousness of their mission?

She did not wish to think of the mission. Tonight she didn't want to think of evil wizards or soulless monsters or anything else unpleasant.

"Thank you. It's a lovely gift." And perhaps the only tangible thing she would ever have from Joryn. Keelia admired the bracelet for a moment longer, and then she stared into the flames. The magical fire danced, spellbinding and oddly beautiful.

"Do the Caradon kiss?" she asked.

Joryn turned his head and looked down at her. His brow wrinkled slightly. "What?"

"Kiss? Do you kiss? It's a very simple question."

He looked puzzled. "There are kisses of greeting and farewell."

"Show me," she insisted, and then she caught herself. "I mean, will you please show me what you mean?"

He sighed, but leaned down and kissed her cheeks, one and then the other, before backing away from her. "Like that."

"Oh."

"You sound disappointed."

"I am. The Anwyn marry and live with humans, women for the most part, and they kiss often. They seem to enjoy kissing their mates on the mouth."

"Is it a part of your sexual rituals?"

"Not necessarily. Sometimes they kiss in front of other people, when they're fully clothed and hours away from any opportunity to be alone." She squirmed. "Besides, my mother told me . . ." She stared into the fire, almost swept into a trance by the way the flames swirled.

"Your mother told you what?" Joryn snapped.

What did she have to lose at this point? Why not be totally and openly honest? "My mother lived as a human before coming to the Anwyn. She was my age before she knew that she was Queen, that she had Anwyn blood. She gives great weight to a kiss between a man and a woman, and she told me often that while I have no say in who my mate is destined to be, the love to come is real, and I will know that love by his kiss."

Joryn scoffed. "Love is for humans, and from what little I have seen and heard on the subject, it is fragile and elusive."

"You and I both claim lowland humans among our ancestors," Keelia said. "Are we really so different from them?"

"Yes," Joryn answered decisively. "Caradon and Anwyn blood are both dominant, as you well know, and that blood overcomes our lowland heritage and its in-born weaknesses."

"Surely there are some among the Caradon who know love," Keelia argued. It seemed to her that every species could, and should, enjoy love among those who were mated. Of course, most Caradon never did settle down with one partner.

"Some claim to," Joryn said.

"You sound skeptical."

"I am."

"You don't believe in love at all?"

"I imagine some might think it to be real when they are in the grip of an especially strong passion."

"But not you."

"Not me."

She had been a skeptic herself at times, but she had her parents to remind her that love was real. She had seen again and again how wonderful real love could be.

"In that case, you don't have anything to lose by kissing me," she said, trying to keep all emotion out of her voice.

Joryn stared down at her. The firelight flickered on

his face, and something in her chest leapt. "I just kissed you."

"You kissed me on the cheek," she protested, "as you would an old woman or a kindly uncle. I would like a kiss on the mouth."

"Are you going to order me to kiss you?" A quick smile bloomed, and that dimple she rather liked appeared in his cheek.

"Of course not." He wouldn't obey her if she did, so what was the point? "It's just that I have often wondered what it's like, and with the creatures roaming these mountains and the coming confrontation with the wizard, and the uncertainty of what tomorrow might bring for either of us, I might never have another chance to find out." She caught his eye. "Have you never kissed a lover?"

"Not on the mouth."

"Why not?"

"It isn't necessary."

"Must all things be necessary?"

"Yes."

"So, you give a kiss no importance."

"None."

"Then what would it hurt to kiss me, so I might know the sensation in case this is my last chance?"

"You're very persistent."

Keelia smiled. "Yes, I know."

Joryn sighed and mumbled something about the endeavor being pointless, but he did lower his mouth toward hers. His lips were upon hers quickly, where they brushed across her lips and then began to move away.

Keelia sighed. "Not like that." She grabbed his face in her hands and pulled him back, planting her mouth on his fully.

For a moment, that was the extent of their experiment. They pressed their mouths together. His lips were firm but also warm and gentle. Not dry, but neither overly wet. She moved her lips very slightly, rubbing them against his. In answer, his lips parted.

Something odd happened to her, inside and out. Suddenly she was hot, aroused, itchy, trembling, and oh, it felt wonderful. She couldn't kiss Joryn hard enough, deep enough, or long enough. Her chest contracted, her stomach danced. Her entire body reacted to the kiss.

She flicked her tongue out and traced the line of Joryn's lower lip. His intake of breath was telling. He might not admit it, but he liked the kissing, too. His breath and his heartbeat and even his scent shifted subtly. He was affected in a deeply physical way by the joining of their mouths.

Keelia could not believe the depth of her reaction. Her breasts ached, and deep in her belly there was a telling heaviness. They'd been kissing for mere moments, and already she was spiraling out of control. It was like going into her fertile days, when a Queen's heat descended upon her, only it was not the proper time.

She didn't want to find release in a trance tonight. She wanted reality. She wanted Joryn.

"So close," she whispered against his mouth. "And still I see nothing of you. Not the past, the future, your thoughts. Nothing." She wanted to know whether or not they would be able to save Joryn from becoming like the monsters who had attacked them, and she did still wonder if he might be her mate. Other than that, it was surprisingly pleasant not to be forced to deal with his thoughts as well as her own. There was usually a certain amount of control necessary when she was in the company of another person, but with Joryn she could be relaxed. She could allow her mind to wander where it would.

And it did wander, to wonderful places and warm possibilities.

Joryn cupped her head and pulled her forward, so they were kissing again. He gently forced her mouth to open wider, and his tongue flickered against hers. Feeling decidedly unsteady, Keelia stabilized herself by placing one hand against Joryn's side. She could feel his heart beneath the skin. It beat fast and hard, just as hers did. Her hand dropped to the waistband of his trousers, and her fingers deftly unfastened and opened the band so she could touch his skin.

"You should remove these trousers so they have a chance to dry well before morning," she said, surprised at the breathless quality of her voice.

"You're trying to seduce me. Again," Joryn said hoarsely.

Keelia's hand snaked well into the opened trousers and encircled his erection. "As you can see, the removal of your clothing isn't necessary for seduction. I'm only thinking of your comfort." She stroked once, and then removed her hand. "Besides, we are only kissing. You've made it clear that you don't wish to lie with me." Though his body very clearly said otherwise.

"I don't want to encourage your ridiculous fantasies that we might be mates for life. That is not my way." In contrast to his words, which seemed distant enough, his hand cupped one breast and the thumb brushed against her nipple.

Keelia's breath caught at the intense and unexpected

sensation, and she rocked against the Caradon, wanting more.

"What if your way is wrong?"

"What if *your* way is wrong?" he countered. His hand slipped down and delved between her legs, where she was wet and aching. He stroked, and her body responded by arching and quivering. "What if there's nothing between a male and a female but need and pleasure and release, and it does not matter who touches you to stir your natural desires?"

Keelia closed her eyes and leaned her head back. He had touched her this way before, in reality and in dreams. But it had never felt quite like this. It had never been so intense and true. She was beyond the point where she could stop, and if he stopped . . . what would she do? He would not accede to her commands, he had already made that clear. Would he make her beg? It was wrong for a Queen to be made to beg for anything, but at the moment she would gladly plead for what she needed.

She thought about begging, but her pride interfered and she hesitated. "What if you are wrong, and it's true that one male and one female are meant to be together to the exclusion of all others? What if there is something more between those who are meant to be mated? Something you cannot understand or explain."

Joryn sighed and laid her down so that she was on her back. The coolness of the stone floor felt good against her overheated skin. The heat of his body over hers felt even better.

"I thought we were only going to kiss," she whispered as he whipped away his trousers.

He lowered his mouth to hers and kissed her again. The kiss had changed dramatically. It tasted of desperation now. It was deeper. Harder. More invasive. "Is that what you want?" Joryn asked as he abruptly ended the kiss. "Mouth to mouth only?"

"No. You know what I want, Joryn." It was a simple statement, without commands or pleas. Her body shook. It trembled so deeply she wondered if Joryn could see the effect he had on her. He could surely feel it, as his body was pressed closely to hers.

He did not offer her his throat, and she did not offer hers. This was not a moment of bonding spiritually, but of sexual gratification alone. Unless he accepted what she believed to be true, Joryn would never offer her his throat in that ultimate gesture of trust and love.

When he pushed inside her trembling body, she did not care.

In dreams and trances, she had experienced the sensations of having a man inside her, but in reality her body was untested. She was a virgin, and then she was a virgin no more as Joryn thrust deep. There was a tiny moment of pain that made her gasp, but the pleasurable sensations were much more intense than the pain.

Her body stretched to accommodate his girth and length, and soon they found a rhythm that suited them both. In spite of their fervor, the rhythm was slow. Keelia knew if she moved quickly, this would soon be over, and she didn't want it to be over. She wanted it to last. The connection, the ripples of sensation flitting through her body, the heat she and Joryn shared, his body on and inside hers. She wanted it to last for as long as possible.

Sex with Joryn was like the dreams and yet it was also

unlike her fantasies. This act was genuine and powerful, and it went far beyond a simple easing of need. Her entire body was involved, and she felt very much like she did when the change to wolf came to her. Tension in her body rippled and shook, as if lightning flashed in her blood, and the heat . . . the heat was beyond anything she had ever known or expected. Her breath would not come, and her body reached for Joryn's with a fierce desperation she had not expected. She not only wanted him, she *needed* him.

She opened her eyes and looked up into his face. He moved faster now, and so did she. Completion was just out of reach, teasing her, guiding her moves and the way she clutched at Joryn. Her legs rose up higher and encircled his back, and he drove deep to touch a place that had, until this moment, been untouched.

Fire warmed and reddened his eyes, but Keelia was not alarmed. She saw, out of the corners of her eyes, flames dancing on air all around their joined bodies. She did not care. Nothing mattered but the motion of his body and hers, the pleasure that danced just out of reach . . .

Completion came with a crack of her body and a scream that was torn from her lips. Joryn's release came on top of hers, and the heat increased inside and around her. Maybe he would turn her to ashes by making love to her. At the moment, she would gladly trade her life for ashes in exchange for an experience like this one.

Keelia began to relax, to catch her breath once again. She opened her eyes to find Joryn staring down at her, his eyes red with fire. Flame on the air still danced around them in the tight confines of the cave. Not everywhere, but enough to light the dark cave as if it were daytime and they were warmed by the sun. She smiled, but Joryn did not.

"Outside," he said, rising up from her languid body with an unnecessary swiftness.

"But it's still raining."

He took her hand and hauled her to her feet, and then guided her very quickly to the cave's small entrance. They walked past the fire he had created and into the night.

The rain shower felt good on her overheated skin. Keelia closed her eyes and lifted her face to the rain, spinning about in pure joy. Joryn did not dance. He stood in the downpour with his arms out and his palms up. After a moment of no movement at all, Keelia danced to him. "You did not tell me that you lose control of your gift when you have sex." She laid her hands on his naked chest, splayed her fingers, and leaned into him.

He said nothing, and when he looked at her, the fire in his eyes was dimmed. Almost gone.

Finally he said, "Perhaps I did lose control, but I was not alone."

"I did scream rather loudly, didn't I?" Keelia was too satisfied to think of anything but what she and Joryn had just shared. They had troubles aplenty, and tomorrow they would have to deal with them again. But not tonight. Not now.

Joryn turned slowly and presented to her his back. Four long gashes marred his perfect, muscled skin, and Keelia gasped. "I did that?"

"Yes."

"With my . . . claws?"

"Yes."

He had already begun to heal, and Keelia placed one

finger against a recently healed gash. In her dreams she never lost control, but this was not a dream, and Joryn had aroused her to a place she had not expected. "I'm sorry." She kissed a just-healed wound, and then licked the skin. "I'm so sorry. I might've hurt you."

"You didn't."

"But I might've—"

"I don't care, Keelia. I swear, right now I don't care about anything but the way you make me feel."

She rested one palm against a very nice, rain-slick butt cheek, and circled the other around to discover that Joryn was growing hard once again. She stroked, and pressed her breasts against his back. The scratches she had made with claws she had not known she'd unsheathed continued to heal.

He was the one. Joryn, a Caradon, was her mate, the man who was destined to be hers until the day they died. He was hers for a lifetime, and given the circumstances, that lifetime might not be a very long one. Shouldn't she make the best of it, whether he believed they were meant to be or not? The rain poured over her as she touched and stroked, as she tried to memorize every edge, every curve, every dip and muscle.

The storm was forgotten as Joryn turned and lifted her into his strong arms. Her arms went around his neck, her legs snaked around his waist.

How could he deny that they were meant to be? She was tempted to offer him her rain-dampened throat here and now, but it would not be right for a Queen to make such an offer first, no matter how she felt at this incredible moment. No, when the time came, Joryn would offer her his throat, and she would take it. Only then could she offer him her own.

So she took his wet hair in her hands and kissed him deeply, in a much more human offer of supplication. He entered her once more and, with the rain pelting their bare bodies, set new sensations into play.

8

Joryn didn't tell Keelia that he'd never before lost control while engaged in sex. It was easy to evade the subject when it came up, as she was easily distracted once they became lovers. One touch, and she dismissed everything else from her mind. Once he took her mouth, all questions were forgotten.

He continued to diligently set aside the preposterous notion that he and the Anwyn Queen were meant to be mates. When the battle they were destined to fight together was over, if they won—and he was not turned into a soulless monster—she would return to her people and her City, and he would return to his studies and his freedom. There were many other females who would make fine lovers in the future. Perhaps they would not be so beautiful, or so enthusiastic, or so valiant. Perhaps they would not call his fire to the surface, as Keelia did.

Perhaps they would be boring and uninspiring and forgettable, but he *would* have his freedom.

There were less than two weeks until the next full moon, and they had not yet found the Caradon wizard who possessed the stone which must be destroyed. Keelia led the way as if she knew where she was going, but in truth she was moving forward with only her admittedly impaired magical senses to guide her. His life was literally in her hands, and he followed her without question.

And he wasn't sure why. It wasn't in his nature to follow anyone mindlessly. Joryn questioned everything; he trusted no one.

They left the forest behind and moved upward on a rocky slope. He did not know where they might sleep tonight, or if they would sleep at all. For the past three nights they had not slept much. They napped when rest was necessary, but since the night of the storm they had not truly slept. They had found a better way to pass the night.

Keelia reached a plateau and stopped. Again, Joryn could not help but think that she looked very much like a Queen, in spite of her travel-weary state. With the blue sky above and beyond her and the majestic mountains beneath her feet, she looked like Queen of the world.

At first he thought she'd stopped for a moment's rest, but when she turned to face him, her expression was one of puzzlement and concern. "I'm not sure which way to go," she said softly. "There are two possible routes from this point, but I can't see clearly which is the right path."

"Will they both lead us to the wizard?"

"Yes."

"Then what difference does it make?"

She paled. "One will get us to his cave in time. The other will not."

Joryn nodded. He had accepted death the moment he'd been bitten. True, he did not want to die, but if it was meant to be, then there was nothing he could do to save himself.

He could save his soul, however. "Remember your promise."

Keelia's hands balled into fists. "As if I could forget! That damned promise is on my mind night and day, and I wonder if I can make myself do what you have asked me to do if it becomes necessary."

"If I am cursed to become a monster and you do not kill me, then you not only betray me by breaking your promise, you doom me to live out my life as a soulless beast. Remember that if you question again what must be done."

She did not cry, but her lower lip trembled. She fought tears, with her jaw rigid and her lips thinned.

"You need rest." He took her arm and led her to a rock outcropping, where he forced her to sit. "When you have regained your energy, you will know which path we should take."

She nodded, but her expression was less than certain. "I do not wish to think about failure at this moment."

"Neither do I," Joryn agreed.

"We will find the wizard and destroy the stone before the next full moon." She bobbed her head decisively.

"You command it," Joryn said with a smile.

"I do," she said seriously. And then she smiled a little.

He sat beside her, and Keelia laid her head in his lap. She made herself comfortable in a place that should be very uncomfortable, and sighed. "Maybe I just need a quick nap. I'll doze off, and when I wake, the correct path will be clear to me."

"Yes." With his fingers, Joryn brushed Keelia's tangled red hair away from her face.

"After I have a nap, if the way is not evident, then we will have sex. Sometimes an orgasm clears my mind."

"Really? It befuddles the hell out of mine."

She turned her head so she could look him in the eye. "Ah, does our sexual union make you question the rightness of our bond? Do you wonder if perhaps I am right and we are truly mated in a manner which goes beyond what you have accepted as true?"

Yes.

"No," he said firmly, even though his mind whispered otherwise.

"Then we will not speak of it again. Today." With her head resting on his thigh, she boldly teased him, her hand tracing and cupping the erection beneath his strained trousers. "Do you know it is said that there are none more sensual than Anwyn Queens?"

"Oddly enough, I never heard that from a Caradon," he teased, though in truth, he could not deny that he had never met another like her.

She was not offended. "Until I met you, until we became lovers, I thought I was doomed to be different, as I am in so many other ways. I thought I would be a virgin Queen, never to know a real man's touch, never to know what it's like to be so caught up in true ecstasy that the rest of the world fades away." She licked her lips. "Never to know the touch of my mate."

"I am not . . ."

He sometimes forgot how strong she was. Her size and build were deceiving. But when she forced him onto his back and straddled him, he was reminded.

"If I found you in the company of another woman, I would have her beheaded."

"Beheaded? Isn't that a little harsh?"

"Not when it comes to the sanctity of a Queen's mate."

"I am not . . ." He stopped suddenly and squinted at her. She looked so sweet and beautiful, but she was the Anwyn Queen. "How many people have you had beheaded?"

She pursed her lips for a moment, then answered, "None, but it is within my rights to so order if I deem it necessary."

"And if I desired another woman, you would do so."

"Yes." She squirmed against his hips, rubbing her body against his erection, and he knew there would be no sleep for her or for him. Not for a while. "If I desired another male to please me, would you not order his death if it was within your power to do so? Think before you answer, Joryn. Do you, in any part of your heart, consider me to be yours?"

Unfortunately, he did.

Fortunately, he knew how to end Keelia's probing questions without answering them.

ON HORSEBACK, WITH A SMILE ON HIS FACE, CIRO watched from the end of a narrow dirt-packed street as his Own rushed into the sleeping village. Weapons raised, screams bloodcurdling, they descended on the simple wooden houses with a mindless fury. He had made them wait for this moment, insisting that they march slowly onward, insisting that they not rush carelessly from one village to another. Their first attack had been weeks earlier, and since that time they'd grown stronger. More of his Own had been called to join him, and those who had once been farmers or merchants or beggars were becoming a fine army. His legion.

Tonight they were hungry, and there was nothing more fearsome than Ciro's Own when they were *hungry*. The villagers wouldn't have a chance. They'd awaken from their sleep to find warriors of a sort they had never imagined hovering over their soon-to-be dead bodies.

They would bring him what he needed, when a portion of their fury had been sated. They would bring him a woman, preferably. Someone young and tender and not entirely innocent. He would take her blood and her soul, and then he would be stronger.

Diella dismounted and walked down the middle of the street. The former empress, caught in the body that had once belonged to an almost innocent girl, held a short sword in one hand. It swung there comfortably, and more than a little restlessly. She was ready to do battle with the first villager who crossed her path.

Ciro closed his eyes as the first shouts rose. When he concentrated, he could see what was happening through the eyes of his Own. He could see through Diella's eyes when he wished. For now, he tapped into the one consciousness that connected his Own. He saw and felt the excitement and blood lust of all the soldiers as they prepared to slaughter the villagers in their beds. He did not see all, but images flitted through his mind, hazy and quick. More than the images, he felt the frenzy of his soulless Own. He felt their collective hunger.

It was rather like sex, he decided, to be so completely and totally joined. There was a rush of emotion, a surge of pleasure. Yes, this was good.

Unexpectedly, Ciro felt a slash of pain in his midsection. One of his soldiers had been stabbed. Ciro's fury rose to the surface. In a fair battle there was always a possibility that one or two soldiers would get sloppy and be harmed, but this was not a fair battle, and he could not stand to lose even one soldier before he marched on Arthes. Not even *one*.

Another of his Own cried out in pain, and Ciro felt that agony in his lower back, as if a sharp knife had slipped deep into his flesh. And then another . . . this time across the throat. In the midst of the pain, Ciro saw a flash of something that stole the last of his contentment.

Green. Not just any shade, but a sentinel's green. His father's soldiers were here.

Resistance came not only from the soldiers, but from the villagers themselves. They'd been waiting . . . *waiting* . . . for Ciro and his Own to arrive. These villagers were not caught unaware, as the others had been. They were well armed and prepared for battle, as much as such simple people could be.

Simple people taught and led by the emperor's soldiers.

When the pain became too much, Ciro disconnected from his Own. Some of his soldiers were running toward him, escaping the battle they had not been prepared to fight. They'd come to this village in order to slaughter the unsuspecting in their beds, not take up something resembling armed combat.

Diella swung her short sword at a man dressed in brown when he tried to hit her on the head with a sturdy length of wood, missing her head by inches. She did not miss when she lashed out with the sword, and the man dropped.

Villagers fell here and there, and so did Ciro's Own. His soldiers had no souls, they were willing to do anything he asked of them, but they were not the finest of fighters. If determination alone were enough, they would be sufficient, but they needed skill. They needed proper training.

Half a dozen of his Own placed themselves between the resistors and their lord and master, protecting Ciro—who needed protection much less than they did. Since the demon had taken possession of more of him, he had become almost indestructible. Wounds didn't hurt him, and they healed quickly. The blood he shed was no more than an annoyance.

If they separated his head from his heart, he imagined that would do him in for good, but nothing else would kill him. No, the Isen Demon would survive in this body it had taken.

One quick sentinel fought his way past the protective soldiers on Ciro's left. It would be easy to turn and run, since Ciro was on horseback and the sentinel was on foot, but the prince did not run from anything. He waited as the sentinel struck down one soldier and then another before breaking through the guard and rushing toward Ciro.

Ciro's lack of movement or resistance gave the sentinel false hopes. The lad rushed fearlessly forward and thrust his sword upward, trying to pierce the rebellious prince's gut with the end of his long blade.

Ciro caught the tip in his hand and halted the process, catching the sentinel by surprise. Blood seeped from between Ciro's fingers, but he felt no pain. He whipped the sword away, and then reached down to grab the sentinel by his green shirt.

The sentinel tried to fight, but Ciro touched the lad's

mind with his own and ordered compliance. *Relax. Come to me. You are mine now.*

It was no effort at all to take what he needed.

He did not taste the soul and blood of a young woman as he had originally intended, but the young man who died an ugly death atop Ciro's horse sufficed. His skin was tougher, his blood not so sweet, but Ciro was nourished.

The sentinel's body discarded, Ciro called his Own and ordered them to retreat. He could not afford to lose another soldier. He had already lost too many on this night, and he needed to be as strong as possible when he marched on Arthes to take the throne from his father.

He sent the assigned meeting place into the minds of his Own, then turned and led his horse into the darkness.

In moments, Diella joined him, once again riding her own horse. "That was a disaster," she exclaimed.

"Yes. Yes it was." Ciro's voice remained low and calm.

"They were waiting for us. They *knew* we were coming. How?"

There was no way they could've known that he would choose that particular village on this particular night. No, it wasn't possible.

"I would suspect they've prepared every village between here and Arthes for possible attack."

Diella sighed. "That's annoying. What are you going to do?"

Ciro chewed on the possibilities for a moment. "My army needs training. They're eager, but not skilled. Passion will only get you so far when you're fighting a skilled soldier."

"You're going to stop marching to Arthes in order to *train* your army of slobbering idiots?"

He was tempted to reach out and slap the annoying

woman with the back of his hand and send her flying, but he didn't. The Isen Demon insisted that she still had a part to play, and he was not to harm her.

"Yes," Ciro said calmly.

Diella wisely decided to remain silent as they lost themselves in the darkness of this disappointing night.

The demon had told Ciro that many had important parts to play in the taking of Columbyana, and the rest of the world as well. A dark magic interfered with the psychic abilities of those who might issue warnings about what was coming. Carefully chosen magical beings—wizards and witches, for the most part—worked their own darkness in all corners of the world. A bitter, hungry wizard deep in Caradon Territory; an ancient witch working her spells in a swamp hut; a seemingly innocent girl in the Mountains of the North, a girl who would take a life in the name of the demon . . . they all had their parts to play, just as he did.

Take the throne.

Take his beloved.

Make the child.

Those were his tasks. He cared little for the tasks of others until the Isen Demon insisted that he listen.

ANWYN QUEENS WERE RENOWNED FOR THEIR SEXUality, and had been for as long as Anwyn history had been spoken and written. Keelia had long ago decided that she was not like other Queens in this respect. Yes, when her fertile time descended upon her, she was obligated to relieve the desire that gripped her, but she had never been tempted to take a lover, and in between these episodes she was quite content to sleep alone.

If she survived this ordeal, she would never be content to sleep alone again.

Joryn had insisted that they stop to sleep for a while, and Keelia had reluctantly agreed. Her visions were becoming fuzzy. Was it tiredness that affected her abilities, or was the fact that they approached a dark wizard dampening her talents even more?

For a while, she did not want to think about darkness or wizards or coming full moons. She'd shed her gown soon after they'd stopped, and now she made quick work of removing Joryn's boots and trousers. He had built a small fire hours ago, caught their supper and cooked it, and insisted that she rest.

She could not sleep, not yet.

Their bed was hard, but she didn't care. Joryn made a nice pillow.

She had decided to accept that he was her mate, no matter how impossible it seemed. Everything changed in time. It had once been thought impossible for an Anwyn Queen to have a daughter, but Juliet Fyne had proved that belief wrong. Keelia's mother had given birth to not one daughter but *two*. Keelia could and probably would have daughters as well as sons, and so would Giulia. What other supposedly indisputable fact might be wrong? It was possible that nothing they believed to be a certainty was in fact certain, even the belief that an Anwyn's mate could only be another Anwyn or a human female.

"We have much in common, you and I," she said as she pressed her hand low on Joryn's belly.

He laughed. "We have nothing in common. Nothing at all."

She circled her fingers around his penis and he grew quickly.

"All right," he said lightly. "We have one thing in common."

"We both change with the full moon," Keelia said.

"But not into the same animal," he argued.

"We both heal more quickly than humans."

"Perhaps it is a human trait that they heal slowly."

"We both have magic."

"But they are very different types of magic."

Keelia stoked him gently. "We have shared dreams, have we not?" Dreams of sexual liaisons that seemed almost real, dreams they had shared before they became lovers.

Joryn sighed. "You are relentless."

"Yes." Keelia rested her head on Joryn's stomach, and as he tensed beneath her and rocked his hips, she slid slightly lower so she could flick out her tongue and taste him. He lurched beneath her, and she heard his sharp intake of breath. "I am relentless when I know I am correct."

She took a bit more of him into her mouth, and whipped her tongue around. She rose up slightly, slowly. "When will you admit that we are mated? When we stop the wizard's work and save you and the others, when we have fulfilled our duties to our people, we will remain together."

"Can we not discuss this at another time?" he asked.

Once again, she flicked her tongue against his erection. "I wish to discuss it *now.*"

He groaned. "You do not play fair."

"Why should I play fair when playing unfairly is so much fun . . . and so wonderfully effective?" She trailed the tip of her tongue down his length and back up again. Slowly. "You are mine, are you not?"

"For now," he admitted.

"Forever."

"There is no forever, Keelia. There's just *now*."

"Maybe. Maybe not." She sighed and continued to play with her lover. "There is a custom among the Anwyn, a custom of offering the throat to one you trust and love above all others. Do the Caradon have such a custom?"

"It's a foolish man or beast who bares his throat," he said. "One bite, and life's blood spills."

"One kiss," Keelia countered, "and a bond like no other is formed." It was a bond she longed for.

Joryn knew how to play unfairly, just as she did. He rolled her onto her back and took a nipple deep into his mouth. He spread her legs and stroked, as a man who knows a woman's body well might. Even though he was very well aroused, he did not rush toward the end of the encounter, but instead took his time. He kissed not only her breasts but the insides of her elbows, which were oddly sensitive; her belly, where she quivered; the insides of her thighs; the bud at her entrance.

And then he drew slightly away. Not far, never far. "Have you ever offered your throat to anyone?"

"No," she sighed. "I am Queen." That should be explanation enough, but she wasn't sure it would be. A Queen did not kneel to others, or receive commands, or offer her throat.

"You are wise to be cautious. Who needs anything other than the moment we live in? We must embrace each day as if it is our last. Now is fine, isn't it? Now is enough."

"I want forever," she whispered.

"But *now* is fine." He covered her body with his and teased her by barely entering.

"Why do you deny what is so obvious?" she argued, even though her breath would barely come to her, and she was hurtling beyond all rational thought. It was so obvious to her that this was more than just sex, and it must be clear to Joryn as well. Why did he fight her?

He did not answer, but again barely entered her and then withdrew. Her body shook, and the last bit of her will vanished. "Yes, yes, you are right, Joryn," she whispered, arching against him. "Now is very fine. I need nothing else."

With that he thrust into her, deep and hard, and she shattered. Her cry echoed off the rocks around and above them, and a moment later so did his.

He didn't always lose control when they made love, but tonight, again, small fires leapt around them. Since they were not in the confines of a cave, he was not concerned. The flames would die down in time. They always did.

She had not lost control of her shape-shifting abilities since that first time, though she did often check his back for scratches, just to be sure.

The light he created illuminated his face nicely. She reached up to caress his cheek. "If I was swept up in the beauty of your precious *now* and told you that I love you, what would you do?"

He did not hesitate in answering. "I would turn my back on you," he said gently. "We cannot allow the falseness of romantic love to come between us. What we have is good, Keelia, but it won't last. It is not meant to last. We'll succeed in our mission and go our separate ways, or else we'll fail and you'll kill me. Don't ruin the only good part of this endeavor we have set for ourselves with talk of forever, trust, and love."

"If this is the only good part, then it is because it's the only good part you will allow." He was still inside her, and yet he argued that this was no more than a casual coupling.

Keelia accepted that she had little choice in the matter. She couldn't command Joryn to feel more than he did. Was it possible that as a Caradon he was incapable of love? No, she didn't think that was the case. He was capable of feeling more, he just didn't. All she could do was continue to enjoy what they had, or else sever their sexual relationship until he came to his senses and realized that she was right and he was wrong.

But they didn't have the time for such foolishness. Since she could not see into him, she could not know if he'd be saved or not. If that was the case, they didn't have weeks and months and years to define and explore their relationship, they had days. Precious days and a few precious nights.

Even joined, she could not sense anything of him. She did not know if he cared for her or only for the pleasure she provided. She did not know why he was so determined to save his people. She knew nothing, and it was alternately refreshing and maddening.

Keelia took a deep breath and rested her hands on his hips. "And you say I'm stubborn."

9

DURING A TOO-BRIEF NAP, JORYN DREAMED THAT
Keelia offered him her throat. When presented with the
pale, delicate column, he lunged for her flesh and bit.
Hard and deep, and without hesitation.

In mountain cat form he'd done battle with other animals, and he'd gone for the throat in more than one
life-and-death struggle. As a man he had never bitten
anyone, much less gone for a woman's neck with a killing
chomp. And yet in his dream he was a man, not a cat,
and still he attacked. He bit down. He devoured her.

It was Keelia's ridiculous talk of trust and love and
forever that spurred the nightmare.

In sun-lit reality, she moved forward with determination. In harsh afternoon light her hair was snarled and her
clothes were torn, but she continued to move with the
grace and dignity of a Queen. He would do well to remind himself often that when this was over, she'd return

to the palace of the Anwyn Queen, where she'd be waited upon by an endless number of servants, and her commands would always be followed without question. Each day a finer gown would be provided for her, and talented maids would wash and scent and style her hair, which would not dare to snarl beneath the Anwyn crown.

If he occasionally suspected that he felt more for her than he should, it was because he was very possibly going to die in a few days. If they did not find the wizard and destroy his enchanted stone, then Keelia would be forced to kill him. It was no wonder that he preferred getting lost in her body and her nonsensical ramblings about forever and lifetime mates to dwelling on the possibilities that awaited him.

What she spoke of was fantasy, which at the moment was much better than his reality. It was true, he had never before thought binding himself to one woman was a *fantasy*. It fell more into the nightmare category. Again, he wrote those occasional thoughts off to the venom coursing in his blood. The cursed toxin had changed him somehow. He was no longer himself.

Yes, better to blame his odd, rambling thoughts to the bite of a monster than to consider that they might be the result of a woman's heartfelt passion.

Keelia turned to look at him as she took a sharp turn in the rocky path. No matter what her situation or her mood, she was always regal. Not untouchable, perhaps, but definitely unlike any other woman he had ever known or ever would know. Maybe he was drawn to her simply because she was unlike other women. What man wouldn't be intrigued by her? What male wouldn't want to become the lover she had dreamed of?

Joryn could so clearly picture the fine, feminine throat she had offered in the dream that had stayed with him all day. Like the Anwyn, the Caradon put great significance on such a gesture, though he suspected that among his people the offer was made less frequently than among the too-trusting Anwyn. To offer one's throat was akin to offering one's very soul to another for keeping.

He did not have to worry about his nightmare of a forever woman coming true. While Keelia might offer her body willingly enough, and even hint at offering her heart, this was not a woman who would ever offer him, or any other man, her throat.

THE GRANDMOTHER PACED IN HER PARLOR, attempting—and failing—to discern exactly where Joryn and the Red Queen were located at this moment. She had thought they would be here by now, but they were not so late that she should be concerned.

And yet she was concerned, mightily so.

Druson had visited her often in days past, as anxious as she about Joryn's mission.

"The bracelet you fashioned from the ancient silver, you said it would protect Joryn from the Queen," Druson said, worry evident in his voice.

"I lied," Vala said crisply. She never could've made Joryn understand and accept why his thoughts were dark to the powerful seer. Perhaps she would be able to explain now, if she had the chance.

Druson was apparently shocked by her answer. "But, why? Did you give Joryn no defense against the Anwyn Queen? Did you send him out there . . ."

"Joryn needs no defense against the Queen," Vala said, impatiently interrupting her disappointed student. "The bracelet has served its purpose."

"Which was?" Druson asked crisply.

"To send those who searched for the Queen astray, to hide Joryn from those who would kill him for touching their Queen." The Anwyn army who had attempted to recover their beloved ruler had made so many misguided turns they were nowhere near the woman they sought. There was still much magic in the silver, but from now on whatever magic existed there was of Joryn's making. Joryn and the Queen.

Vala continued to pace in the room which suddenly seemed too small for her and one overly anxious student.

"They should've been here by now," Druson said.

"Yes, that's true."

"Where are they, Grandmother?"

"I don't know."

Druson clenched his fists. "What do you mean, you don't know? I thought you saw everything?"

"Not anymore," Vala whispered. "As the darkness grows stronger, my gift dims." She had so much to tell Joryn and the Anwyn Queen, but they had not come here as quickly as they should've. She did not think they were dead, but in truth she did not know that with any certainty. She no longer knew anything with any certainty.

"I'm going to search for them and bring them to you," Druson insisted. "Surely I can detect the scent of an Anwyn Queen in Caradon Territory."

Vala did not trust Druson entirely. He had always wished for more magic than he possessed, and that desire made him prone to jealousy of those, like Joryn, who had been born with great gifts. But he was her student, and while he wanted more than he'd been given, he had not yet chosen a dark path. He simply had not chosen a path of goodness, either.

"Perhaps that would be best," she said, surprising him. Judging by the expression on his face, he had expected resistance. "Find them and bring them to me. But no matter what happens, you must promise me that you will not harm the Anwyn Queen."

"What if she's killed Joryn?" Druson snapped. "What if she's the reason he did not return to us?"

"She did not harm him," Vala said softly. If she knew nothing else, she knew that to be true. "She would not. And whether you like the fact or not, we still need her."

Druson huffed at that, but did not argue.

A soft knock on the door surprised Vala. The fact that she was startled was evidence of her weakening gift. No, the gift was there, but she was no longer able to access it as she should. She was tired. Tired of the constant battle, the constant vigilance.

Druson was not surprised, but he did seem annoyed as he went to answer, throwing open the door with more energy than was necessary. "I told you to wait," he said tersely.

A soft female voice answered. "It's getting cold, since the sun set. Can I come in? Please?"

Not only a female, but a human one. Why on earth would Druson bring a lowland human here?

When the girl entered the room, Vala understood. Small but nicely rounded, fair of face and with a thick fall of silky black hair, the girl was quite beautiful. Like most males, Druson was a fool where women were concerned.

The girl grinned at Vala, and dimples flashed on full, pink cheeks. "I'm sorry to intrude, but it is rather cold outdoors." Her gaze flitted to Druson and she gave him a seductive smile. "For someone who has no Caradon blood, that is. I didn't expect it to be so chilly here at night this time of year, but then we are very high in the mountains." She continued to walk toward Vala, and when she was close, she offered her hand in a human custom which was usually reserved for their males. "It is a pleasure to meet you, Grandmother. Druson speaks very highly of you."

Vala did not see the danger until it was too late. While the girl offered her right hand, her left remained hidden in the folds of her voluminous skirt. At the last possible moment, that left hand swung up and sliced through the faded cloth of a simple dress and into Vala's old flesh. She felt the bite of the cold metal, gasped, and dropped to her knees as Druson shouted, "No!"

Too late. Druson was always too late and too slow.

Above Vala, the girl continued to smile sweetly. "That should take care of you, you interfering old bitch." She leaned forward, still grinning, the bloody knife still clutched in her hand. "I should tell you, before you die, that all your efforts have been wasted. You have actually helped things to unfold as they should, and for that the Isen Demon thanks—" The girl's hateful speech ended when Druson yanked her up by the hair, deftly took her knife from slender fingers, and spun her around to slit her throat with her own weapon.

The Grandmother felt a rush of unexpected relief. It had taken her death to bring it about, but Druson had finally chosen his path.

Vala sighed as her most inadequate student dropped

to his knees to examine her wound. All Caradon had the ability to heal quickly, but a killing wound could not be mended fast enough to save the injured. It was the way of the world, and could not be changed.

"Don't bother with attempts at doctoring," Vala said. "The wound will kill me very soon."

"No," Druson said, but the truth showed in his eyes. He knew she was dying. "I'm so sorry, Grandmother. I didn't know she would . . . I couldn't even imagine . . ." He sighed, and then his breath caught in a soft gasp. "All I saw was her pretty face and the way she smiled, and this is where it leads. I am the worst of fools."

Vala reached up and touched Druson's cheek. "There is no time for apologies. You were a poor student for most of your life, but you have something the others do not possess with such intensity. Will. Desire. Ambition. You have always longed for power. Heaven forgive me, I am about to give you everything you've ever wanted."

"All I want right now is for you to heal."

She ignored her student and moved her hand to his forehead. What she was about to do would either kill Druson, drive him mad, or make him incredibly strong. Others among her students were better suited for this gift, but she had no choice. She had to pass her gift to Druson, or let all her knowledge die in this small hut, long before the battle was done.

She let loose her powers, bundling her energies and her knowledge in bright white light and forcing that light from her soul, her mind, and her heart into Druson. He gasped, as she had known he would, but he did not move away or cry out. She held him in place with her power, with *her* will and ambition. More than a thousand years of knowledge poured into a young man who had not been built for such a gift. He had chosen the right path when he'd taken the life of the murderous girl who'd bewitched him, but would he stay on that path? Would he use this gift as it was intended to be used?

Would he survive this infusion of knowledge for which he had not been made?

She felt the energy draining from her, traveling at great speed from her mind and heart into those of an unprepared lad. A man to most perhaps, but in her eyes still an untested lad.

When the transfer was complete, Druson stared at Vala with widening eyes. He felt the power within him, but he did not know how to control it. Not yet. She patted his cheek. "I give this gift to you as it was given to me long ago. In time, you will be able to access all the powers I have given you."

"I don't understand," he whispered.

"From now on, you will be called Grandfather."

It was with a touch of relief that Vala passed her gift and her burden to her worst student, and with peace she slipped away.

KEELIA FELT AS IF SHE ITCHED ALL OVER. IT WAS MORE than the excitement of moving closer to the wizard and his blasted stone; it was more than wondering if they'd find the wizard in time.

The timing was not quite right—she was weeks early—but there was no denying that she was going into her fertile time.

If she had sex with Joryn once it descended, there would be a child, without question. Her child would be half-Anwyn, half-Caradon, and fatherless if she could not save Joryn. How would she explain that to her son or daughter? *Sorry, dearest, but I had to kill your father before he turned into a monster and murdered us both.*

Would the child turn to wolf or mountain cat with the coming of the full moon? That would not be known until the child was twelve or thirteen years old, unless she could somehow see the child's future in a way she could not see her own or Joryn's. Perhaps the eyes would tell. Green eyes meant cat, gold eyes, wolf. But even that was no more than supposition on her part. She simply did not know. Such a half-breed was unknown and unthinkable.

If it came to be, how would her people accept a prince or princess who had Caradon blood? She knew the wilder species to be kinder and smarter and more like the Anwyn than she had ever believed to be true, but could she convince others of that truth? Or would she and her child be shunned?

The questions nagged at her as she led the way from rocky path to green, from sunshine to welcomed shade. As the days passed, she and Joryn spoke less and less. They felt the weight of what was coming, they sensed the uncertainty. At night they made love and slept close and did not speak of their fears or wishes. Such discussions seemed useless, a waste of their precious breath.

These days should be filled with fear. She should be miserable. Her entire life had been one of ease and privilege, the life of a princess, the life of a Queen. But she was not at all miserable. There was purpose in her heart, and the nights with Joryn were everything she had always imagined a loving relationship should be. Perhaps he claimed not to love her, perhaps he said he would turn his back on her if she dared to speak the word, but still . . . there was beauty here. There was unspoken love.

She turned and waited for Joryn, and when he was beside her, she resumed walking up the leaf-strewn trail. "Do you have children?"

"No." He did not seem horrified or pleased, simply casual and uninterested.

"But you have told me yourself that there were many women . . ."

"I was very careful."

"Hmmm."

"What does that mean, this *hmmm* sound?" he asked.

She tried to remain pragmatic and logical, though she felt neither. "Since these were women with whom you did not have a bond, women you . . . left behind, I suppose, then how do you know there are no children?"

"I told you, I'm very careful."

"Why? Why do you care if you leave a woman you will never see again carrying your child? It's not as if you'd ever know with any certainty, since the sexual relationships are temporary."

He stopped. "Oh, no. You can't be. It's not the right time for you to conceive; even I know that."

Keelia sighed. "And yet you sound aghast at the prospect."

He grabbed her shoulders and looked down at her, and she saw the flickers of fire in his eyes. That fire spoke of anger or passion. "You know some of the details of my gift, but you do not know all. Tell me you are not carrying my child."

"What do you mean, I don't know all?" She knew enough. If his talent was a hereditary one, he was wise not to scatter little fire starters across the land.

His grip relaxed. "It doesn't matter. Why are you asking these questions now? Are you . . ." *Now* he sounded horrified.

She had told him she never lied, and that was the truth. "No, I am not. I am a day, perhaps two, from going into my fertile time, however. The episode will last three days. If you touch me during that time, we will make a child."

"Then we will refrain from sex during those three days."

He sounded so logical, which was what she was trying to be. "You have never seen an Anwyn Queen in her fertile phase. It may be necessary for you to restrain me."

For a moment he was speechless. "I . . . I can't."

"Then use your little trick on my throat and render me unconscious."

"I can't keep you unconscious for three days!"

Who was being illogical now? "You have already kidnapped me, rendered me unconscious, and imprisoned me. Why is this any different?"

"Because I know you now. Things have changed."

"You would prefer to ask me to tell my child that I murdered his or her father?"

Joryn blinked hard. "What I ask of you is not murder, Keelia, you can't—"

"No matter what word you prefer, the outcome is the same. Would you have me kill you while your baby grows inside me? Would you force me to tell our son or daughter that I was obligated to take your life so you would not become a monster? A child of our making would be faced with enough difficulties without that additional burden. To be . . . to be . . ."

His face relaxed and the expression became calm. No, more than calm. Numb. Cold. "Little steals your tongue.

Shall I finish for you? You do not wish to bear a Caradon child."

Her lips pursed tightly. "Don't be ridiculous."

"Is that what I am? Ridiculous?"

Keelia threw her hands in the air. "I don't understand your problem! You said yourself that you do not wish to make a child. Surely you can see the hardships such a child would face. If not, then is your reticence a product of your hatred for my people? Are you simply disgusted at the idea of fathering an Anwyn babe?"

She waited for Joryn's quick denial, but he remained silent for a few long moments, and then he said in a lowered voice, "That's part of it, I suppose."

She'd made many concessions for her Caradon lover. She had ceased issuing commands, she had stopped trying to convince him that they were meant to be mated, she was trying her very best to save his life! And all this time, he despised her for the blood that ran through her veins.

Neither of them wished to create a half-breed child in an uncertain world and still . . . it hurt. She turned her back on him and began to climb once again. Knowing the truth would make it easier to keep her distance when she wanted him but could not have him. Knowing he was disgusted by the idea of her carrying his child would help her to maintain her dignity when her body demanded release.

No, during heat her body demanded more than release. It was fertile and demanded to be nurtured. The trance state which offered her release had done nothing more than keep her from going mad. It had never been sufficient. It had never been enough.

With Joryn so close, how would she manage to keep her hands off him? She glanced back to see him following at a greater distance behind than was usual. He did not wish to speak to her further, apparently.

A Queen should not suffer because a common Caradon magician thought poorly of her people, but as she climbed the mountain—still intent on saving him if she could—her heart broke a little.

JORYN HAD ALWAYS EMBRACED HIS FREEDOM, SO HE had never before spent more than two nights with one woman. By that time he was always ready to move on. After all the nights he'd spent in the embrace of the Anwyn Queen, he should be mightily tired of her. Tired of her red hair, her slight body, her gold eyes, her pale skin, the way she cried out when her pleasure came, the way her body fluttered into his, the way she touched him.

But he was not at all tired of her, which made it difficult to keep his distance, especially now.

Though Keelia insisted that she did not want him, the way she looked at him said something entirely different. She watched him with hooded eyes filled with her own special fire; she moved with an increased sensuality. She licked her lips. Slowly.

They stopped for the night, and Keelia quickly removed her tattered gold gown. She sat upon a grassy slope and assumed the position he had seen her take once before, crossing her legs and closing her eyes, dismissing him entirely. Her breaths came evenly and deeply. Her eyelashes fluttered and her cheeks grew pink. She sighed.

He knew this look; he had come to adore that expression on her beautiful face. Somehow, she was having sex without him.

In no time at all, she threw her head back and moaned. Her body twitched, her lips parted slightly, and she gasped.

Joryn had vowed to stay away from the Anwyn Queen during these three days, but his body had not received the message, apparently. He was hard, and his hands itched to grab Keelia and wrap her legs around his hips. He longed to bury himself inside her.

Moving slowly, she rose to her feet and looked squarely at him. Her gaze dropped, so that she could see very well how she affected him. Once again, she licked her lips, and then she smiled and took a sensuous step toward him.

So this was the Anwyn Queen in heat.

"That was pleasant, but it was not entirely enough," she said. "You know what I need, Joryn. Give it to me."

He had to remind himself that she was not in her right mind. Not now, not for the next three days. If he left her with his child growing inside her, what a disaster that would be. Would she hesitate in taking his life, if it came to that? And if they survived with their souls and their bodies intact, would the child bind them together forever?

The word "forever" still terrified him, and so did the idea of making a child. He had allowed Keelia to think that he was appalled at the idea of fathering a half-Anwyn baby, but in truth it was the fear of spreading his gift that held him in check.

An untaught child who could open doors into the land between life and death could cause disaster for himself and those around him. He might take friends there to play with the spirits and never return; he might bring unwanted spirits back with him into this world, where they could wreak havoc.

An untaught child with his gift might start an unchecked fire that would open a doorway that could never be closed.

Even though Keelia reached down and grabbed him, Joryn controlled himself. "From what I just saw, you don't need me at all."

"But I do." She stroked. "Visions and fantasies suffice when you are not present, but why should I settle for an unreal, unnatural fantasy release when you are *here*." She squeezed to make her point. "I command you to fuck me, Joryn."

He had a sudden vision of those claws of hers springing to life at an inopportune moment. Perhaps he should appease her for now.

"I cannot deny the Anwyn Queen when she commands me," he said, wrapping his arms around her.

She smiled, and her grip lessened. Her body slithered and pressed against his, and he felt a deep tremble pass from her body to his.

"Lie down," he whispered.

Keelia did as he commanded, lying on a bed of soft grass. When he did not immediately join her, she crooked one small finger at him and grinned widely. She knew she was irresistible. She knew no man would walk away from such an offer.

Joryn lowered his body so it was pressed to hers, and Keelia wrapped her legs around his hips. She was right *there*, wet and hot and tight and trembling. Her fingers speared through his hair, and she held on forcefully.

"Don't make me wait any longer, Joryn," she said breathlessly. "In my dreams it has always been you . . . always you, before we met, before we formed our union in fact. Reality is so much more wonderful than my dreams and visions, I don't know how I will ever again be satisfied with anything less." Her eyes glowed, and her hips rocked against his.

Joryn's entire body shook. He wanted this woman in a way that went beyond anything he had ever known. His body was drawn to hers in an explosive and undeniable way, and at this moment he could almost believe that she was his mate. His lifelong, bonded by the soul, *mate*.

He reached out and cupped her breast, and she trembled. His hand raked up to her cheek and he caressed her there. And then his hand slid to her neck, and he pinched her in a soft and vulnerable spot where he had pinched her once before.

She realized what he was going to do a split second before he pressed the proper nerve; he saw that knowledge in her eyes. And then she was limp and motionless. Sleeping, for all intents and purposes.

For how long? Normally she would be unconscious for several hours, but would her condition affect the length of her oblivion?

At least he could be honest with her while she was out. He spoke to her bare, limp body while he grabbed up her gown and began to tear strips from the hem. "You would be satisfied to know that I am in great pain, and that this is a tremendous sacrifice for me. I swear, Keelia, you make me question everything I have ever believed to be true. You make me wonder if it isn't possible that there is a lifelong mate for me, and . . . and if perhaps it isn't you."

He took her hands in his, crossed her wrists, and bound them securely together. His fingers brushed the silver bracelet she always wore, the bracelet which had once been his. He liked seeing it on her; he got some odd satisfaction from looking at the ancient silver against her pale flesh. "I have never known a woman like you, but then I have never known an Anwyn female, or a Queen, for that matter."

He bound her ankles together as well, but tried not to make the bonds too tight. She had incredible strength to call upon, so he had to be careful to restrain her well without hurting her.

He did not want to hurt her.

When she was well bound and still sleeping, he settled down beside her, wondering if he'd pass the next three days in pain. He could relieve himself in a solitary manner, and probably would before the night was over, but he had a feeling that sad release would be a temporary fix which would not last, no better than Keelia's visions.

Visions of him, she said. Visions she'd had long before they met.

Any man might wonder whether or not everything he'd ever believed might be wrong, when confronted with a vision like the Anwyn Queen in her fertile time. She was meant to be incredibly desirable. She was intended to be irresistible. There was probably some sort of Anwyn magic at work here.

But in truth, he'd begun to doubt his beliefs long before her heat had begun.

"Sometimes, when I allow my mind to wander, it does seem that you are entirely mine." Anwyn or not, Queen or not . . .

A ridiculous notion for a man who would most likely not live to see the rise of the next full moon.

SITTING IN THE MASSIVE CHAIR IN HIS MAIN ROOM IN this series of caves, Maccus closed his eyes and inhaled deeply. She moved closer, his Queen. She was drawn to him as he had known she would be. All was coming together just as he had been promised.

She would be here soon, well before the full moon by his reckoning. When he took a deep breath, he could almost smell her. It had been suggested that he wait for special conditions before making her his own, but Maccus had never been patient. He had never been good at waiting. A few of his servants would make certain that the Red Queen came to him more quickly than she might on her own. There was no need to take the chance that she might not arrive in time.

A stream of blackness, a sliver of a dark cloud, rose up out of the rock a few feet away. It was in this way that the Isen Demon always appeared to him. When the time was right, they would be one, as was intended, but for now they operated in concert rather than in perfect unity. That unity would come, as the demon grew stronger and as Maccus himself grew in strength.

The Red Queen would give him that strength.

The demon had no voice, and still Maccus heard the censuring words. In his mind, they echoed.

She is to be bathed in the blood of her lover when you wed her.

"Yes, I remember that instruction."

The wedding must happen beneath the full moon,

*when she draws the power of the animal into her blood.
Do not touch her until that moment. Do not touch her!*

Damned demon had been reading his mind again. It was more than annoying when that happened, but he imagined that when they were joined, it would be even more so. Such was the price for a power beyond all imagining.

"I will wait as you command," Maccus promised. "I will be . . . patient."

See that you do. With that, the wisp of black smoke was sucked into the earth once again.

Maccus could—and had—defied many more powerful than himself and succeeded, but he was not foolish enough to deny the demon. Promises had been made; a pact had been formed. There was no turning back now . . . not that he was at all tempted to do so.

With the demon absent, Maccus closed his eyes again and reached out for his Queen. *His* Red Queen.

10

KEELIA'S SLEEP WAS DEEP, AND FOR THE MOST PART ALL was black and quiet. Now and then she drifted toward consciousness and heard a familiar voice. Joryn's voice. He said things Joryn would not say, so she decided the words were part of a dream. Odd, since she had not dreamed at all the last time Joryn had rendered her unconscious. Not that she remembered, in any case.

She woke slowly, gradually coming to understand that she was being carried. Not gently, as you might imagine a Queen would be borne, but draped over Joryn's shoulder like a sack of meal and horribly jostled as he walked and climbed at a quick pace. A moment later, she realized that she was naked, and that her hands and feet were bound.

Her insides fluttered insistently.

"What are you doing?" she asked, trying to make her voice cold, and failing miserably.

"Don't pretend you don't remember exactly what happened, Your Persistent and Very Naked Majesty."

She'd wanted Joryn desperately, and she'd done her best to get him. The priestesses who'd seen to her training since the age of fifteen had told her she would be irresistible when she set her mind on seduction, but apparently that was not the case. In this way, as in so many others, she was a failure as Anwyn Queen. She was different from all those who had come before her. For as long as she could remember, she'd been told that she was special and powerful and unique. She would give anything to be more like the women who had come before her; women who had not failed in the simplest of tasks.

She wanted Joryn now, but did not find herself in the best position for another attempt at seduction. Just as well, since that attempt would likely also fail.

That didn't mean she wanted him any less. Joryn's skin against hers was wonderfully seductive. Always, but especially now. Draped over him as she was, she felt him everywhere, and her insides fluttered again. His skin was so close, she could not help but inhale his arousing scent. That scent alone was enough to make her quiver deeply.

She pressed her bound hands against his bare back in order to steady herself, and to feel his wonderful skin. All she wore was the silver bracelet he had given her, and it brushed against his nicely muscled back just as her fingers and palms did. Her thumbs raked against a particularly attractive muscle; the tips of her fingers swayed.

The heat of her fertile time had always been strong, but now that she knew what it was like to have a true lover, now that she understood the depth of the sensations

of making love, the heat was beyond strong. It was daz-
zling. It was unstoppable. She closed her eyes, and imagined Joryn pushing inside her, again and again.

Her hands balled into fists, and she moaned. Her
body lurched slightly.

Joryn sighed. "Not again."

"Yes, *again*," Keelia snapped, forcing her mind away
from the fantasies of love. "How long was I unconscious?"

"All last night and through the morning. The sun is
high in the sky at this hour."

Less than a full day. Two more full days, plus a little
more, before this need eased into something more manageable.

"Stop for a moment."

Joryn's answer was a harsh burst of laughter.

"Please," she said softly. "This is a very uncomfortable position. I only wish to stretch my aching limbs."

"Your commands didn't work, so now you're going
to try begging?"

"I did not beg!" Keelia insisted. "I simply said please.
It's not the same as *begging*." No matter how desperate
she felt, she would not be reduced to pleading for relief
of any sort.

Joryn did stop, and he very gently placed her on her
feet. She could barely move at all, since her hands and
feet were bound, but that didn't stop her body from re-
acting when she looked at her lover. Small insistent ex-
plosions throughout her body demanded that she take
what she needed from this man. She had survived many
fertile times without feeling quite this way. She'd medi-
tated, and dreamed, and visited her own unreal world,
but she had never been tempted to demand that a man

ease the pain for her. Even now, she did not want anyone else to lie with her. True, no one else was *here*, but even if she had her pick of any brawny Anwyn or this Caradon, there would be no choice at all. Joryn was hers.

"We could make love, and right before you—"

"No," Joryn interrupted. Then he laughed again, with that harsh bark. "Keelia, I want you to listen to me very carefully."

"Of all the things I want to do to you, listening is very low on the list," she said honestly.

He took her by the shoulders and made her look him in the eye. "Do you remember how the one beast who held on to his soul fought for it? Do you remember how he battled for what was right, for what was his?"

"Yes," she whispered.

"You must fight now, Keelia, and dammit, so must I."

"Because you hate the Anwyn."

He opened his mouth to answer and then clamped it shut again. "What difference does it make why I fight?"

Tears welled up in her eyes but did not fall. She was so certain that he was the one, and he dismissed her for her Anwyn blood, just as she had once dismissed him because he was Caradon. With nothing but desire clouding her mind, that detail seemed so unimportant. Why could he not see that her blood didn't matter?

"I must be very pathetic to you, needing something only you can give me and suffering for it even though I know you despise me for what I am."

"I do not despise you."

"Any other man would give me what I need."

Joryn reached out and touched her face. He did not know how dangerous that simple caress was. "We were brought together for a momentous cause, Keelia. We are here not as man and woman, but as Caradon and Anwyn. We are meant to fight the evil that has infected my people and will soon infect yours if we are not successful. I will not deny that I have very much enjoyed our time together, when we have set aside our calling for pleasure on occasion, but that does not mean there can be anything more. Whether I am saved or not, I cannot leave a child with my gift behind, and you cannot go back to your people carrying a half-breed babe."

"But—"

"You know I am right in this."

Keelia closed her eyes and swayed. "You don't know how strong this desire within me is."

"I think I do," he responded.

He did want her. Perhaps she wasn't a complete failure, after all.

"You are right in all you say, but right now I can't think of anything but what my body needs. It's never been this difficult for me," she confessed. "I'm always anxious and twitchy during the fertile days, but the occasional trance takes care of the problem for me, at least for a few hours. Last night, it didn't help at all. I turned around and there you were, and even though I had just experienced release through my vision, at the sight of you I hurtled beyond control." She sighed. There was only one solution. "You must make sure I'm unconscious for the entire three days."

Joryn shook his head. "No. You need to eat and drink, and—"

"I can survive two more days without food and water, but I can't survive this!" Her claws began to emerge.

Joryn didn't back away from her. He reached out

and clamped his hand on her wrists. "Stop," he whispered. "Control it. I know you can, Keelia. I know you can. You have the strength and the bravery to fight anything. Even this."

The claws retracted, and she felt a small sense of control in her traitorous body. She wanted to forget who she was and become nothing more than an animal intent on making sure the species survived.

Which species?

But Joryn was correct. She was not here for herself, but to stop the dark magic that had dared to invade her mountains, and Joryn's. She took a deep breath. "All right. May I put on what's left of my frock?" There was likely not much of it remaining, since she recognized the strips of gold fabric that had been used to bind her hands and feet.

"As much as I would love to cover your distracting nakedness, I can't figure out how to get the gown onto your body without untying your hands." Joryn gave her a pained smile. "I didn't plan very well last night."

It wasn't as though he hadn't seen her naked before, but when he carried her and her skin brushed against his . . . well, any amount of clothing would be better than none. "Next time you render me unconscious, you can untie my hands and put my clothes on and then re-bind my hands. It won't be easy, since I will not be able to help you at all, but—"

"I'll do it."

They rested for a moment before continuing on. There was little dried meat left in his pack, and Joryn didn't dare leave her alone to hunt for meat, so he fed her sweet, wild berries, slipping small pieces into her mouth and waiting while she chewed and swallowed. He held the wineskin of water to her mouth, and administered a few drops at a time. Those simple and necessary gestures seemed to Keelia to be madly intimate and arousing. His fingers so close to her mouth, his care of her so tender.

She fought for control, as the beast who had helped them defeat the monsters had fought, reminding herself that if he could endure great pain to hold on to his soul, she could fight the surge of desire she felt whenever she looked at Joryn, or when his fingers brushed against her lips as he fed her.

No matter how she fought, the desire continued to build until she felt like she would scream, or break the bonds and attack him. She could escape from these bonds, but she was not quite that far gone. If she remained conscious, however, there was no telling what she might do.

Joryn ate quickly, and then made as if to touch her throat. She instinctively lifted her hands to cover the vulnerable spot. "Before you do that, can I have a moment?"

"A moment for what?"

Release, sanity, false love. "A moment of meditation."

He groaned. "Do you know how hard that is to watch when I can't touch you?"

"Turn around or shut your eyes," she suggested. "I must do *something*." She closed her eyes and began to take long, deep breaths that would put her in a trance-like state where she could have a false visualization of what she needed so desperately.

She very quickly found herself in a meadow as usual. Joryn was beside her, naked and smiling and wonderfully aroused. In her fantasies he loved her very well. He did not tell her she wasn't good enough for him, or cringe at the idea of giving her a child. He did not talk of duty or darkness or death. No, in her fantasies, he gave her everything she wanted. In her fantasies, he obeyed all her commands.

JULIET WAS CERTAIN THAT HALF THE ANWYN ARMY and her three eldest sons were searching for the missing Queen, but she refused to wait for them or turn away from the path on which she knew Keelia had walked. Her psychic powers had been adversely affected by something of late, but she fought for knowledge and chased down the trail she instinctively knew her daughter had taken. Ryn did not question her or suggest that they wait for assistance.

"We are deep in Caradon Territory," Ryn observed without slowing his step.

"Yes, I know."

"Have you given any thought to the prophesy? Is that why we are here?" She could hear the worry in his voice. He had always been concerned about the foretelling of the union between the Red Queen and a Caradon lover. She didn't think an entire day had passed since Keelia's birth that Ryn had not given the dreaded prophesy some thought.

"I don't know," she said honestly. "Perhaps."

"So you will be warned," Ryn said with an uncustomary glint of steel in his eyes, "if we find our daughter with a Caradon, I will kill him." His words were calm, but the threat was a real one.

Juliet was guided by her magical instincts, but soon her Anwyn senses told her just as strongly that Keelia had been along this path. Days old, the scent was unmistakable. Ryn caught the scent, too. She knew by the way his step increased and the glint in his eyes grew harder.

It wasn't only Keelia's scent that guided them, but that of a Caradon male.

JORYN HAD NEVER CONSIDERED HIMSELF THE SELF-sacrificing sort. He enjoyed his independence, even though he studied rigorously with the Grandmother and did what was expected of him when she asked. It was his obligation to refine the gift he had been given. When called, he had not hesitated in the mission on which his teacher had sent him, but he had always known that when his duty was done, he would go back to his old life. He spent time honing his magic and always would, but he was not wedded to any schedule, and when he grew tired of studies and exercises, he was always free to leave the Grandmother and the other students and explore other regions of the vast Mountains of the North. He'd even ventured into the valleys below, mingling on occasion with the humans there. If he was very careful, they never knew that he was different.

But he never stayed long in places where he did not belong. He always returned to the mountains he considered his. It was invigorating to run and sleep beneath new skies, to wake not knowing what each day would bring.

Watching Keelia yearn for him and not touching her was definitely an acute form of self-sacrifice. Like her, he had to dig deep within himself for control during these long days. When he faltered, he imagined a half-breed son or daughter with his gift, growing up in The City without the proper training, without being taught the necessary control. Perhaps if he survived, if they really did find the wizard and destroy the stone, he might consider Keelia's notion that they were meant to be together.

If any woman could entice him to sacrifice his beloved freedom, it would be this one.

Tomorrow her fertile time would be finished, thank the gods. The inconvenience of the timing had cost them dearly; the journey was considerably slower than it had been, since he had to carry her unconscious body and the way was not always an easy one.

He reached a plateau, and while Keelia had directed him as to which way to go, she had not told him there would be a fork in the path. He didn't know which path to take, so he gently laid her on her back and took the opportunity to rest.

She looked peaceful enough, lying on the grass unconscious. There wasn't much left of her dress. The hem now hit her well above the knees. Short women didn't usually have such nice legs, in his experience, but hers were fine—as was everything else about her. Yes, if any woman could tempt him to change his life, it would be her.

It wouldn't be long before she woke. When that happened, he'd feed her, allow her to relieve herself if it was necessary, ask her which path they should take, and then render her unconscious again.

There was much more at stake than his personal freedom. He'd do well to remember that fact when he was tempted by her.

He heard her breathing change before she opened her eyes. She came awake not with a start, but languidly, as if she were lying in her own soft bed instead of on the hard ground.

"Why did we stop?" she asked, her voice lethargic.

"There's a fork in the path," he explained. "I wasn't sure how to proceed."

Keelia sat up, graceful even though her hands and feet were bound. She studied both ways, and a small wrinkle appeared between her eyes. "One leads to the wizard, the other leads to . . ." Her head tilted. "Death. One path to victory, one to the end. One to the stone we seek, one to a great fall."

"Which is which?" he snapped.

Keelia's eyes met his, and he saw the worry there. "I don't know. If you would open yourself to me, if you would stop hiding, maybe I could see your future and in that way I would realize which is the right path."

Joryn started to explain that he was not hiding from her, and then he realized the truth of what she said. She'd been right all along. He was holding back. Subconsciously at first perhaps, but still, thanks to his magic, he had the ability to keep his thoughts from her.

His inborn magic, or a mate's right?

Keelia looked down at her bound hands. "Maybe the bracelet still comes between us. I never should've put it on. Take the blasted thing off and toss it over the cliff, and then perhaps I will be able to see what lies ahead for you."

Joryn reached out and attempted to gently slide the bracelet from her wrist. With the bonds there, crisscrossed over the silver, the task was impossible. He drew away after a cursory attempt, as he could not bear to touch her any longer. She was much too tempting, even now.

"Perhaps later."

Keelia lifted her hands. "You can untie me. I'm fine, truly. The difficult time has passed. I think we handled it quite well, don't you?"

He reached again for the golden bonds, relieved that he would no longer have to carry her, but he stopped before he actually touched her hands. "You said the fertile time would last three days. It's been two and a half."

She sighed dramatically. "Fertility is not an exact science, you maddening Caradon. Perhaps the length of time was shortened because the heat came early."

"Perhaps you're lying to me."

Her eyes widened. "I have told you many times, I do not lie!"

"Not even to get what you want?"

She pursed her lips. "What makes you think I still want you?"

The too-quick beating of her heart; the telling pink flush on her skin; the sparkle in her golden eyes as she tried to deny what she felt.

He was so intensely focused on Keelia, he did not see or hear or smell the beasts until it was almost too late. There were three of them, and they screeched as they attacked, two rushing around a bend in the path, one leaping from a ledge high above. Joryn spun and stood in one smooth motion, drawing his knife and placing himself between Keelia and the monsters who had once been Caradon and were now unnatural things which did not belong in a decent world.

They surrounded him in a half-circle, one straight

ahead, one to the left, one to the right. They looked almost amused. All three wore stones around their necks, stones which lay against flesh that was alternately furry and fleshy. These were not innocent Caradon who had been bitten against their will, but three of the original beasts who had chosen to be this way. These were the creatures who were spreading the venom.

The one in the middle spoke, with great difficulty. "Ya d'not b'long here." His words sounded muddy, since his snout was misshapen, but his intent was clear enough.

"Neither do you," Joryn responded. Such creatures did not belong anywhere on this earth.

"We will tak the keen and let you liv," the beast said. "Mof aside."

"No."

"The keen will be ourzz sun enuf no matter what you say, und so will you." His eyes dropped to the site of the bite, even though his torn trousers covered the area, and even if they had not, there was no longer a scar or a scratch to mark the injury. "Fur days, and you'll becum one ov us. He is anxious to haf you, yust as he is anxious to haf her."

"We will never be with you." Joryn wished heartily that he had freed Keelia when she'd asked it of him. Now that the beasts were here, he did not have time to cut her bonds. Before he was done with that simple task, the three mutant beasts would be on top of him, and on top of Keelia.

"Yur will departs wif yur soul," the beast explained. "There is great freedom in what you will become, broder. Freedom and strenk and puwer."

"I am not your brother."

The beast grinned, showing sharp, yellowed teeth. "Yu will be."

At once, the attention of all three of the beasts was ripped from Joryn to Keelia. He knew why without turning to look, since he heard her step in the dirt and also heard what sounded very much like a growl deep in her throat.

When Keelia stood beside him, Joryn glimpsed a creature very much like the ones who had intruded upon their camp. She was not human, but neither was she wolf. She possessed claws and wicked teeth, but continued to stand on two feet.

He barely took time to recognize that she had freed herself quite easily and quickly, and probably could've done so at any time in the past two and a half days. So why hadn't she?

Keelia and the Caradon beasts moved forward at the same time. They were more interested in her than they were in him, so two focused on her. They wanted her, but why? One beast, the monster that had been standing on Joryn's left, tried to stop him from interfering in their taking of the Queen.

These creatures who wore the stones were more intelligent than the others he'd faced. The one he battled fought smarter, protecting himself from Joryn's knife thrusts and going for the torso with his own short-bladed weapon. Only one hand was capable of grasping a knife handle, since the other was more paw than hand. That paw possessed wicked claws.

Beside him, Keelia was little more than a blur, attacking with her claws and drawing blood, seemingly unafraid of the knives and claws the attackers wielded and dodging with great ease and grace their attempts to wound or grab her. She leapt out of their reach with an unexpected strength, seeming to fly out of their range and then just as easily dip back in again to attack.

From the thing's muddied words, it seemed that they wished to take Keelia and leave him alive, since he would soon be like them, but they were brutal in their attack. They went for crippling wounds rather than ones which would kill, but they were far from gentle. They would be satisfied to leave here with a badly wounded prisoner.

With a jump to the side and a quick thrust, Joryn was able to kill the beast he fought. At the same time, one of the mutants who battled with Keelia fell. She swiped out, and the thing was dead before he hit the ground. Faced with taking on both of them, the monster in the middle, the one who had spoken, ran. Keelia made as if to follow, but Joryn stopped her. He laid a stilling hand on a furry red arm, and instantly—*instantly*—she was woman once more.

"Let him go."

"But he will tell the wizard where we are and that we've defeated them, and he'll send more of those things to attack us!" she argued, turning to face him. She was so beautiful. Moments ago she had been a monster much like the ones who had attacked, but now . . . she was once again the woman who had bewitched him. She was the woman who made him question everything he had believed to be true for so long.

Anwyn were the enemy.

No woman was worth the sacrifice of his freedom.

He could never be satisfied with the same woman, day after day after day.

He could tell her none of that. Not now, not ever.

"Yes," Joryn said. "The beast who escaped will no doubt go directly to the wizard." A smile bloomed on his face. "And we will follow."

II

THE ATTACK ADDED EVEN MORE URGENCY TO THE MISsion they had set for themselves. Apparently the wizard wanted her, and they fully expected Joryn to become like them when the full moon rose. The wizard and his monstrous soldiers knew too much. They knew that Keelia was coming, that Joryn had been bitten.

Keelia experienced a chill. Perhaps it was no mistake that Joryn had been bitten and they'd survived the initial attack. Perhaps everything that had happened to this point was a part of the evil wizard's plan, and they were walking into a trap.

Why did the wizard want *her*? It made no sense.

As she walked along an almost flat slice of trail, Keelia attempted to remove the silver bracelet. She did not want to toss it away, since it was all she had of Joryn, but if the simple piece was somehow interfering in her ability to see what lay ahead, then she had to be rid of it.

The bracelet had conformed to her wrist too well, and would not release. The wide band of silver hugged her small wrist and would not budge. Joryn seemed to have forgotten about the discussion they'd been having before the attack. He hadn't mentioned the bracelet once since they'd moved away from the site of the ambush.

Eventually, Keelia stopped trying to twist the bracelet off. Joryn had put it on her; perhaps it was required that he be the one to remove it.

Darkness fell long before Joryn said it was time for rest. All afternoon they'd followed the path the fleeing Caradon beast had taken. The correct path, they hoped. On this patch of flat land, Joryn built a small fire. The fire might give away their location, but he didn't care. "Let them come," he'd said as he built the fire.

Keelia had told Joryn that her fertile time was over. In truth it was waning, but it was certainly not *over*. She still wanted him, but she no longer felt as if her body was hurtling beyond control. Even though she did not lie, she believed this small falsehood to be justified. She was tired of being unconscious, of being carried, of being denied.

If they were not able to end the curse in time, the man she loved would become a monster . . . unless she did as he insisted and took his life before that happened. What if this was her only chance to know what it was like to hold the man she loved during her fertile time? What if this was their last, their *only*, chance to create a child?

Her gaze was drawn up to the growing moon. Four days until it would be full again. Four days, and if they did not destroy the wizard's stone, then Joryn would die.

She didn't like the possibilities that whirled in her

head, but if it became necessary, she would kill the man she loved to keep him from becoming like the things who had attacked them. It would take great strength and it would hurt beyond all imagining, but she would not allow the man she loved to lose his soul and become a monster.

Oddly enough, just weeks ago she had not thought "monster" and "Caradon" to be so very far apart.

Joryn stretched out on the ground close by her, but he did not sleep. Keelia wondered if he would ever sleep again. She scooted closer, but not so close that she could touch him. Yet. If she allowed her falsehood to continue, she could have everything she wanted. Joryn; pleasure; his child. No matter how desperately she wanted him, she wouldn't allow a falsehood at the root of their union. It just wasn't right.

Keelia offered him her arm. "Can you remove the bracelet from my wrist? I tried, but it won't cooperate with me."

He barely touched the silver, and she knew, even though she could not read his mind, that no matter how difficult it made their journey, he did not wish her to peek into his mind. Eventually he made a halfhearted attempt to twist the silver band off, but it would not move.

His hand dropped away. "Perhaps it is not time for the bracelet to leave you."

"Perhaps you do not wish for me to know your thoughts, no matter what the cost might be."

He remained silent, not bothering to deny her accusation.

"I did lie to you a little," Keelia said when the silence stretched too long.

Joryn did not seem surprised. "About what?"

"My fertile time isn't entirely over. Almost," she added quickly, "but not entirely."

"Do I need to tie you up again?" he asked, half joking, half pained.

Keelia toyed with the hem of her skirt . . . what was left of it. "I don't think I have enough fabric remaining to fashion new bonds. Sorry." She scooted a bit closer and reached out to touch his hair. "Would it truly be so horrible to make a child with me? Do you hate the fact that I'm Anwyn so much that the idea of giving me a baby disgusts you?"

He groaned a little. "Nothing about you disgusts me, Keelia."

"Are you bothered by the fight this afternoon? Are you frightened by the fact that when I changed in part, I was very much like the Caradon beasts?"

"No," he said quickly. "You're nothing like them."

She moved so close that her leg rested against his. He was warm and hard and wonderful. "Then why?"

He grinned, and she could see the pain in that smile. "This is more difficult than denying you when you were demanding and throwing yourself at me, and trust me when I tell you that wasn't at all easy."

"I did not throw myself at you," Keelia said as she draped her leg over his and placed her head against his arm. "I only made it clear in every way possible that I needed you. Only you," she added.

His body wanted hers, that much was clear. And still he fought against her.

"I could tell you that my heat is over and we can lie together without making a child, but that is not so. The most fertile time has passed, but to make a child is still possible."

He glanced sideways at her. "Possible or assured?"

"At this time, possible. Perhaps even probable. But not assured, as it would've been yesterday."

He held his breath, then sighed. "It's a chance we can't take, Keelia. Your Anwyn blood doesn't bother me, not anymore. In the beginning it did give me pause, but . . . no longer. I like you. I admire you. You're beautiful and passionate and amazingly brave, and no matter what happens, I'm glad that my path led me to you for a while. But to leave behind a child with my gift—"

"Do you think I can't handle a bit of magic in my offspring?" Keelia interrupted. "I can teach a child to control fire if need be. I can see that he or she is trained by the best Anwyn wizards and priestesses if you are not there to see to the training yourself."

"No matter what happens in four days, I will not be there," Joryn said, and she was reminded that he didn't believe they were mated. Even if she saved him, would he walk away from her? Yes, yes he would. Without a second thought, without a single doubt, he would walk away.

"I don't care," she whispered, and then she touched his cheek and made him look at her. She rose up slightly and placed her mouth near his ear. "I know you don't want to hear this, but I love you. You are the man I was meant to spend my life with. Maybe our time together will be short, maybe it will be long. I don't know. I should know, but I *don't*, and it's maddening."

His green eyes remained calm. "You think you love me because it is your duty as a Queen to make babies, and I am here."

"It's more than that."

"I don't believe in love."

"I do. Maybe I can believe enough for both of us."

He looked away from her, then back again. The fire-light flickered on his face, and she saw a muscle in his jaw twitch. "My gift is more than making campfires and lighting torches, Keelia."

"I know . . ."

"No, you don't!" His voice rose sharply. "You don't know," he said again, more softly.

"I could know if you would only open yourself to me," she argued gently. "Open your mind." *Your heart, your soul.*

"I would have nothing left for myself if I gave every-thing I am to you," he confessed. "If I open my mind to you, I will no longer possess that part of myself which is meant only for me. I will lose my freedom, my dig-nity, my honor, if I give everything I am over to you."

"So you won't lie with me when we might make a child, and you won't allow me to so much as peek into your mind."

"No."

Anger replaced desire. "You would prefer to be alone in all ways until death comes for you, whether it comes tomorrow or in four days or in forty years."

"Yes."

She knew she loved him then, because he broke her heart with that one word. No one had ever dared to hurt her this way before, and she was unprepared for the sharpness of the attack. After slowly untangling their legs, she scooted away from him, "Fine, then."

"Tomorrow when you're sure you won't conceive, we will—"

"No," Keelia said sharply. Joryn wasn't the only one concerned with dignity and honor in this relationship.

"I want all or nothing from you, and it looks as if you are not willing to part with anything near *all*."

"Keelia . . ."

"Do not try to sweet-talk me," she said as she continued to scoot away from him. She moved away until her hip met rock. "You've made your wishes clear. We will do our best to destroy the wizard's stone, and if we cannot accomplish that mission, I will kill you before the rise of the next full moon."

Joryn tried to jest. "It sounds as though I've made that possibility a bit easier for you."

She wanted to say *yes* in a very definitive voice, but couldn't.

WHEN THE NEXT DAY ARRIVED AND KEELIA WAS VERY obviously not in her fertile time, Joryn might've tried to seduce her. He thought about it. He was still in pain from need, and he certainly still wanted her. It seemed he always wanted her. But she had actually said she loved him, and that alone was enough to cool his ardor. Best to maintain this distance he had created in the name of remaining childless.

If only he didn't want her so much.

He could not dismiss the way she had leaned in last night and whispered in his ear. In the dreams she had often whispered words he could not decipher, but he'd known that they were important words, a message of great weight, words that would change his life. *I love you* couldn't be the message he'd dreamed of. It did not carry the import he'd known her dream whisper to have.

Following the trail of the mutant Caradon was easy enough. The creature stank to high heaven, and the scent permeated everything. Joryn could only hope that the beast was leading them along the path to the wizard, and not along the path to death. A great fall, Keelia had said. There were certainly a number of possibilities for great falls as they climbed higher in these unfriendly mountains. At times the trail they followed was not much wider than the width of one foot, and a slip at the wrong time and place would send a careless traveler to a nasty death below. Keelia made her way with the grace he had come to expect from her, and a strength that continued to amaze him.

When they reached a wider section of the trail where death did not await with every misstep, Keelia relaxed visibly. Her breathing changed, and her limbs relaxed, as much so as was possible given the circumstances. There was very little left of her gown, and in actuality it could no longer be called more than a rag that barely covered her breasts and her belly and the tops of her thighs.

He rather liked it, but the garb did nothing to cool his ardor.

"When I get home, I'm going to have a bath straight away. A long, scented, bubbling bath."

It was good to think of what might come later if they survived. "I wouldn't mind a bath myself," he said. "And something to eat that didn't come straight from the tree or charred from a campfire."

"Redberry pie," Keelia said dreamily.

"Hunbeast stew."

"Bread still warm from the oven."

"Roasted, seasoned *tilsi*."

"Aunt Sophie's chicken and dumplings."

"Greasy fried tubers."

Keelia wrinkled her nose. "I don't care for fried tubers."

"More for me," he said, as if they would ever share a meal when this task was done. No, he would return to the Grandmother, his chore completed, and Keelia would return to her throne, where she would be waited upon and adored for the remainder of her life.

There were times when he was certain that Keelia would never appear less than queenly, no matter what the circumstance. But it was also easy to forget, now and then, that she was a Queen. It was more than the ragged clothes and tangled hair that sometimes made her appear less than regal; it was the way she attacked this chore. The way she was determined, as any soldier would be. She was a remarkable woman, but he could never tell her so.

Unaware of his thoughts, she continued the conversation. "I will gladly burn what is left of this dress, and order five others made to take its place. Usually a gown is disposed of if it is marred by one small stain, or the tiniest of tears. This"—she picked at the ragged hem—"is appalling. My mother would be dismayed to see me this way."

"It doesn't matter what you wear," Joryn said. "You're still Queen of the Anwyn, and a beautiful woman as well."

Keelia glanced back at him and raised her eyebrows slightly. "If you're trying to sweet-talk me, save your breath. I have not changed my mind. I demand all or nothing, and you have chosen nothing."

"I was speaking the truth, not attempting to sweet-talk you."

"Good," she said dispassionately as she returned her

gaze to the trail ahead and changed the subject. "I have begun to feel a bit anxious since we came off the narrow ledge. Do you sense anything different?"

"No." But then he had no psychic powers. "Perhaps you feel anxious because we're moving closer to our destination."

"I hope that's all it is," she said, lifting her eyes to study the rock face to her right. "I don't think any other Anwyn or human has ever been this deep in Caradon Territory."

"Likely not," Joryn agreed.

"That knowledge makes me feel a bit lonely. Maybe a bit lost." She studied her surroundings, continuing to move forward. "I am consumed by the certainty that I don't belong here."

Yes, you do. You very much belong here. Joryn dashed that thought aside with force.

It was late in the day when Keelia stopped. They would travel a bit farther before camping to attempt to sleep, but they could not continue on endlessly without rest.

Keelia didn't immediately sit to rest her weary legs, but rounded a boulder where she could have a moment of privacy. Joryn did not know why she continued to be shy about some things when she was anything but shy about others. Still, he did not chide her for hiding from him for these brief moments during the day. He made himself comfortable on the hard ground, sitting at first, then lying back to stretch out and gaze up into the darkening sky.

Three days now until the full moon. Joryn felt the passing of each day as if it flew by much too quickly. He was not afraid of death. Thanks to his gift, he knew without doubt that the afterlife was real, that death was not the end. There was the Land of the Dead for those who had earned reward, and a less pleasant destination for those who had done evil. The land in-between, the land he was able to visit on occasion through his fiery doorway, was for those who had not yet earned either reward. Their fate was uncertain, but it wasn't as if the land in-between was an unpleasant place.

He had done no evil in his lifetime, unless kidnapping Keelia counted as evil. As his intentions were honorable, he did not consider it to be so.

Joryn wasn't afraid of death, but he did feel as if this life was not done. Not yet. It was too soon for him to go to the Land of the Dead or the land in-between. He was not ready. There was wine to be drunk, and sights to see. Lessons to learn and laughter to share. There were women to love, though at the moment he could think only of one.

He watched the boulder, waiting for Keelia to appear. Deep inside, he was beginning to wonder if perhaps she might be a part of the life he was not ready to leave. Not forever, but for a while . . . for as long as they enjoyed one another's company. They'd had little opportunity for laughter, and he wanted very much to take her in a large, soft bed. He wanted to feed her that redberry pie, and dance with her to soft music, and take her to beautiful places she had never been.

As if a Queen of the Anwyn would agree to such a temporary relationship.

Where was Keelia? She should've joined him by now. She needed rest, but they did not have time to linger here for very long. Three days until the full moon. Three short days.

"Keelia?" he called, sitting up and dismissing his ridiculous fantasies. "Is everything all right?"

All remained silent. If she was back there enjoying herself in one of those maddening trances that left her flushed and shaking . . . no, she didn't mind if he watched that particular activity. Perhaps she knew how frustrating it was to witness such a delicious spectacle and not touch, and she enjoyed torturing him.

She did not answer his call, and he strained to listen.

He heard nothing, nothing at all.

Joryn jumped up and ran for the boulder, wishing fervently that he would find her there lost in a trance where she could experience release without him, but knowing in his heart that it would not be so. He no longer heard her, smelled her, *felt* her . . . How could this have happened so fast?

Behind the boulder, he found exactly what he had known he would find.

Nothing. Keelia was gone.

KEELIA TRIED TO STRUGGLE, BUT SHE COULD NOT move. She tried to scream, but no sound would leave her throat. A dark cloth of some sort covered her head, so she couldn't see anything either. She had been tossed over a large, hairy shoulder, and while it was similar to the position she had been in when Joryn had carried her, this harsh captor did not bother to be at all gentle about it. She was jostled mercilessly.

No wonder she had felt such unease this afternoon. The kidnapper had been watching for a while, waiting for an opportunity to sneak up behind her, drop a heavy, silencing talisman around her neck, and grab her.

Even though her psychic talents had been tainted, she could see some of the creature who had magically immobilized and grabbed her. The thoughts of the kidnapper were jumbled and sharp, and entirely unpleasant. He hated all those who were not like him. He most especially hated *her*, but he had been ordered not to harm the Anwyn Queen. Someone—someone of whom the soulless creature was afraid—had plans for her.

The mutant Caradon hadn't wanted to harm her—at least not too badly—when he and the others had attempted to kidnap her before. The three beasts—including this one lone survivor—had been ordered to take her alive, and unharmed if possible. The talisman she now wore had been in his possession all the time, only he had not had the opportunity to use it, not until now.

The beast had realized all along that she and Joryn followed. The thing had led his prey to precisely where he wanted them to be, and then waited for the right moment to attack them.

No, he'd waited for the right moment to attack *her*. The thing was quite certain that Joryn would soon be like him, twisted inside and out, soulless and existing only to serve its two masters—the wizard and the demon.

They had not been alarmed by his scent, because his stench was everywhere. He had planned well, this soulless creature had. Either that, or the wizard had armed him with a variety of plans for any contingency.

If she could unsheathe her claws, she could fight. But like everything else, they were frozen. Useless. All was numb.

If she and Joryn had built the kind of mental connection Anwyn Queens and their mates were supposed to possess, she could reach out to him now and call for help, but there was no connection beyond sex and their joint determination to stop the wizard who had created the mutants who threatened their mountains. Nothing more. Nothing at all. She didn't know if it was the bracelet or Joryn himself that interfered. Maybe it was both. Maybe they were one and the same in some way she did not understand.

Even though he'd been ordered to deliver her alive and preferably unharmed, if this creature had anything to say about the matter, she wouldn't have long to live. His hate of her was painful to experience, gut-wrenching to taste. His hate was not reserved just for her, of course. Hate permeated his misshapen body and his bitter mind. It filled the hole his soul had once possessed. Keelia shut down her ability to connect with the creature, sure that such bitterness would harm her if she wallowed in it for too long.

They had been traveling for a long while when the creature spoke, his voice muddy as it had been before. Each word was an effort, she knew, and yet he felt it necessary to speak to her. Even though his words were less than perfect, she had no trouble understanding him.

"T'ey vnt you badly, my mysters do. Bof ov dem haf great plan fur you." He cleared his throat and spat. "I hope you dis'ppoint dem, Anwyn Keen. Meybe iv yu annoy my mysters, dey vill gif yu to me to dispose ov." He spat again, harder this time. "I vuld like dat," he said dreamily.

Apparently the trail that would've led her to death by a great fall would've been the right choice, if this was the path to the wizard.

* * *

THEIR CAMP WAS ISOLATED, AND STILL CIRO MADE sure his legion operated properly, as an army should. Some soldiers kept watch on all perimeters, while others trained for the arduous battles to come.

Training—with strict orders not to kill one another—did not sate their need for blood, and they were growing hungry again. But they were not ready. Not to take on experienced soldiers or armed and vigilant villagers.

Ciro's tent was positioned in the center of camp, where anyone who thought to attack would have to fight past every soldier of his growing army, his devoted Own, to reach him. More of his Own came to him every day, and with each addition his army grew stronger. Even though he was anxious to continue on his journey, he knew it was not yet time.

Diella entered his tent as if it were her own. Ciro grit his teeth. He would be so glad when the time came that he could kill her outright. She was an annoyance, and she behaved as if she were still empress when her time was long past. She was merely the spirit of a long-dead empress trapped in a stolen body, and for some reason the demon wanted her to remain alive. For now.

"I'm bored," she said as she sauntered toward him.

"That's hardly my problem," Ciro responded.

"Surely you're not entirely happy to be sitting here when there is so much to be done."

"The demon will tell me when the time is right for us to make the next move."

"Yes, I'm sure it will."

Diella boldly sat on his knee, reaching into her pocket to withdraw a healthy portion of the drug Panwyr. At the sight of the gently sparkling brown powder, Ciro's mouth began to water. His brain pounded and his eyes could see nothing else but the offering on her palm.

The Isen Demon had been addicted for a long while, and Ciro had become addicted soon after the demon had joined with him.

"This will help us to pass the evening, will it not?"

Diella took a small pinch of the drug and sniffed it up her nose. Her cheeks, even the scarred one, went rosy, and her lips parted with a satisfied sigh.

Ciro took the drug from her palm, inhaling it as she had done. All worries about the battles to come melted away. When he was not thinking about taking his father's throne, he had room in his mind only for Rayne.

Beautiful Rayne, who would be his empress. Beautiful Rayne, who would bear his son.

Diella took his face in her hands, and he allowed her to do so. "So young," she whispered. "So handsome." Her fingers raked through his hair. "Such fair, lovely hair. Like an angel." One bold hand dropped into his lap and she sighed. "So large."

In the back of his mind, Ciro knew that Diella was not the one for him, that he should save himself for his beloved. But he did not tell the woman on his lap to stop, not when she fondled him, not when she freed him.

Diella roughly freed one breast and all but shoved it in his face, and Ciro did not mind. He was tempted to bite into the vein there, to take just a taste of her blood. But he did not bite. He squeezed hard, and laid his lips on the swell of young flesh, unable to stop himself. The drug swirled through his blood and made the world a fine place. There were many colors, here in his tent, colors which had taste and smell.

The power that surged through him was almost overwhelming, and he finally gave in to his impulses and raked his teeth over a tempting blue vein. He took a sip of blood, no more.

Diella's attentions became more ardent, and she stroked him forcefully and with demand. No one demanded anything of Ciro, not anymore.

No one but the Isen Demon.

The demon whispered inside Ciro's head. *She is mine. Take her for me.*

"But she's not . . ." Ciro stopped speaking and shut his eyes tight. His words were slurred. His thoughts were not. *She is not Rayne.*

Open your eyes.

He did so, and gasped at the sight so near. It was Rayne who leaned down to kiss the side of his neck, Rayne, with her dark hair and flawless face and perfect body who lifted her skirt and straddled him. It was Rayne's bare breast slightly stained with blood.

It was beautiful, pure of soul Rayne who took him into her body and offered him womanly heat and much needed release.

He had not known that an untried maid could be so bold and enthusiastic.

In the back of his mind, a dark voice whispered. *Mine. Mine.*

And then . . .

Ours.

12

"Gently, gently," a deep and pleasant male voice ordered as Keelia's captor tossed her to the ground. Her limbs were still useless, and she could not speak even to cry out in pain. She dropped to the ground limply, utterly defenseless.

She sensed a presence beside her—a presence very different from the rough and unkind creature who had kidnapped her.

"I'm sorry for your discomfort." The voice was low and reassuring, gentle and intelligent. Equally gentle hands removed the hood from her head, and she saw the wizard from her vision, the one who had enchanted the stone that had created the soulless monsters.

He lifted her head with great care and dropped yet another talisman around her neck. It was smaller than the binding talisman, and hung from a dainty silver chain. The stone was swirling gold and deep purple, and seemed to be alive in the way it sparkled and churned. At first Keelia was alarmed, but a rush of peace descended upon her.

The wizard seemed so kind. Perhaps her visions of him as an evildoer had been wrong. Perhaps her visions had been twisted by the same power that had dampened her psychic abilities. Nothing about him alarmed her, not in any way.

He was dressed in a flowing dark purple robe, and a very pretty silver and gold medallion lay against his chest. It wasn't a crude talisman like the ones the beasts wore, but was a very attractive piece of masculine jewelry. The two metals, one warm and one cool, were blended together, intertwining in fascinating swirls.

His hair was long and black, without even a hint of curl or wave, and it hung well past his shoulders. His eyes were green as emeralds, but there was a touch of something else blended with the green. Black, perhaps. Deep, endless black that she could very easily fall into. The eyes were odd, but his face was decidedly handsome. He had a wonderful smile. Keelia's heart leapt, and in that moment she knew she had been enchanted in some way. By the newest talisman perhaps, or by the eyes, or by some other spell he had used upon her. She tried to fight against the unnatural forces that affected her, but it was so hard. It would be so much easier to drift into the mindless oblivion he offered, rather than continuing to fight.

The wizard saw her uncertainty and his smile dimmed. "I have dreamed of this moment for so many years. Before the Isen Demon promised you to me, before I knew it was possible that I could actually have you for my own, I dreamed of bringing you here."

Keelia tore her eyes from the wizard's face and studied *here*. Purple-tinged wizard's light, along with ordinary lanterns and candles, illuminated this cave which was much more than a cave. She saw a number of naturally formed doorways which would lead to other rooms, or to an exit perhaps. The ceiling was high above, the smooth stone floor covered here and there by woven rugs. Like the Anwyn homes which were built into the mountain, this cave had been fashioned into the finest of dwellings. There were many furnishings, and some of the walls were covered by colorful tapestries. Having made the difficult climb, she wondered how they had come to be here.

Magic had been used in some cases, she imagined, but not in all. Some of the pieces had simply been constructed here. The wizard had been building this home for many years.

For her.

"Promise to behave yourself and I will remove the binding talisman."

Keelia wasn't sure how she was supposed to make such a promise when she couldn't move or speak.

The wizard reached out and grasped the stone that had immobilized her. As he lifted the stone and moved it past her eyes, she noted that it was different from the one the creatures wore, different from the one that now lay against her chest.

Again she realized she had been enchanted, so she fought. Inside, where the wizard could not see, she did battle with herself. A part of her saw this man as handsome and kind. She instinctively thought of him as a friend, one she could trust with her darkest secrets and her very life. But she knew this was not true. No wizard who used his gifts to create twisted monsters was kind. No man who used his magic for darkness was her friend. She fought very hard to retain her senses, but it wasn't easy. In fact, it would be very easy to drift into the world this wizard had built for her, to allow herself to be sucked into what he offered her, body and soul. It would be very much like falling into the blackness she sometimes saw in his eyes.

In doing so, she would lose herself. Keelia breathed deep and prepared to strike as soon as she was able. She could kill the wizard and the beast who had carried her here if her moves were well planned. Once they were dead, she could search at her leisure for the stone—given that there weren't more of the monsters waiting around every corner. It didn't matter; she had to try.

The wizard stopped moving while the binding talisman still hung over her head. She was unable to move or speak still, even though the stone was no longer touching her. Did the new talisman have the same effect? Had he simply exchanged one immobilizing spell for another? No, this was different somehow.

"Do you wonder why I have dreamed of you? Why I have gone to such lengths to prepare a home fit for a Queen?"

Actually, she did wonder a little. She had not dreamed of this wizard at all, not in her entire life. She had never so much as glimpsed him in a vision until she reached for information about the twisted Caradon and the reason for their existence.

"My name is Maccus. Perhaps that name resonates in the depths of your soul or in your very heart."

Keelia found that she could shake her head a little. She was still influenced by the original talisman, but as it no longer touched her, she was regaining some control of her body. Her fingers curled. A muscle in her jaw twitched.

"No?" Maccus said. "That's surprising. I did expect that my mate would know me when she saw my face."

Her voice was a raspy whisper as she answered, fighting still for control of her body and her mind. "You are *not* my mate."

His green eyes went hard. The black flecks there seemed to grow. "Do not pretend to be ignorant of your prophesy, my Queen. *Our* prophesy, I should say. The Anwyn Red Queen and her Caradon lover, her Caradon mate. The prophesy as you know it is not entirely correct, of course. Prophesies rarely are easily understood, and through the years they might become distorted."

Keelia held her breath. It was not possible that this evil wizard was her mate. It was Joryn who called to her, Joryn who invaded her dreams.

Joryn who did not want her.

She wanted to fight, but gradually her will faded and even though she did not move, it seemed that she drifted toward the wizard. Perhaps Maccus was right and she was meant to be here, with him. Perhaps he was not as evil as she had envisioned, but was simply misguided. "Distorted, how?" she asked, her voice rasping.

"Our union will not bring peace, my love." Maccus's smile seemed very real again. He truly was quite handsome, and Keelia felt what was left of her will seeping away. No, she felt it being ripped away. For a moment she knew it was some wicked enchantment that made her feel this way, and then she forgot. She no longer wished to harm the lovely wizard, even when he said, "Our great alliance will bring complete and utter chaos."

* * *

MACCUS STUDIED THE ANWYN QUEEN, A CONTENTED smile on his face. He'd waited such a long time for this moment, and she was everything he had hoped she would be.

Still influenced by the enchantment, she seemed dazed. Sleepy, perhaps. Very tired. Exhausted as she was, she looked much better than she had when Eneo had carelessly dumped her on the floor.

The Anwyn Queen had arrived here stained and battered from difficult travels, but thanks to his attentions, she would soon no longer look scruffy and dirty as a common farmer's wife.

He bathed her himself, even though there were servants who could see to her care. She seemed to be alarmed by their twisted bodies, but in time she would come to accept that they were better off than they had been as ordinary Caradon peoples, and she would accept them as her subjects.

It was with great care and admiration that he bathed her body with the finest of soaps and the softest of rags. Poor dear, she had not enjoyed a proper bath in such a long time. She sat in a tub of warm water, her knees drawn up and her head resting against the rim. The water glistened on her fair skin. She was more beautiful, more tempting, than he had imagined she would be.

He wanted her so badly, but the Isen Demon would destroy him if he did not follow the plans precisely. No woman, no matter how beautiful, was worth a demon's wrath. Maccus attempted to remove the crude silver bracelet on her wrist, hoping the soap would make the task possible, but it fit too tightly. No matter. In time he would see it removed, even if he had to cut it off. It was plain. Ordinary. Not at all worthy of a Queen.

When the Queen's body was clean, Maccus washed and combed her hair, taking care not to yank out the fine strands, even though they were terribly tangled.

She was compliant throughout the ministrations, thanks to the talisman around her neck. It was a temporary measure. In short order he would replace it with something more powerful. Something stronger which would ensure that she was entirely his. Already the magic which was obvious in the swirl of energy was slowing. Fading. Soon his Queen's talisman would be nothing more than a pretty rock, but for now it did the job quite well.

When the Queen was clean from head to toe, Maccus assisted her from the tub and dried her body and her hair with a velvety towel. She raised her arms when he commanded it. She turned about at his instruction. She stood very still and allowed him a moment of admiration for her fine, naked body before he continued.

He clothed her in a proper gown. The frock he provided was not the shimmering gold color usually worn by the Queen, but instead was fashioned of a silky purple and blue fabric adorned with pearls. The color of the fabric changed when she moved, catching the light even where there was little. The dark colors made her skin appear luminescent, and her eyes were brilliant when they did not have to compete with the gold of her gown. In deference to her hot blood, the gown had been made without sleeves, and there was a long split up one side of the skirt, to allow air to circulate. Maccus wanted his Queen to be comfortable.

The shimmering purple gown also matched his own

ensemble, as was proper since they were to be mated. They would be in unity in all ways, down to the clothes they wore.

The Queen remained silent, and extremely cooperative. She seemed drugged, she was so lethargic, and he longed to see the sparkle in her eyes and the incredible strength in her fine body. But for now it was important that he keep her in such a state. In short time she would accept him, understand him, love him. Only when that was accomplished would he gradually ease the enchantment that made her his.

Only then would she know her full power, her full promise. How he longed to see that power; to share in it.

But there were steps to be taken, steps that had to be taken in the proper order. The Isen Demon's instructions were very clear. Maccus was to wed the Red Queen in a blood ceremony that would taint her soul, and only then could she be his in all ways. He had heard that Anwyn Queens were quite sensuous, and having bathed his Queen and admired her body, he was quite anxious to discover that sensuality for himself.

But patience was called for. Patience and restraint.

Maccus led his Queen into the main workroom, where he placed her in a chair he'd had built specifically for her. It was a throne fit for a Queen. She would be comfortable there.

Thus far everything had proceeded as planned. The Queen was here and manageable, thanks to his enchantment. Her lover was coming this way . . . and he who touched fire was intent on saving the woman he had allowed to be taken. When he arrived here, the Anwyn Queen would kill her Caradon lover, and bathed in his blood she would gladly and of her own free will wed

Maccus. The children that might've been those of a lowly Caradon with minimal magic would now be Maccus's.

And what children they would be.

The Isen Demon spoke to him, as it did on occasion. *It is not only through death that I take control. Real power lies not in death but in life. My children will rule the world. My offspring will make all others tremble.*

Maccus smiled as his Anwyn Queen dropped her head and dozed off.

Poor dear. She'd had a difficult day.

WITHOUT KEELIA TO GUIDE HIM, JORYN HAD TO trust his instincts alone. This high on the wizard's mountain there were few trails to choose from, and as he continued upward, he believed himself to be on the right trail. Still, he was not entirely certain as he would've been if Keelia had been with him.

He vacillated between being angry and worried. Was she so annoyed with him that she'd continue on alone, sneaking away from him and going after the wizard on her own? Or had she been taken? Kidnapping her so silently wouldn't be an easy task, but neither was it impossible. He'd done it, after all, and he knew that the wizard's monstrosities intended to take her. Why had he allowed her that unnecessary moment of privacy? Why had he not kept his eyes on her every moment of every day and night?

Deep down, he wished fervently that she'd simply left him. In anger, she had slipped away. If that was the case, she wouldn't be in danger. If she'd run from him, she would not be in the hands of monsters or evil wizards.

She was peeved, that was all. She'd slipped away to teach him a lesson, and soon she'd appear with a smile on her face and a haughty, "Worried, Caradon? Serves you right for denying me what I want."

But that didn't happen. He finally admitted to himself that it was not Keelia's way to run when her wishes were not granted. No, she'd face him down, tell him he was wrong, and fight for what she believed in. She would not run. As he accepted that, a chill danced down his spine.

As he climbed endlessly, Joryn felt as if he were being watched even though he heard nothing; smelled nothing other than the stench of the Caradon monsters that was in every rock, in every breath of air. If it was in his power, he would kill them all.

He had begun this task to save the pitiful creatures, and now he valued the life of the Anwyn Queen far more than all the cursed Caradon mutants combined.

He should've told Keelia why he could not take the chance of leaving her with a child, but he'd expected they had more time for such conversations. Not much, but a little more time. A day or two in which to find the courage to tell her . . . or not. The Anwyn Queen was much stronger than his mother had been. Perhaps a child in her care wouldn't be shuffled off into the charge of those who could better handle the growth of an unexpected power. Maybe Keelia would not drop the child into the lap of a teacher, as Joryn had been dumped upon the Grandmother for instruction and care.

Keelia had mentioned the instruction of Anwyn wizards, but she had never said she'd literally give the child away and then depart in the dead of night . . .

Joryn walked up the trail quickly, his aim the top of the blasted mountain. He walked, and ran, and cursed, all through the night and into the morning. He could not forget that his task here was about more than one woman of another species, one woman who called to him as no other ever had. At the moment, stopping the spread of darkness was second in his mind—second to finding Keelia alive and well.

THROUGH THE FOG, KEELIA REALIZED THAT THIS WAS what she'd always wanted. A mate who loved her, a for-ever love, a connection on a soul-deep level. Maccus loved her. He adored her. He would never *ever* leave her. Her bones felt as if they'd gone mushy and her brain wasn't much better, but she knew that much. He'd made this place comfortable for her, down to a soft bed and a chair much like her throne back in The City.

She had no desire to return to The City and her family. Everything she'd ever wanted was right here, with Maccus.

Since coming here she'd slept quite a bit, and when she slept, she dreamed. Annoyingly, she dreamed of Jo-ryn. Joryn who had made her scream in pleasure and in anger. Joryn who had denied her when she'd needed him most. Joryn who had said he would never love her. The dreams disturbed her and she tried to shake them off, but when she dozed, he was there.

He was looking for her.

Keelia awoke with the dream still with her, too clearly and too real, to find Maccus sitting on the side of her bed. She would've moved—toward him or away, she wasn't quite sure which—but she couldn't. She was no longer immobilized but her limbs were heavy. Her muscles were lax. Her heart—numb.

Maccus took her limp hand in his. "I made this for you, darling." He slid a cold silver ring which was enhanced with a large green stone onto the middle finger of her left hand.

"It's very pretty," she said, her voice a bit mumbly. "Does this mean we're married?"

He smiled at her. Oh, he did have a nice smile. "Not yet, my love. This is simply a token of my love and fidelity, my devotion and my desire. Never fear, we will be married very soon." He gently removed the talisman she'd worn since coming here. She noticed, as he took it away, that it did not sparkle as brightly as it had when he'd first put it around her neck. It remained pretty, but the colors no longer danced. For a moment Maccus watched her closely, as if he expected some reaction. Eventually, he relaxed and leaned in to kiss her forehead, as a friend might.

"It's very pretty," she said again, and her mind began to wander. She was a little bit hungry, and still tired. Always tired.

All her life she'd suffered with a strong will. She'd argued with her parents, her sister, her brothers and cousins. She'd always stubbornly fought for what she thought or knew to be right. Strong-willed, her father had said with a mixture of pride and aggravation.

At the moment, she had no will at all. Her will was Maccus's. He would make all the decisions which needed to be made, and she had only to lie here and be adored.

"I want to give you many pretty things," he said, reaching out to caress her cheek. "When you are my wife, every day will be filled with gifts and beauty and love. That's what you want most of all, isn't it, darling? Love. Someone who will always be here for you. Someone who will adore you."

"Yes. How did you know?" It was hard to keep her eyes open, but she managed. This small chamber was for sleeping, but in addition to the soft bed there were wall hangings to cover stone walls, and many, many candles to offer light. There was even a bowl of scented oil burning, giving off light as well as a lovely smell. He had done all this for *her*.

"I have always known, love." Maccus wrapped his fingers around Joryn's silver bracelet and attempted to remove it. He had made the attempt before, and so had she, but the thing would not move. Maccus seemed annoyed, but not terribly so. Eventually he ended the effort.

"When will we marry?" Keelia was anxious for these days of beauty and gifts and endless love to begin. It seemed like a very nice way to live.

"In two days, just before the full moon rises."

Full moon. The words tugged at her brain. Something was going to happen under the full moon, but it hurt to try to remember what that might be. Better simply not to think at all. Better to let Maccus do all the thinking for her.

The horrid creature who had kidnapped her walked into the room as if he had the right to enter her chambers uninvited. Perhaps she was feeling tired and less than determined, but she was still a Queen. Keelia lifted her hand and pointed. "He hurt me. I do not like him."

"Eneo is harmless," Maccus said, taking her hand and caressing the palm.

"He *dropped* me. On the *ground*."

Maccus sighed. "He did, didn't he?"

"Yes." Keelia's eyes were already heavy, and she wanted nothing more than to drift back to sleep.

Maccus left her bed, turned slowly, and faced the creature Keelia did not like. The furry thing began to speak, but Keelia paid the words little mind. She couldn't concentrate very well these days, and the beast's words were garbled. Trying to decipher them would take much too much effort on her part. Maccus was walking toward the thing. He would handle the matter, as he would handle all.

Before she could close her eyes and drift away, the thing screamed. Keelia sat up and squinted, trying to comprehend what had happened. Maccus smiled. The creature's furry arm was oddly twisted. The beast, Eneo, kept grabbing at his misshapen arm and screaming.

"There now," Maccus said with satisfaction. "He hurt you, so I hurt him. That is fair, is it not?"

She should feel sympathy for every living thing, but this creature had attacked her and Joryn; it had tried to kill Joryn and it had kidnapped her. It had *dropped* her on the *floor*. "He is very loud," she said, and then she dropped back to her soft bed. Maccus took the wounded monster from Keelia's chamber, and soon all was quiet again. She drifted back toward sleep and the dreams that were always the same. Joryn was searching for her, and she didn't understand why. It wasn't as if he loved her or ever had. Maccus loved her. She fiddled with the stone of her new ring, even as she dreamed.

DRUSON RAN, HIS MIND RACING AS IT HAD SINCE THE moment the Grandmother had laid her hand on his forehead. He had to hurry. He had to reach Joryn in time. There wasn't much of it to be had. Not much time at all.

He couldn't remember when he'd last slept or eaten,

but that didn't matter. If he didn't get to Joryn in time, all would be lost. All lost.

This was the shortest way. Somehow he knew that to be true. There was much knowledge in his head, and while he could control nothing, now and then a bit of truth simply popped into his mind. He was to take this wooded path to the rocky trail, down and up to unprotected granite and a dangerous trail. If he hurried, he would arrive soon enough. Something had slowed Joryn down. Something, something. Something bad.

Druson knew where Joryn was, but he didn't understand *how* he knew. His mind was jumbled and dancing and too full. Much, much too full. The future, the past, the magical possibilities, the spells, the songs. Why so many songs? He had to share some of this knowledge with Joryn, so he would know what had to be done.

And to think, he had once suggested killing the Anwyn Queen.

One of the songs began to spill from his mouth, one unexpected word after another tumbling out in an odd and beautiful sort of way. He had never known he could sing in tune. The voice was not his own, and yet . . . it was. The song he sang as he ran was of love and tragedy and . . . birds. Why birds? He didn't even like birds.

The Grandmother had always been quite fond of them.

At first, Druson didn't realize that the harsh bark of laughter was his own. He stopped and looked around the wooded path, into the trees, into the shadows, and then he glanced up. The skies were almost dark again.

Two days until the full moon. Hurry, hurry, hurry.

Druson began to run again, his energy seemingly boundless. It was impossible to grasp every thought, every memory, every piece of knowledge in his mind. Some were more important than others, and those were the ones that repeated again and again, so he would not forget.

Save Joryn.

Save the Anwyn Queen.

Save the world.

There it was again, that odd harsh laughter that echoed all around him. This time Druson didn't so much as slow down.

I3

HE WAS LOST. HE'D BEEN LOST SINCE MORNING. BY the gods, he'd been lost for days. Weeks. He'd been *lost* long before Keelia had been taken.

Joryn stopped and turned about, studying the landscape in all directions. This part of the rocky mountain was dotted with caves, but none called to him as being different from any other. None struck him as being the *right* one. Perhaps he needed to climb higher. Perhaps he needed to backtrack and take a trail he had bypassed.

The moon would rise in a few hours, and unless his luck changed, it would be the last night he passed as a man. The curse . . . the infection . . . would claim him, and without Keelia here to take his life, he was doomed. He glanced over a ledge and studied the long drop. Everything he had ever been taught, every fiber of his being, screamed that to take one's own life was wrong. Others who'd been infected had done it, though, and he could not blame them. Had they gone into the Land of the Dead or even into the land in-between, or had they been whisked to an eternal punishment?

He couldn't even consider such an act in any case, not while there was still a chance that he and Keelia could to put an end to the curse.

To take his own life was not only morally reprehensible, if Keelia needed him he could not think only of himself. If there was even a possibility that she was in danger and needed his help, he could not take the cowardly way out. Who would've thought he'd ever put the needs of the Anwyn Queen, or any other Anwyn, above his own?

He hadn't been standing on the mountainside studying options for very long when he heard a distant voice that traveled oddly on the wind. Standing very still, he did his best to place that voice. It approached quickly, but was still a distance away. Joryn sniffed the air. It was difficult to be certain, since the stench permeated these mountains, but he was almost positive that whatever creature came toward him was not one of the infected, though he was Caradon. The wizard, perhaps? Or one of his apprentices who had escaped the curse?

Joryn concealed himself behind a boulder, and kept his eyes on the path. Whoever approached was moving with urgency and great speed. The creature mumbled incessantly. Occasionally what sounded like short-lived laughter reached his ears.

If this approaching climber was the man Joryn sought or one of the wizard's apprentices, then when taken, he could lead Joryn to Keelia. If he could save her before the rise of tomorrow night's full moon, perhaps they could end the curse. If not, then she could take his life as she had promised to do. The wait stretched too long . . . no, Joryn's patience was stretched too thin. If this man could not lead him to Keelia, then what would his next move be? How would he find her?

At last, the approaching man came running around a bend in the path. Though Joryn had grown impatient, he acknowledged that the man's speed was extraordinary, given the slope of the mountain and narrowness of the trail. He took quick stock, judging his enemy while waiting for the right moment to reveal himself and strike. He brought to life a spit of fire on the palm of his hand, and readied to throw it. Joryn would not aim for the creature . . . not this time . . . but would place the fire in his path.

The enemy had long dark hair liberally streaked with gray, but his body was that of a younger man who should not have so much gray in his hair. Head tucked down as he ran, the man mumbled ceaselessly and then laughed, which led Joryn to believe that the scurrying Caradon was quite mad.

When the time was right, Joryn rose from his hiding place and directed the fire in his hand to the ground, startling the runner. The man stopped, and his head popped up. For a moment, Joryn was so surprised he didn't think to immediately extinguish the fire that blazed in the middle of the trail.

"Druson?"

How had the fellow student grown so much gray hair amid the dark so fast, and why were his eyes so wild and so incredibly . . . old?

"Joryn, there you are," Druson replied, his words quick and breathless. "I knew I would find you, I knew I would. Am I too late? Where is the Queen? I can't believe

I once directed you to kill her. I was foolish then. Foolish, foolish." The statement was followed by one of those insane bursts of laughter which held no joy or humor.

Joryn fluttered his fingers and extinguished the fire, then approached Druson slowly. In the past, he had thought Druson to be impetuous and overly ambitious and hasty, but there was very little of the man he remembered in this creature. "What happened?"

Again, that awful laughter. "Where to begin, where to begin? So much to tell. So much to come if we don't hurry."

"Tell me what I most need to know. The rest can wait."

"The rest can wait until we save the Queen. We will save her, won't we? We must. We must." Druson's mad eyes locked to Joryn's. "She is our Queen, too."

ARIANA AND SIAN ARRIVED AT THE ASSIGNED MEETING place a full day early. Tomorrow night she would meet with Merin and whatever army he had managed to build in the weeks since they'd parted. After that . . . well, she wasn't sure what would happen after that. She had intended to have Keelia's psychic counsel before making that decision. Was she meant to remain on the battlefield, taking souls from the Isen Demon in order to weaken it, and healing Merin's soldiers when she could? Or was she meant to return to Arthes and heal the emperor? Both were necessary but she was only one woman, so how was she to decide?

At the edge of their small, secluded camp, Sian came up from behind and wrapped his arms around her. In spite of the circumstances, Ariana smiled. In the midst of chaos, she had found love. In her heart, she took that as a sign that all would be well, even though her logical mind told her that might not be so.

"Looks like it might rain," Sian said, leaning down to kiss her neck and ignoring the fact that they were not alone. The Anwyn soldiers that had been spared from the search for Keelia shared their camp. "Just a little while ago, I was certain we wouldn't have rain for days."

Ariana looked to the southeast, where dark clouds had formed. Those clouds seemed to be bearing down upon them. Odd, since storms usually did not approach from that direction. A flash of lightning danced across the sky, and a crack of thunder followed. The storm was small, and it was most definitely moving closer. In fact, it looked to be moving directly toward them.

"I suppose we should pitch tents tonight, just in case those clouds bring rain." As they looked like they would.

The Anwyn soldiers heard the approaching horseman before Ariana and Sian did. They armed themselves with the spears which were their preferred weapons, and spread out in a decidedly military formation. Ariana waved them back when she caught sight of the rider. It was Taran, the young sentinel she had sent to her mother with a very important and cryptic question. Judging by the expression on his face, he had an answer.

Taran barely slowed down before leaping from his horse gracefully and running toward her. Ariana frowned. How was it possible that the news was so urgent?

Her heart leapt. Something was wrong. Her mother? Her father? One of her younger brothers or sisters? She disengaged herself from Sian's embrace and ran toward the sentinel. "What news?" she asked sharply. "Is my family well?"

Taran nodded, and Ariana's heart returned to a normal rhythm. "Do you have an answer to my question?"

Still breathless, the sentinel shook his head.

"No?" Ariana put her hands on her hips, indignant now that she was no longer worried about her family. Yes, he was young and untested and somewhat naïve, but she had given him a task and in these uncertain times she expected her assignments to be fulfilled. First Keelia, and now this! "Why not?"

Taran took in a deep breath of air and exhaled slowly. "Your mother said she would deliver the message to you herself. I'm so sorry, sister. I could not stop her."

Ariana's eyes jumped to the black clouds that continued to approach. "Mum," she whispered. As a child she had quickly learned that her mother's moods could affect the weather if they were strong enough. It was a magical gift Sophie Fyne had learned to control for the most part, but when the emotions were particularly intense, there were sunny days in wintertime and stormy ones when all around the skies were clear.

Another splinter of lightning danced on air, and Ariana turned from the thunder to look Sian in the eye. She sighed, wondering what the night would bring. "Perhaps you should hide."

KEELIA FELT TWITCHY, EVEN THOUGH SHE WAS TIRED and her brain seemed not to want to function at all. She'd slept away most of her time here in Maccus's home—her home—and yet she was constantly teetering on the edge of exhaustion. The twitchy sensation was new. There had been a time when she would've known what that twitch meant, but not tonight. Tonight it was simply annoying. She did not want to be forced to think. It was so draining . . .

"Is something wrong, love?" Maccus smiled at her. They sat together in the main room, their chairs positioned a few feet apart. It was here, she had learned, that Maccus worked his spells and made magical things happen. Earlier he had asked some of his men—rather, creatures who had once been Caradon—to entertain her, as his betrothed appeared to be bored. One twisted creature had sung a song which made no sense, since his words were not at all intelligible, and another had danced clumsily while Maccus plucked at a small stringed instrument she had not seen before. The melodies he played were quite lovely, but the dance was not at all enjoyable. Even though the beast had tried to be joyful, the movements appeared to be painful and cheerless.

But now they were alone, and as Keelia watched Maccus closely, his expression gradually changed. "What do you feel, dear? I can see that something is bothering you. I know you so well."

Maccus did know her well. He loved her; he would never leave her. She knew that to be true, and yet deep down that twitching tried to interfere with what she so easily accepted to be fact.

"I don't know. Something is wrong."

Maccus left his chair and came to her, kneeling beside her and laying his hand on her thigh. The fabric of her pretty gown shimmered. "Is it him? Is it the one whose gift is fire?"

Keelia's breath caught, and before she could stop herself, she answered. "Yes. Joryn comes."

"He comes for you?"

"Yes." Keelia laid her hand over Maccus's. As a

Caradon he should be warm-blooded like her, but his hand was oddly cold, as if it were made of stone. Her eyes were drawn to the intricate silver and gold emblem he wore around his neck. He never removed it, she realized. That talisman gave him enhanced powers; it made him cold.

"We need to capture him, my love. I know you can reach out and discover for me when and where this Joryn can be taken. Will he sleep tonight? Will he hide? When will his guard drop, and where will he be when that happens?"

Joryn's thoughts and his future had always been dark to her, as if he purposely hid his mind and his heart, but now, now that they were separated and he was no longer attempting to shield himself from her, she could see him well. He was worried. Worried about her, but also about himself and another . . . someone who had changed. Trying to see more made her head ache, so she stopped.

"Tell me, dear," Maccus whispered. "I need your help."

It was as if she had no choice but to help him. No, it wasn't that at all. She *wanted* to help this man who loved her; she wanted it very badly. Keelia rose from her seat and walked toward Maccus's worktable. She grasped an ebony wand in one hand, and took a jar of enchanted sand in the other. Without thinking, she scattered the sand on the table.

Maccus gasped, but he did not chide her or try to stop her, and when she began to draw in the sand, he calmed considerably.

Keelia drew an outline of the mountain the mouth of this cave faced. "When the moon is here"—she drew the almost full moon above the mountain—"and the sky is just turning from black to gray, Joryn will sleep." She moved down the table and drew out a path which led down the mountain. It was as if she knew every twist, every turn, even though her head had been covered when the twisted creature Eneo had carried her to this wizard's home. Her home. "There is a small cave between a rock shaped like a woman's breasts and a steep cliff streaked with pink stone."

Maccus smiled. "I know the place, love."

"He is not alone," she whispered.

Maccus's eyebrows rose slightly. "He's not?"

"No, another travels with him." Her eyebrows knit together in frustration. Part of her wanted to tell the wizard who loved her to stay away from Joryn and his companion, but something else, something very strong, compelled her to assist in their capture. "Take them," she said, "but do not have them killed. Not yet. They have a role yet to play."

"That they do."

"You must tell your soldiers—"

"Our soldiers, love."

"You must tell our soldiers to bind Joryn's hands first. Before he wakes, before anything else, they must bind his hands or else he will use his fire against them. He always wears a dagger in a sheath at his waist, and that should be removed as soon as is possible. He also knows a sneaky trick." She placed a hand at her neck. "If his hands are tightly bound before he knows of the danger and he cannot use any of his weapons then taking him will be easy."

"And his companion? Does he have any weapons our soldiers need to beware of?"

"No," she whispered. "He will be easy to take." Within her mind she caught a glimpse of green eyes touched with madness, and shuddered. "He is an old man. Very, very old."

Maccus put his arm around her, caressing her arm with a gently rocking thumb. Keelia found herself leaning into him. This was where she was meant to be. He loved her; he would never leave her. This was everything she had been waiting for all her life. So why was there a sickening knot in the pit of her stomach?

Maccus allowed his hand to brush against her breast as he made her turn to face him. His smile was contented, and she longed to feel that contentment herself.

"Tomorrow night you will be my bride."

"Yes, I know." She was alternately thrilled and excited and terrified, as if beneath a calm exterior she was continually at war with herself.

"We will make a child."

"It is not my fertile time." She found herself fiddling with the ring Maccus had given her, toying with the stone there the way the wizard toyed with her. Like him, the stone was cold. Icy cold and unnatural.

"That doesn't matter, my love. Tomorrow night, beneath the full moon, you and I will make a very special child. You will wear the blood of the lover you have betrayed, and I will be advanced. I will be elevated, and more powerful than you can imagine. Together we will create an incredible daughter. We will create a daughter who is destined to be the bride of a prince's son. Ciro's son."

"I'm glad," Keelia said, even though Maccus's words brought back the twitch. She found herself moving her twitching fingers from the cold ring to the warmer, oddly comforting silver band on her wrist. *No, no, I'm not glad at all. Don't touch me! Run, Joryn, run!*

But she could not utter a word of protest as Maccus escorted her back to her chair and departed so that he could inform his soldiers where and when Joryn could be found. A single tear escaped and ran down Keelia's cheek, and then she drifted into a deep and dreamless sleep where there was no pain and not a single doubt.

"TROUSERS," SOPHIE VARDEN SAID IN A MOTHERLY one-word scold. "I traveled with Arik and your father for months during the revolution, and I never donned a man's trousers. It's unseemly."

Ariana faced her mother calmly. "I'm not only traveling, Mum, I'm fighting. Trousers make more sense."

At least her mother had harnessed her emotions so that they weren't being drenched by rain. Now and then a fork of lightning lit the dark sky overhead, however.

Ariana had often wondered what the coming days would bring, but she had never imagined this.

Sian approached, and Ariana tried to gently and cautiously wave her husband back. There would be a proper time for him to meet her parents, but not now.

He ignored her, joined them, and introduced himself first to her father. "Sian Sayre Chamblyn," he said. "Honored to meet you, sir."

"Kane Varden."

Ariana watched in horror as her father studied Sian up and down, his eyes finally landing on the choker Sian wore, and then flitting to her throat, where an identical choker lay against her skin. Kane Varden's hawkish eyes narrowed.

Ariana placed herself between Sian and her parents, taking her mother's arm. "Personal matters can wait, and should. The country is in crisis, and I must know if Aunt Liane and her child or children survived."

Ariana's mother sighed and clasped her daughter's arm. "I never thought that old secret would come back to haunt me this way. It seemed best at the time to allow her to go, to take her children and hide herself away. Why is this important now?"

It was best to be blunt, she knew. There was no time for making the dire news pretty and palatable. "Emperor Arik is dying. For all I know he's already dead. He was quite ill when I left him."

"Your sister Sibyl is in the palace," Sophie said.

"Yes, I know. We'll extract her when we warn the emperor . . . if he still lives." Her parents had sent Duran with Ariana when she'd gone to the palace. It made sense that they had provided Sibyl with a suitable escort as well. "Which of the boys accompanied her?"

"Bronsyn."

Ariana sighed in relief. Not all of her brothers had magical abilities, but if Sibyl was in immediate danger Bronsyn would know, and he would remove his sister from harm's way. Sophie obviously shared that same thought. She shook off her maternal worry and continued.

"Prince Ciro—"

"Prince Ciro is lost," Ariana interrupted. "He's been taken over by the Isen Demon body and soul, and he himself is now a monster. If Ciro takes the throne, we are all doomed."

Sophie Fyne Varden was a lover of peace. She frowned as she began to understand the import of the situation. "If it's revealed that Sebestyen had sons who lived, there will be war. Those who always thought that Sebestyen was the rightful emperor will fight for his sons' rights. I know what such a war is like, Ariana."

"Mum, we're already at war. War is here."

Her mother sighed. "There must be another way."

"There is," Ariana said, knowing that Sian would prefer his heritage to be kept a secret, but also realizing that she had no choice if she wanted her mother's assistance. "Arik fathered a child thirty-four years ago. An illegitimate child."

Her mother sighed in obvious relief. "Then when Arik passes, this man—"

"This man doesn't want the throne," Ariana said sharply. "He doesn't want it, nor does he want his mother's name sullied by the knowledge that she was the emperor's lover without marriage." Her lips thinned. "I know that sort of thing isn't important in all circles, but it is important to . . . to this man."

Blue eyes narrowed. "You know him, don't you? Who is this child of Arik's who wishes to deny his true parentage?"

A shout went up, and the sounds of a scuffle alarmed Ariana so that she spun about to see her father and the man she called husband grappling on the ground. While she'd been speaking with her mother, the two men had edged away. Apparently they'd been having their own discussion. Using the abilities Sian had taught her, Ariana sent a stream of energy through the air and plucked away the knife her father drew so smoothly. The weapon skittered away, spinning in the dirt.

"The emperor's son is my . . . my husband, Mum." Sian was her husband in almost all ways, but like him, her father put a lot of weight on the legalities. "The man Poppy is apparently trying to kill."

JORYN AWOKE WITH A START AFTER A VERY SHORT period of sleep. His hands were already caught tightly in those of a mutated Caradon, and in seconds they were securely bound behind his back. Three of the monsters gave his capture their full attention, while one made short work of trussing a very confused Druson.

He should not have stopped, not even for a few minutes. But he'd been on the verge of losing his ability to think clearly, and Druson had been utterly exhausted in mind and body. A few hours of rest had seemed not only permissible, but necessary.

Joryn quickly realized that he didn't have a chance. The creatures were stronger than he, and they'd taken him by surprise. If he'd had the opportunity to call upon his gift of fire, he would've been able to fight back; if he'd had a chance to wield his dagger, he might've at least put up a decent fight, but they had known exactly how to disable him.

How had they found him? The cave he'd chosen for a short period of rest was small and well concealed. It would not have been an easy place to find.

Perhaps they'd had some sort of magical help from the man who'd cursed and directed them. Had the wizard known all along where he and Keelia were? Had they been walking into a trap from the beginning?

The creatures dragged a tightly bound Joryn out of the cave and into the almost-dawn of his last day on earth. Another waited for their exit, a smug creature Joryn recognized as the mutant who could speak. One arm was sloppily immobilized, as if the monster had been wounded and then hastily tended.

Joryn's ankles and hands were trussed so tightly he could barely move. He was dragged along the ground, and one of the monsters kicked him repeatedly with a large, somewhat hairy foot. After a while, the creature who had been waiting for them to exit the cave spoke, his words muddy as before.

"I don car if you hurt hm, but don kill hm. It is not hsss time."

The monster above Joryn grumbled and growled, and then delivered one last kick.

Joryn twisted his head to see what was happening to Druson. The man who was now the Grandfather, a spiritual leader who should be protected by all Caradon, was dragged unceremoniously from the cave by the single creature who had bound him. He screamed and then mumbled in confusion. Most of his words were unintelligible, but now and then Joryn caught a word or two that made some sense to anyone who might be listening.

The wizard could not know what his beasts had found. Druson possessed powers and knowledge even he did not yet realize, and for him to fall into the hands of someone who would use that knowledge for evil was unthinkable.

"Say nothing," Joryn instructed, shouting to be heard above the creatures' delighted growls and Druson's latest scream of protest. "Say *nothing*!"

Druson's eyes caught Joryn's, and in spite of his obviously fragile mental state, he nodded in agreement. Perhaps his friend was not entirely insane, after all.

"The Red Keen wus right," the creature in charge said. "She tuld uz where tu fine yu, so clear dat a chile could've foun' yu an' yur frien'." His furry nose wrinkled. "She wus wrong 'bout yur frien's age, but I spose e'en a great seer iz 'lowed a mistake now and den."

He must be lying. Keelia would not have betrayed him. Not unless . . . Not unless they'd tortured her. Hurt her. They'd forced her to betray him somehow.

The creature above kicked once more, this time with Joryn's head as his target. Just before darkness descended, one thought rang in Joryn's brain.

What had they done to Keelia?

14

At last all was relatively peaceable. Ariana had explained to her parents that she and Sian were married in her heart and mind, and when the time was right, they'd also marry legally. Her mother understood. Her father, like Sian, seemed to place a lot of importance on legalities.

She should've known that the first thing her father would ask Sian was if he'd done right by his daughter. The chokers had been a dead giveaway that something was going on. Now she'd have both her father and Sian pushing her to take the next step.

It was difficult to explain to anyone that she didn't want to say her vows in the midst of war, but wished to wait until she was surrounded by harmony and untarnished love. Right now, Ciro and his Own tarnished everything in Columbyana. The more Ariana learned to manipulate energy with her magic, the more she appreciated the importance of energy. It was present in all things at all times, and it was always flavored in some way. Dark, light, and everything in between.

She wanted to marry Sian, but not with this flavor to the world.

Merin's army was much larger and well armed than it had been just two months earlier. Tonight was their assigned meeting time, and although it was early in the day, the soldiers had begun to arrive. Alone, in small groups, in organized militias, they came. Some were on foot; others rode fine horses. All were solemn and prepared to fight against an evil they had never imagined before this moment. With each coming, she felt the hope in her heart grow. All was not entirely lost as it had once seemed to be.

Merin approached her as he had often during the morning. Without greeting or preamble, he spoke. "I have news from a recent arrival, sister. Ciro's army has been camped four days' hard ride from here, apparently training, after being defeated in a small village on their way to Arthes."

Hope. "So, he's not made his way to his father yet."

"No, thank the heavens. If the emperor did not succumb to his illness since our departure from the palace, then he lives and the capital city remains ours."

But for how long? If Ciro took the palace, it would be very difficult to get him and his men out. Those who did not understand what he had become might even support his position there as Arik's only son. Well, only legitimate and *known* son.

Sian did not want to be emperor. He did not even want others to know of his true parentage. But if Sebestyen's sons were not found, what choice did he have?

There were still many hours of the day remaining before the sun set and the full moon rose. In that time, more soldiers would come. More trained and untrained fighters ready for battle would join the side of right.

Did Ciro's army grow as well? Ariana did not possess her cousin's psychic powers, but she suspected that was the case.

"COME, LOVE, AND SEE WHAT WE HAVE FOUND."
Keelia allowed Maccus to take her arm and lead her to a small, pleasantly chilly chamber in the cave home she now thought of as her own. Two men were imprisoned there. A man with dark hair liberally shot with gray, a man she did not know, was shackled. Heavy chains that were anchored in the wall were attached to leg irons, but his hands were free.

The other prisoner was familiar to her. Joryn was more staunchly restrained than his companion, with his hands and his feet immobilized. His face and arms were cut, and blood stained his brown trousers. He looked at her so hard, she felt that odd twitch once again. Looking at him made her dizzy, so she closed her eyes.

"Does he frighten you?" Maccus asked, concern in his voice.

"Yes," she whispered.

"In order for us to do what must be done, you must look at him, love. You must not let him make you afraid."

Joryn spoke, his words soft. "Keelia, what have they done to you?"

She did not open her eyes, but those words touched her inside in a place that was sleeping. Sleeping or dead? She could not be sure, but there was a numbness inside her that tingled at Joryn's voice. She had once thought herself in love with him.

"Open your eyes," Maccus ordered, and Keelia obeyed. It was as if she had no choice. "Look at the man we have captured."

Her eyes scanned him from head to toe. Yes, she had loved him once, but no more. He'd refused her when she'd needed him. He'd told her he could never love her. Maccus loved her.

"Keelia," Joryn whispered, and her heart twitched.

"Speak again, and I will have your mouth stuffed with rocks and bound with the skin of your useless little friend." Maccus nodded at the other prisoner, the one Keelia did not know.

Joryn's lips thinned and his mouth clamped shut. He wanted to speak, but would not for fear that Maccus would do as he threatened. The prisoner remained silent, but a distant voice whispered in her head. She had to strain to hear the words.

Snap out of it, Keelia.

Joryn's voice was almost real, but his mouth didn't move, and Maccus obviously heard nothing. In fact, the wizard continued to speak, taunting his prisoner.

Keelia answered silently. *Snap out of what? I am well. I am more well than I have ever been.* Something deep within her recognized that as a lie.

You're enchanted. You're not yourself. I can see it in your eyes.

My eyes are fine.

Your eyes are dull and distant, Joryn insisted, still inside her head. *They are not the eyes I came to love.*

Love?

Yes, love. There was a bitter tone to those words, even in thought. He did not want to love her, or anyone else.

Why can I hear you inside my head?

For a moment there was no answer, and then a terse, *Because I am your mate, Keelia. Because we are linked in all ways.*

Maccus is my mate. Again, a warning tingle suffused her body. *Tonight we will make a child beneath the full moon.*

Joryn yanked at his chains, but they did not come loose. *Impossible. You have the power to remain human beneath the moon, but this mad wizard does not. He will be in mountain cat form. Besides, your fertile time has passed.*

He said it does not matter. He will be elevated, and I will conceive.

Elevated? How?

I do not know.

Keelia, I . . .

The creature Keelia disliked so much entered the small room, and she was distracted. The voice in her head ended abruptly.

Maccus smiled at his servant. "I believe it is time. The moon will rise in a few hours."

Eneo bowed curtly, and when Maccus offered his arm, the mutant took it. When Maccus nodded once, the creature bent his head and bit hard into his master's arm. The wizard flinched, but he did not cry out. He closed his eyes and smiled as Eneo drew away.

"I can feel the poison coursing through my blood."

Keelia felt frozen. Numb, twitchy, and frozen.

Elevated. This man who said he loved her would turn

into a monster beneath the full moon, and then they would be wed and mated.

The voice in her head returned, loud and insistent. *Run, Keelia. Run!*

But she did not run. Her feet were frozen, as was her heart. She closed off the voice that tried to warn her, and retreated into the numbness where she felt safe and protected. She fiddled with the ring Maccus had given her, and when he leaned down to kiss her mouth, she did not protest.

But for a moment, just a moment, she smelled and tasted the prisoner Joryn, not the wizard who had promised to wed her when the moon rose.

IN ALL JORYN'S IMAGININGS, HE HAD NEVER CONSIDERED that the end would come so very badly. He was prepared for death. He had always been prepared for death. But to be imprisoned this way, helpless while Keelia was enchanted by the wizard and Druson was teetering on the edge of madness, was more horrible than a battle to the death.

He and Druson were alone in a prison not all that different from the one he'd prepared for Keelia, what seemed like a lifetime ago. He had not chained her, however. He had never mistreated her.

Shortly after the mutant creature had bitten Maccus, the wizard had led a horribly compliant Keelia from the chamber. In all the time Joryn had known her, she had never been compliant. In the early days he had thought that trait to be a failing on her part, but now he longed to see her fire and determination and stubbornness come to life.

Druson had been silent, as ordered, but now that they were alone, he spoke, his words for Joryn's ears alone. "We don't have much time," he whispered urgently.

"I know," Joryn snapped. "What do you suggest?"

"We must escape."

Joryn sighed. His friend and only ally had become entirely simpleminded. "How?" If Druson possessed the Grandmother's gifts, then perhaps he could free them somehow. It was clear, however, that the now magically advanced Druson had no idea what to do with his powers.

"We must save the Queen."

Joryn looked over at his friend, the Grandfather who sat so still and useless on the cave floor, and tried to still his mind. Panic would not help. What he needed was reason from Druson. What he needed was help. Maybe if he led the conversation, some kernel of usable knowledge would be revealed.

"You said she was our Queen, too. How is that possible?"

Druson looked up. His eyes still startled Joryn. They were ancient, as the Grandmother's had been, and yet his face remained young. Young, and terrified. "Long ago, we were one. Caradon and Anwyn were one, and we shared these mountains as a united people."

"That's not —"

"Possible?" Druson had apparently picked the word from Joryn's head. "As we are now, no, but we were not then entirely as we are now. We were powerful shapeshifters who embraced nature and unity and peace. Most could transform into two or three animals. A few had a limitless power of transformation. Some even had the power of flight, and large birds flew over these mountains, soaring high."

A fanciful tale or a true telling of long ago? Joryn couldn't be sure. "What happened?"

"War," Joryn whispered. "Two brothers of high station both loved the same woman. The brothers fought over her, and they divided the people. Where there was once harmony, there came bloodshed. The people were divided, and the peace that had sheltered us vanished. No, it didn't vanish; it was eaten away, one tiny bit at a time, until there was none left.

"There was a very powerful witch in these mountains who lost all her sons in the senseless battle, and when she buried the youngest, she cursed us all. She cursed us to be forever separated and weakened and . . . and incomplete, but forever is not really forever, and we are coming back to one again." Druson lifted his hands to Joryn. "But all is not decided. Who will our people be in the years to come? Who will rule our hearts and minds and souls? The decision comes down to one powerful woman and two men."

"Keelia," Joryn whispered.

Druson shook his head, and then said, "Yes. You should've given her a child when she asked," he chastised. "The Queen knew, deep inside her soul, that your child growing inside her would be the first step in healing our people and the Mountains of the North and the very world. Her child will fly again, as we once did, but if it's his child, too, then all is ruined."

"Ruined?"

"Ruined to the very core. He says chaos," Druson whispered, "but I say destruction. I see nothing where Caradon and Anwyn once lived. I see death and disease where once there was life and beauty." Tears ran down his face. "I see too much, Joryn. Too much, too much, too . . ."

"Calm down," Joryn said, his voice surprisingly composed, considering the situation. "These powers of yours are very new and untested. How sure are you that all this you see is truth?"

Druson laughed madly. "I wish I thought I might be wrong, but I'm not. I'm not wrong, Joryn. We must save our Queen."

The efforts of seeing so much had apparently exhausted Druson. His eyes rolled back in his head and he fainted, falling limply and landing hard on the stone floor, leaving Joryn to contemplate how he might escape this seemingly inescapable situation.

CIRO WATCHED HIS SOLDIERS WITH A HINT OF PRIDE. With training, they had improved greatly. The next villagers who were foolish enough to fight back would regret their decision and wish for a quick death.

While his legion ate, Ciro sat and watched them as if they were his beloved children, and dreamed. It was odd that the Isen Demon inside him allowed him to dream, but it was decidedly so. He dreamed of power and blood, and he dreamed of Rayne.

The real, true Rayne, not the illusion Diella sometimes created. Ciro thought of Rayne as she had been when he'd last seen her, chained in the basement of her father's home. He tried to reach out to her with his mind and spirit, as he could reach out to his Own, but his beloved's pure soul kept her from him. He could not touch her mind, not yet. The time would come.

He had been smitten with Rayne at first sight, even before the demon had revealed his plans for them. He wished he had lain with her before departing, but the demon had been very insistent that the time was not yet right. A particular infusion of power was necessary, and while the demon grew stronger every day, that particular strength was not yet theirs.

There were a number of instructions to follow in creating his son. The stars were to be aligned just as the demon instructed, and Rayne was to be pure when he planted the child inside her.

Thanks to the whisperings of the Isen Demon, Ciro realized that his son was not the only special child. Other special babes were planned by the demon. One was a daughter soon to be created, a daughter who would wed the son of Ciro and Rayne and stand beside the dark ruler as the world changed and shifted into a long period of darkness.

Ciro realized that his own reign would be filled with battles against those who continued to foolishly seek the light, but when his son and the soon-to-be-made girl-child ruled, there would be no more light in the world.

In the years to come, there would be other children created with the demon's special touch and assistance, but the initial three were the key to victory.

Ciro's son.

The girl-child of the mountains.

The bastard Diella carried.

Ciro had come to despise Diella, who sauntered toward him as if she were of higher station, as if she were not as much a slave to the demon as any of the others. "Is it time to begin our journey again?" she snapped.

"Do you think your legion is ready for what they might face on the road?"

"You are anxious to take the palace?"

"Yes," Diella snapped. "I did not wait in filth and pain for more than a quarter of a century just to sleep on the ground and rut with your filthy soldiers. I want a bed, and handsome sentinels, and pretty clothes, and all the Panwyr I desire, and I want slaves to cater to my every whim."

Another man might wonder if the child Diella carried might've been fathered by someone else, but thanks to the demon, Ciro knew that the newly created child inside Diella was his. His and the Isen Demon's. She didn't even know of the child's existence, and he would not be the one to tell her. Not yet.

In times past Diella had repulsed Ciro, and he'd refused her advances. The demon had been leading him, making him wait for the moment when the stars were aligned correctly and the power of the demon was strong enough for what needed to be done.

"That sounds very much like the life you had before your emperor husband killed you," Ciro countered.

Diella's eyes went hard. "Sebestyen didn't kill me. The coward tossed me into Level Thirteen and allowed the vermin there to do the job for him."

Ciro was glad he had scarred the face of the young body Diella had taken for her own. She was more trouble than she'd been worth thus far, but the demon insisted that she had a maternal purpose yet to serve, and so he could not kill her. Perhaps after the child was born . . .

"So," she continued. "Is your legion ready?"

"If anyone else spoke to me in that tone, he'd soon be my supper."

Diella grinned. "But you can't make me your supper, can you? The Isen Demon owes me for all I've done on its behalf, and it will not allow you to hurt me."

Did she really think the demon would allow her to live as a *favor*? She did not understand her master at all, if that was the case.

He wanted, so very badly, to kill her. *When we are finished with her, she will be yours*, the demon whispered deep in Ciro's mind.

"We march for Arthes in the morning," he said, his voice calm as he imagined how he'd dispose of Diella when the time came.

THE TIME FOR HER WEDDING WOULD SOON COME. The day was growing darker, and Maccus had instructed his servants to prepare a special site beneath the stars for their vows. Keelia studied the place, squirming in the heavy black gown that Maccus had insisted she wear, and fiddling with the ring he had given her.

Here, well beyond the walls of the cave, they would be bathed in moonlight. Smallish rocks formed an almost-perfect circle around a clearing, and there was an altar of sorts in the center of the circle. The altar was also made of stone.

Keelia had always imagined that there would be flowers at her marriage ceremony, if she ever had one, but there were no flowers here. The clearing was stark, decorated only by an arrangement of long-dead leaves still attached to their severed tree limbs.

She heard a commotion and turned to watch. Ten

servants—ten mutants—led the two prisoners toward the circle. Her heart leapt as she caught sight of Joryn's face, even though she knew he did not love her, knew he did not want her, knew he had never intended to stay with her. If he now insisted they were mated, it was in an attempt to save his life.

When she experienced doubts, she was suddenly washed in that welcomed numbness that allowed for no pain.

Don't let him touch you.

Shouldn't you be begging for your own life?

I don't care about my own life.

But he cared about her? That did not fit with what she knew; it certainly did not fit with what Maccus told her.

I'm going to create a child tonight. A special child.

Joryn jerked against his bonds, but he did not escape. *No!*

He loves me.

I love you.

There was that twitching again. The silver band grew warm, reminding her of the moment Joryn had slipped it onto her wrist. *No, you don't.*

Maccus told his servants where to place the prisoners. No one seemed to pay the prisoner with graying hair much mind. He was always crouched and often mumbled, and never put up any sort of a fight. He was constantly befuddled. Keelia had thought the man to be ancient when she'd first had a vision of him, but only his eyes were old. His eyes and his mind. Apparently he was insane.

Her betrothed, who was dressed in black as she was, came to her once the prisoners were in position. Maccus placed his hands on her shoulders and smiled. "Soon, love, we will be married."

Keelia attempted a smile, but it didn't quite work. Joryn was trying to talk to her. She did her best not to hear him, but the words kept coming. She was able to ignore some of what he said, but whenever he said that he loved her, the words were loud and clear. Those words worked their way past everything else.

If she told Maccus that Joryn spoke to her in a way no one else could hear, he would silence the doomed man. So why didn't she tell? Why didn't she betray the secret conversation?

Everything inside Keelia told her that Maccus was right for her, that he loved her, that their life together would be perfect. He said he was her mate . . .

Chaos.

But she did not share this secret connection with him. She could not see inside Maccus's mind. Of course, she had never really tried.

While her betrothed told her that the time for their joining would soon be here, Keelia tried to peek into his mind. Nothing. She tried again, and soon realized that he had not blocked her abilities. There was nothing within him. Blackness. Emptiness. A dark void . . .

But why should she worry about such things? The numbness began to creep upon her again, offering welcome respite from the turmoil of her mind.

Maccus pressed a dagger into her hand, forcing her fingers to curl around the handle. It was not plain, like Joryn's dagger, but was set with pretty stones that seemed to be alive. The weapon was pretty, but it was also evil. She felt that evil, and it made her palm itch and burn. Maccus turned her about and forced her to stand before Joryn, who was tightly bound to a stake at the edge of the circle.

"Wait until he changes," Maccus instructed. "As soon as the transformation is complete, you are to drive this blade into his heart. Do you understand?"

"Yes." Keelia touched the tip of the blade to Joryn's bare chest. "I understand."

"You are to use your powers to retain your human form, and once I am fully elevated, we will be wed."

"Keelia," Joryn whispered aloud. "Don't."

"Beg all you want," Maccus said sharply. "She's mine now. In a very short time the Queen will be entirely mine, and you will be dead." He smiled. "When you're elevated, the demon will take your soul, so when you die, it will already be lost to you. Lost forever. Yours is a powerful soul, and he awaits it with much anticipation. You will feed him well. You will feed us all."

Maccus glanced down at a bound Druson, who all but cowered in the dirt.

"Leave him alone," Joryn commanded.

"I will for now. For some reason, the demon wants him to see everything that happens here tonight."

Darkness came too quickly, and the full moon shone down in bright, silvery rays. Joryn felt the shift in his blood; he felt the pain of a transformation which was usually painless. The wizard was caught in the throes of transformation, too, writhing and pulling at his clothing.

Keelia stood before him, the tip of her knife resting over his heart. While he could still speak, Joryn said, "I love you, Keelia."

"Liar. You're only saying that in a vain attempt to save your own life."

"No. This is not a life I want to lead." Already his

voice was changing, growing deeper and rockier, more indistinct. "Remember, I asked you to kill me if I became like them. Kill me, and then run, Keelia. Run away from these monsters."

"They are not monsters," she said, but her voice sounded less than certain.

"Do you remember how the creature we found by the stream fought for his soul?"

"Yes," she whispered.

"I plan to fight for mine, and I want you to fight now, too. Can you do that, Keelia? Can you fight?"

Her lips parted as if to form an answer, but no words came out. The other mutants were busy watching their master and his transformation, awed and reverent as the man who had created and led them became one of them. Druson mumbled incoherently and twitched. Soon he would shift himself into the familiar form of mountain cat. Perhaps when that happened, he could escape. Someone should escape this nightmarish horror.

"I love you," Joryn said again, but this time he was too far gone and the words made no sense. So he spoke to her with his mind, something he had fought against for the entire time he'd known her. He had never wanted to be this close to anyone, and now that closeness was all he had left that was good and right. *I love you. Fight, Keelia. Fight!*

Joryn felt his soul slipping away. No, not slipping, but being grabbed and pulled. The demon was trying to yank his soul from him. Such an outrage was the most unnatural of atrocities. He grit his teeth and fought.

It would be so easy to just let his soul go, but like the creature by the stream, Joryn wrestled to keep it within

him. The battle was painful, as if the soul considered
this twisted body to no longer be its home.

The wizard at the center of the stone circle stopped
writhing and stood tall. His face was grotesquely caught
between mountain cat and man, and his hands were
claws. His black shirt had been torn, but still hung on a
torso that was part skin and part fur.

Maccus spoke, his words muddy but clear enough.
"Finish it, love. Bathe yourself in your lover's blood so
that we can be wed and create our special daughter."

The tip of the blade in Keelia's control barely cut
into Joryn's skin.

15

FIGHT. IT WAS A SIMPLE-ENOUGH WORD, AND KEELIA had done her fair share of fighting in her lifetime—most specifically in recent weeks. So why was it so hard to fight now?

Her eyes were drawn down to the ring on her finger; the ring Maccus had placed there. The green stone swirled and danced in a way a rock should not. Her glance shifted to Maccus; he was grotesque, but a part of her thought him handsome and powerful and hers. A part of her could not wait to be his bride.

It isn't real, Keelia. He's bewitched you somehow. Fight, please, My Beautiful and Brave Majesty.

The graying prisoner changed into a mountain cat, but not before shouting once in that gruff voice that came between man and cat, "You don't need your hands!" The large, powerful cat—his fur mottled black and gray— quickly fought off its bonds and ran, escaping while

Maccus's servants had their attention on the Queen and her task.

Her task was to kill her lover and wear his blood to her wedding.

Fight.

A drop of Joryn's blood sprang onto the end of the blade she wielded. She could feel him fighting, not for his life but for his very soul.

"Finish it, love," Maccus said, his words rough and ill-defined but crisper than Eneo's had ever been. "This is one task I cannot take on for you. This duty is yours, and yours alone. Do as I command, love, and complete freedom will follow."

Freedom from what? Thought, right, love, judgment . . .

"My will is yours," Maccus whispered. "Kill him, adorn your face and arms with his blood, and then come to me."

The silver bracelet on Keelia's wrist warmed and tingled. It reminded her of who she'd been before coming to this place; it reminded her of who she'd been before another's will had become her own. It reminded her that Joryn was right. She'd been bewitched.

Feeling as if she were fighting against gravity and time itself, Keelia yanked her hand down and away, releasing the dagger so that it fell to the ground. She dropped to her haunches and swung her hand fiercely at the nearest rock, slamming the wrongly alive stone of her ring against the rock with such force that it shattered and died.

Instantly, she was free of the wizard's enchantment, and he knew it. He cursed and reached for her with deformed paws, but she was able to roll out of his reach.

Others moved in to assist their wizard master. There were so many of them! Maccus and his soldiers outnumbered her, and Joryn was still tied to a stake.

Was he? Did the Joryn she loved still exist within that twisted body? Yes, she knew he did. She felt his struggle. She had promised to take his life if this happened, but she couldn't even think of that now, not while it was possible that she could save him.

And she could save him as long as he continued to fight.

Maccus and his monsters came near, but they did not move forward to harm her. They still needed her, and they still had hope that she could be used as they intended. Used to bear a monster. Used to rule these mountains at the side of an evil, twisted wizard.

"All your magic is caught in the things you possess," she said, rising slowly to her feet. "All your bewitchment is in stone and metal, in silver and pretty gems." She ripped the damaged ring from her hand and threw it to the ground. "Do you have any talents of your own? Any talents that reside inside you? No, you need spells and talismans and objects to hold the temporary magic you create. None of it is yours to own. You're a vessel for a demon and nothing more."

In anger Maccus lashed out at her, but she moved quickly and his claws missed her. He quickly contained his rage and drew away.

"We could have such power, you and I and our child," he said. His lips were malformed, but she understood him well enough. The medallion he always wore around his neck hung against a furry portion of his chest, and she studied it for a moment. In her time here he had never taken it off. It was precious to him. That was where his magic rested, she realized. Now that her mind was clear once again, she knew many things.

She glanced at Joryn, at the creature who had once been Joryn. She knew it was him thanks to the streak of red fur that started at one ear and traveled back. And she knew it by the flame in his eyes.

Step back, he ordered, and she knew instantly what he planned to do.

Not yet.

The fire in his eyes grew brighter. *Now!*

Keelia rushed toward Maccus, not away. She reached out, knowing she had one chance, and no more. Needing an infusion of strength, her hand changed in an instant, and an appendage that was part human and part wolf grabbed for the medallion Maccus wore and ripped it from his neck.

He howled as she dropped to the ground and rolled away with the medallion clasped in her hand. She felt the small stone that was built into the backside of the metal, and she knew this was the stone she had come here to claim. Without ever looking at it, she turned the medallion about and swung her arm mightily. She smashed the cursed medallion, stone side out, into one of the rocks that had been used to form her wedding site.

Maccus shrieked, but the inhuman sound changed before it was done. He and his soldiers returned to their human forms, as Caradon all over the world were now changing. Though Keelia's gifts remained less than they had once been, she felt the shift to the pit of her soul. It was momentous. Painful and startling and unexpected.

Something other than the creatures howled in outrage. The demon who'd orchestrated the design of the atrocities, the evil thing which had planned her marriage to a monster, felt pain as well. It was weakened and startled and defeated. Not permanently, perhaps, but this was a battle it had lost.

Keelia realized with sadness that returning the creatures to their Caradon selves did not return their souls. Those who had not fought to hang on to their souls, as Joryn had, would remain monsters of another kind, but monsters without the strength of mutated bodies and the guidance of the Isen Demon.

An angry wizard and his men rushed toward Keelia, but she was not afraid. This was not her time to die; she knew it with all her heart.

Down!

She obeyed Joryn's silent command and dipped down, covering her head with her arms and making herself small. He didn't have much time. Some of the enemy soldiers were already slipping into their feline forms, and Joryn would soon follow. There was a full moon overhead after all, and he would not have much of a window between his short time as a mutant and his transformation to his wildest form. As a cat, he had no gift of fire. As a cat, he could not save them.

But the time he had before the change was enough. Without using his hands, he called upon a wild and furious fire that burst into Maccus and his soldiers, instantly consuming them in flame. They screamed as desperately as they had when the curse had been ended, trying to escape the inescapable for a moment or two. Then all was silent as they fell dead, one after another dropping to the ground.

Keelia grabbed the dagger she'd thrown aside, the dagger with which she'd drawn her mate's blood, and she began to cut Joryn's bonds. Before she was finished, he began to shift. All was silent as he transformed into a yellow mountain cat with a streak of red down one side.

With her heart in her throat, Keelia dropped to the ground and wrapped her arms around the mountain cat's neck. She had almost killed him. She had held a knife to his heart and drawn blood. She had betrayed him, giving away his location to Maccus, telling the monsters how to restrain him . . . allowing him to be brought to this cursed place for sacrifice. He had every right to kill her, here and now. If he felt that was right, she would not fight back.

But he did not attack. He allowed her to rest her head on his neck and hold on tight.

"I never thought I'd willingly hug any kind of a cat, much less a Caradon," she said, trying to make her voice sound lighthearted and hide the tears that dampened her face. She could still feel a connection with Joryn, but it had changed, as he had. His thoughts now were primal and uncomplicated.

Joryn was not entirely dark to her. She knew that, man or cat, he would not hurt her. He would not leave her.

As the moon moved across the sky, Keelia gave in to the call of the wolf and allowed herself to change. Wolf and cat ambled away from the smoldering bodies of Maccus and his soldiers, to escape the horrific scene and rest farther down the mountain.

JORYN AWOKE TO FIND KEELIA'S NAKED LIMBS ENtwined with his own. They were safe; he was a man again; she was his.

The ground beneath them was rough, but he did not care. He rolled Keelia onto her back, waking her. She sighed and wrapped her legs around his hips, and then he was inside her.

As sexual liaisons went, he was not at his most finessed. He needed Keelia with a desperation he had never before experienced, and he practically cried out at the sensation of her body accepting his. Their joining on this morning was fast and hard and over too quickly. While he was inside her, fire danced on air around them. In the past the loss of control had alarmed him greatly, but not today. Not today.

Sated, Keelia sighed and ran her hand down his side in a possessive motion he found he liked very much. "So," she whispered. "What now?"

"I don't know," Joryn said honestly. "Do we need to decide at this moment? We've done what we set out to do. There will be no more monsters."

Keelia's expression was suddenly solemn. "There will always be monsters. Even those beasts who were freed last night, those who have returned to their original bodies, remain soulless and evil. They will not have the strength they once had, but they are still enemies to be fought in days to come."

"Don't we get even a quick victory celebration?"

She raked her fingers through his hair. "I think we just did."

He thought of all that Druson had said while they'd been imprisoned, and wondered if it might possibly be true. Had Anwyn and Caradon long ago been one people? Was Keelia not only Queen of the Anwyn but also Queen of the Caradon as well?

Would they create a child who could fly?

He wondered if Keelia could still read his thoughts, but if that was the case, she did not reveal it. Perhaps the intensity of the situation had created an atmosphere where they could communicate without words. Perhaps it was an ability she could turn on and off, and at the moment the ability was inoperative. He tried to slip into her thoughts, but if she knew he was reaching out to her, she didn't show it.

Maybe their mental connection was an ability that would come and go, and he'd never know when she might be peeking into his head.

"I need to make my way back to The City," she said, and there was a touch of sadness in her voice.

"I imagine your army is still searching for you."

"Yes. How will I ever explain what's happened? They'll think I've gone entirely mad if I tell all."

With her bare skin against his, he didn't want to think about her returning to her Anwyn palace and him returning to . . . to what? The Grandmother, his teacher, the woman who had cared for him most of his life, was dead. Druson really *was* entirely mad. The idea of returning to The City of the Anwyn with Keelia was still impossible to comprehend. Whether he could believe that they were mated or not, there was no place for him there. In truth, there was no place for him anywhere.

All that was left for him was the blessed freedom he'd always loved, an independence which now seemed oddly desolate.

He did not wish to think of such a life, so he leaned down and took a nipple into his mouth, suckling deep. He touched Keelia, he teased her, he made her moan beneath him, and then he made love to her again. More properly this time. Slowly, deeply, and with a desperation as true and real as before, he claimed the Queen as

his, even though he was not yet sure how he would be
able to keep her.

KEELIA SLEPT AND DREAMED OF FLYING. SHE HAD
wings in the dream, and she soared above the valleys at
the foot of the Mountains of the North and then turned
up, exhilarating in the rush of the wind on her face as
she soared higher and higher until she was flying above
the mountain itself. Heavens, it felt so real. She could
feel the wind in every feather of her wings; she experienced the power of the welcome wind against her face.

She woke not as pleasantly as she had earlier. She and
Joryn were no longer alone. His strange friend had found
them, and he came bearing a plain cloth sack of clothing
and food he'd collected from the wizard's caves.

"Get dressed quickly," the man Joryn called Druson
said, his voice too fast and high to be normal. "If they
find you naked, they will be displeased. Hurry, hurry!"

Keelia took the purple sleeveless gown Druson offered her. At least he hadn't retrieved the heavy black
dress she'd left lying near Maccus's body. For himself
and for Joryn, he'd stolen dark purple trousers and
matching vests.

For a moment she studied the bracelet, which remained on her wrist. This plain piece of silver had kept
her from losing all of herself to Maccus and his wicked
enchantment. It carried within it a part of Joryn, somehow, and though she could not explain how precisely, it
had saved them all.

"Who's coming?" Keelia asked as she dressed. She did
not attempt to rush the process, since Joryn had seen her

naked many times, and Druson seemed not to care that she was unclothed. His mind was definitely elsewhere.

"You know, you know, they'll be here soon."

"Do they mean us harm?" Keelia asked, not terribly afraid. She had her claws and Joryn had fire, and in addition to the clothing, Druson had taken a fair number of knives from the wizard's cave, including Joryn's plain but serviceable dagger.

"Not you, My Queen," he said reverently.

My Queen. Odd for a Caradon, other than Joryn, to address her as such.

And even odder, when she was dressed, the graying Caradon presented himself to her and dropped down to one knee, placing one hand over his heart and bowing his head. "I am yours to command, My Queen."

Keelia ordered the odd Caradon to rise, and he did. "Do they intend to injure Joryn?" she asked, since he had made it clear she was in no danger. She tried to see who was coming, but her mind was blank. Whatever dark magic affected her abilities, it had not died with Maccus. Not entirely. She still saw some of what was to come, but certainly not all.

"Oh, yes," Druson said with a nod of his head. "They most certainly mean harm to Joryn. You must protect him. He is still necessary."

"Thanks so much," Joryn said dryly. "When I'm unnecessary, you'll allow them to do away with me?"

"If it is the proper time—" Druson began.

"Do you know when these enemies will reach us?" Keelia asked, interrupting the Caradon. It would be impossible to climb in the cumbersome skirt, so she gathered up the fabric of her gown and tied it so that the hem stayed well above her knees. In this way she'd have some freedom of movement.

"Oh, yes," Druson said. "I know. Come. This way."

"You didn't say when . . ."

But Druson was gone, scampering down the path that led away from Maccus's cave.

EVERYTHING HURT SO MUCH. HE BURNED EVERY-where. Every inch of his skin, his face, his eyes. Maccus lifted his head from the ground to see the bodies of his soldiers around him. They had died in agony, but for some reason he had not. Then again, perhaps he *had* died and then had been restored to life by the Isen Demon.

Even taking a breath hurt, but Maccus did breathe. His clothes had been burned away. His skin had likely once been as black as that of his fallen soldiers, but as he watched, it repaired itself. New skin grew, quickly and almost painlessly. He was not finished with his task; that's why he was not dead. That's why the Isen Demon saw to his repair.

Not yet able to walk, Maccus crawled over to the glint of metal that caught his eye. The stone in the center had been destroyed, but the metal work of the medallion was untarnished by flame. He lifted the broken chain, then lay there in the dirt and repaired it with fumbling, pained fingers as his body repaired itself. When that was done, he lifted the medallion and placed it over his head. Instantly, he grew better. Stronger. The speed of his recovery increased dramatically, even though the talisman was damaged.

He lay in the dirt and felt himself heal inside and out.

What had gone wrong? The whore had been his; he'd known it. He'd felt it to the depths of his . . . well, if he'd had much of a soul, that's where he would've felt it. She'd been so easy to charm, so simple to enchant and make his. What had broken through the enchantment?

At this moment the whore of a Queen should be in his bed, pregnant with his child, begging him to fuck her again and again.

Instead she had ruined everything.

No, not everything.

The Queen and the child could still be his. There were two nights of the full moon remaining in which to accomplish his goal. Two nights in which he could make her his bride and give her the child which was required as repayment for all the powers he'd been given.

He could still do as he'd been instructed, and live to rule these mountains when the Isen Demon's infection spread so dark and deep no one could think to stop it.

IT WAS ALMOST SUNSET AGAIN, AND THEY HAD NOT found anyone along the way. No threat at all, no one for which they had to "hurry."

They came to a small spring-fed pond, and it was there they planned to camp for the night. When it was almost time for the moon to rise, they would store their clothing in a small nearby cave . . . as there was no more close by to be stolen, bought, or borrowed . . . and change as was in their nature.

Druson disappeared, as he often did, and Keelia stripped off the purple gown. She hated to make use of anything that was connected with the wizard Maccus, but it was a pretty dress. It was the custom for the Queen to wear gold, but in an odd way it was nice to see something darker and more flattering against her pale skin.

Still, she would burn the gown as soon as she had the chance. It had the stink of Maccus and his bad magic in the very fibers of the fabric. The custom of always wearing gold could be easily changed, if she wished. She had a feeling that would be the least of the changes coming to her world.

Keelia waded into the pond, glad of the sensation of refreshing water against her skin, and dipped down to immerse herself. Summer was fully upon them, and even here high in the mountains the air was too warm to suit her. She longed for winter, when the snows came and the cold winds howled and there was ice in the very air she breathed.

She longed for many things. Winter would come; it always did. Other things she longed for were not so assured. Joryn was her mate, and he should be King. He should sit beside her, as her father had sat beside her mother. He should rule with her, help her, love her, give her babies. Would her people accept him? Would he accept them?

The moment Joryn stepped into the water, she knew it, even though he was silent and her back was to him. She smiled, and let the sensation of his presence wash over her. If she could do so, she would forever protect him, just as Druson said she must.

With his gift of fire, how was it possible that he might need her protection? Perhaps Druson was as daft as he sometimes appeared to be.

Joryn wrapped his arms around her and pulled her back to his chest. It was very nice, just to be held. Just to be close. There was so much she had to say to him, and she didn't know how. She didn't even know where to begin.

She turned and wrapped her arms around his neck. "Have I told you yet that I'm sorry I almost killed you?"

"No," he said, seemingly unconcerned.

"I'm sorry." She kissed his chest, there where the tip of the knife had touched him. There was no mark to show her where that injury had been, but she knew exactly where she had cut him. She had no doubt. "I'm also sorry that I told them where to find you."

"You weren't yourself."

"No, I wasn't."

"You came around quite nicely in the end."

"Thanks to you. When you told me to fight, the word stuck in my brain and worked past all the bad magic." He'd also said he loved her, but that had been when his life was in danger. He hadn't mentioned love since, and she wasn't sure that she could. Or should.

He laid his mouth over hers and kissed her, deeply and completely. She began to melt against him. Into him. Did he still doubt that they were mated? That they were meant to be? When his hand delved between her legs, she forgot everything else and began to soar, just as she had in her dream. She soared toward joining, pleasure, unexpected love. So it was with great effort that she drew away from Joryn and asked him to wait.

"If you continue, I'll soon not be able to think clearly, and there's something that must be done. Now is as good a time as any," she said.

"Not thinking clearly is sometimes a good thing," Joryn argued as he reached for her again, playful and lustful.

Keelia danced out of his reach. "There will be time

for that later, but for a moment, just for a moment, I'd like you to stand very still."

His eyebrows arched slightly. "Is that an order?"

She smiled. "No, it's a request."

With the water hitting him at the waist, Joryn stood as she'd directed. He crossed his arms over his chest and remained motionless as she'd asked. A breeze lifted one lock of damp, dark blond hair, but beyond that he was very still. Keelia took a step closer to him, and he smiled.

"Don't move," she reminded him as she stepped within reach. The water lapped at her skin, and she had a moment's doubt about what she was about to do. If he turned his back on her, what would she do? She'd be humiliated, and a Queen should never invite or even allow her own humiliation. But she was not only Queen, she was a woman. She approached Joryn in that way, as a woman.

When she stood so close her breasts almost touched him, Keelia tilted her head back so she was looking Joryn in the eye. She'd seen those eyes red with fire, dark green with desire, dancing with laughter. For a long moment she held that gaze, without attempting to reach into his mind, without touching him in any way. He would never know how difficult this was for her, how important.

Keelia dropped her head back slowly, offering him her throat in an unmistakable gesture. Her head was thrown so far back, all she could see was blue sky.

For a long moment all was silent. She didn't think either of them even breathed. A new slice of fear stole her breath. What if he refused her? What if she offered him everything she had to give, and he walked away? Maybe he had not forgiven her after all.

And then Joryn's mouth was there, pressed against

her throat, kissing gently as he muttered her name again and again.

He lifted her up, his skin slick against hers, and then he was inside her and she held on tight and rode him, all the while with his mouth on her throat.

And then it happened, with a force that knocked the breath out of Keelia and made her gasp. They were connected to the pit of their souls, and she not only knew Joryn, she *was* him. She knew what it felt like when he buried himself deep inside her body, she knew the pleasure he felt, the worry, the commitment, the love. She felt the air in his lungs and the taste of her skin, and she even felt the fire that always slept within him.

They found release together, shuddering and gasping, holding on to one another in more ways than she had known possible. He was a part of her, a life mate in all ways.

Now all they had to do was survive whatever threat was coming their way.

Coming, coming . . .

Here.

Keelia's psychic abilities had been uncertain and unstable of late, and still she was angry that the internal warning had come so late. If Druson was right, it was up to her to protect Joryn.

There was no time to discuss the miracle that had just taken place. She took Joryn's hand and led him toward the pond's edge. "Where is Druson?"

"Hunting. There's no need to worry that he'll—"

"The threat he warned us about, it's close. Very close."

They left the water behind and stood on dry land, quickly pulling on their clothes while searching the landscape for a threat of any kind. Keelia continued to hold on to Joryn's hand. The link was not the same as it had been while they'd been joined, but it remained, solid and unbreakable. He was hers, and she would protect him.

"I don't need protection from a woman," he said.

Keelia smiled. Joryn was inside her still, and he didn't even realize it. He didn't realize that she had not spoken the words he responded to aloud.

The sound of scrabbling rocks drew her attention to the right, and she placed herself in front of Joryn. Her claws could be unsheathed in a heartbeat, and she was ready to use them if need be.

He placed a hand on her shoulder. "I can protect myself, Keelia," he said tersely. "And you."

"Maybe we were meant to fight together," she said. "Like we did when we defeated Maccus."

Keelia allowed Joryn to stand beside her. She held her breath as the threat moved closer, running up the slope, heading directly for their camp. Closer, closer . . .

Here.

A mass of fair hair and tanned skin came over the rise, and once again Keelia threw herself in front of Joryn.

He protested and tried to move her aside, but she would have none of it. She lifted a hand and asked him silently to contain his powers. He didn't have a chance to ask why before she spoke to the intruder.

"Hello, Father."

16

IN THE END, JORYN HAD TO EITHER ALLOW KEELIA TO
protect him, or use his gift for fire against her father.
There had been a time when he would not have hesitated to attack a large Anwyn brute who rushed toward
him with deadly intent, but things had changed.

Everything had changed. As dark of night and the full
moon approached, he stood with Keelia and her parents
and a muttering Druson, who made no sense at all. The
Grandfather didn't cease his constant nonsensical mur-
murs, but no one was listening to him.

"We don't have much time." The pretty red-haired
woman, Queen Mother Juliet, looked very much like
Keelia, only she was a few years older and her hair was
curly instead of straight. Their eyes and the shape of their
faces were much the same. "Keelia is the only one of us
who won't transform tonight, and I cannot rest easy until
I know that my daughter is safe."

"She's safe," Joryn said, doing his best to assure Keelia's mother . . . and her glaring father, Ryn.

Druson's words became a bit clearer. "Not safe. Not yet. He still needs her to do what he wants done."

Joryn put a hand on his friend's shoulder, trying to comfort Druson and end the babbling. "The wizard is dead."

The Grandfather shook his head. "No, not dead. Not dead!"

Juliet's brow wrinkled with worry. "Perhaps we should listen to him." In spite of her words, she seemed uncertain. "If the wizard was the cause of the disruption of my abilities, as well as those of others who have my gift, and he's now dead, then why have my gifts not returned in full force? I see some things, but not all. Is it possible that this . . . this Caradon is correct?"

Keelia nodded as if she understood her mother's concern. "Perhaps someone or something else is to blame for the interference we're experiencing. I know Maccus is dead. I saw him die."

Druson ran both hands through graying hair. "You're not listening to me!"

Ryn had no patience for humoring an obviously insane Caradon seer. "That's because you're not making sense. I can barely think for all your rambling. Shut up!"

Joryn glanced at the horizon. There was no time to share with Keelia and her parents what Druson had told him about the past history of Anwyn and Caradon. He wasn't even sure that it was true, but if it was . . . they all needed to know. Everyone needed to know, but such explanation would have to wait until morning.

Druson worked at making his meaning clear, enunciating each word. "We cannot let the wizard have her! I will die for my Queen, but—"

"*Your* Queen?" Ryn said gruffly.

Druson pounded a fist against his own chest. "*My* Queen, you barbarian."

The big man looked as if he had been slapped. In his mind the Caradon people were the barbarians, not the superior Anwyn.

Druson had been mentally off, and scattered, and yes, very near insane. But he had not been violent. He hadn't even fought against Maccus's soldiers when the proper time for fighting had been presented. So Joryn—and everyone else present—was surprised when Druson grabbed Keelia by the back of her gown and dragged her away from the group and toward the cliff's edge.

"You don't understand!" Druson shouted. "Our Queen is special, she is unlike all others but she does not yet know the depths of her power. The forces of our ancestors are hers, but she cannot see. The future of all rests with her, it rests inside her and she does not *know*."

"What don't I know, Druson?" Keelia's voice remained calm. "Tell me."

"You are now as we once were. You have unlimited and untapped abilities beyond what is known to our people or any other. And yet your power sleeps, because you have not reached for it." Druson dragged Keelia closer to the cliff's edge, glancing back and down to test the distance he'd fall if he made a misstep. Joryn had looked over that edge earlier. It was a tremendous and almost straight plunge that would take anyone who went over it into the green valley at the foot of the mountain.

"Watch yourself, Druson," Joryn said calmly as he took a step toward his friend. "Don't stand so near the edge."

Druson laughed harshly. "You don't understand. I tried to tell you, but you don't understand." He looked at Keelia. "She does," he whispered. "If not, she soon will."

Without warning, Druson called upon all his strength to push Keelia to the edge, and over. She flailed, but she hadn't seen the move coming, and she dropped over the edge with a horrifying scream. Druson backed away from the edge and laughed again, but there were tears in his eyes. "Now she will know. Now she will see."

Joryn did not hesitate. He ran toward Druson, passed by the insane Grandfather, and leapt from the edge of the cliff, following in Keelia's path.

KEELIA'S PANIC DIDN'T LAST LONG. HER BREATH WAS stolen away by the fall, and then she found it once again. She was terrified, and then suddenly she was not. This was so much like her dream, it felt as if she had been here before, with the wind on her face and in her hair, and the air catching and holding her body as she fell.

She heard the fabric of her gown rip, and was not concerned. Her arms were guided back, her head up, and it felt so natural, so right. The wind caught her hair and what was left of the gown, and then it caught something else.

Her wings.

Directly below, a flash of flame caught her eye. Between her and the ground, a large circle of fire appeared and grew. She had wings which kept her aloft, but had not yet learned to control them well. She couldn't move out of the way of the flames fast enough, nor could she catch air with her wings and rise away from the fire. Even as she attempted to shift her unwieldy form out of the way, the circle of flame grew larger and larger, until she knew she could not possibly miss it.

A shout from above caught her attention, and she clumsily rolled her body, wings and all, to see Joryn falling toward her. The appearance of wings had slowed her down, and he'd shaped his body to have as little wind resistance as possible, so he continued to rush toward her. The flame was his doing, she understood, but why?

They both tumbled toward the earth at an alarming rate of speed. They were both going to plummet through the fire and into the valley below if something didn't happen very quickly. Could she catch Joryn and learn to use these newly discovered wings in time to save them?

His voice rang in her head. *Hang on.*

When Joryn reached her and snapped his arms about her, she obeyed. She hung on to him with all her might. Linked, wings fluttering, hair entangled, they fell into the fire . . .

And instantly landed on a soft bed of grass.

Amazingly, she and Joryn lay on the ground. Keelia felt as if she'd fallen a few feet, no more. How was that possible?

Keelia quickly regained her breath and sat up slowly. She and Joryn were surrounded by a collection of stunned and annoyed and amused people. No, not *people*, she realized as she looked at them. Spirits. Those who were dead but had not yet moved on.

One peaceful spirit smiled at her and nodded his head. He bowed to her, and when he lifted his head once again, she looked into his eyes and recognized the creature from the battle by the stream, the one who had fought for his soul. And won.

An older woman with long white hair and a well-lined, serene face approached. Keelia instantly knew that the fate of this one's soul was not undecided, as many of the others were. There was a pure white glow about her that made Keelia smile. The older woman had come here for the express purpose of speaking to Joryn. She'd been waiting for them to arrive.

Keelia reached around to touch the wings that had sprung from her back. Joryn caressed a feather that had sprouted in her hair, one of a few that were mingled with the red strands, and Keelia wondered what else about her had changed.

"Only the eyes," Joryn answered, as if she had spoken aloud.

His eyes were drawn to the woman bathed in white, and he jumped to his feet. "Grandmother."

The old woman smiled. "I'm simply Vala now. What was the Grandmother now resides in Druson. You must protect him."

"Druson pushed Keelia over the edge. She might've been killed."

"He knew she would not." She shook her finger at Joryn like a censuring mother might. "You were told not to use this doorway. Things in your world are not as they should be. The dark magic which is at work in your world disrupts all energy, even that which creates these doorways."

Here in this place, Keelia's gifts were at full strength. It had been so long since she'd experienced a powerful rush of knowledge, she was stunned. How could she not have known months ago that her talents had been tainted?

Because she could now see so much of Joryn, Keelia knew what doorways the old woman spoke of. She also knew that Vala held the answers to many questions. Their time here was short, and she wanted as many of those answers as she could collect. Keelia scrambled to her feet, feathers and all.

Joryn smiled. "You scold me for using the doorway, and yet you are here to speak with me. It's not as if I could allow Keelia to fall to her death."

"She might've gained control of her wings," Vala argued.

"Or not."

Keelia hated to interrupt the easy banter, but she had too many questions to stand by and wait patiently. "I don't understand any of this. Where did these wings come from?"

The old woman reached out and patted Keelia's face. Her touch was peaceful. Heavenly and welcome. "They come from inside you. You see so much of others, and yet you do not see that which rests inside yourself. You have the power of all the creatures of the earth. They need only to be unlocked. Freed. Experienced."

"But . . ."

"Joryn and Druson know the rest. They will tell you all that you need to know." Vala turned her attention to Joryn. "The wizard is not dead."

"I saw him die."

"He is *not* dead. He will try to claim the Queen before the cycle of the full moon ends. You must stop him, Joryn, or else all is lost. Do not allow him to touch her. Do not allow his poison to infect the mountains we love. Now go, before you're both trapped here. You'll do the world no good resting in the land in-between."

Joryn nodded. "Where will the doorway lead us?"

Vala smiled. "As always, the doorway will open on the same place where you entered this world. That is as it must be."

Keelia fluttered her new wings. They had entered this world in midair.

DRUSON HELD HIS BREATH AS HE WATCHED. WHAT IF he was wrong? He didn't think he was wrong, but what if he was? Behind him, Keelia's mother screamed, and her father bellowed. They both ran to the edge after Joryn leapt into the air, but they did not follow. The large Anwyn grabbed Druson with large hands which would soon be paws. Druson was moments away from death, but he had no regrets. He'd done what needed to be done.

He glanced up into angry golden eyes. "Look," he said softly. "Look, look, *look*."

The old Queen was already watching, and it was her word that saved Druson from a quick death at massive Anwyn hands. "Wait." A stilling hand came up, and Druson did not die.

The Anwyn and his mate looked over the edge and saw what Druson saw. The Queen sprouted wings, large wings that slowed her descent. The circle of fire appeared, and Joryn shaped his body in a fashion that allowed him to reach Keelia. He caught her, or she caught him, and they fell through the fire.

And disappeared, for the span of a heartbeat or two.

When they reappeared, the Queen's wings were spread wide, and Joryn held on to her, in essence riding on her back as they glided into the valley below and landed.

It was time for the full moon transformation, for him and for the Anwyn pair beside him. Druson felt the shift begin. Unlike the Queen, they could not control the shifting from human to animal and back again. He managed to voice one warning before the change robbed his ability to speak.

"Tonight beware the black cat who wears metal at his throat."

THE GROUND RUSHED UP QUICKLY, BUT NOT DANGER-ously so. Keelia did her best to control the wind with her wings, but flying was a skill she'd need to practice in order to perfect. Joryn's weight on her back did not help matters any, but this was the only way for the two of them to make it safely to solid ground.

She landed hard, and Joryn rolled off her back and away, shifting to mountain cat as he whirled across the grass.

Keelia did not shift. Her wings retracted, and she took a deep, calming breath. A moment later those wings were gone, though she suspected—no, she *knew*—that she could now call upon them as she called upon her claws. Falling, finding her wings, entering the world between life and death, speaking with the white witch who was no longer Grandmother, exiting that world with Joryn on her back, and making their way safety to the ground . . . it had all happened in a matter of minutes. Perhaps two.

While she lay on the ground trying to catch her breath, the blond cat sauntered over to her and sniffed at her throat, then her hair, then her cheek. He only wanted to know that she was all right; she knew that as she reached out to stroke Joryn's head.

"Now I understand why you're afraid to make a child who might have your gift for fire. It isn't simply fire at all." Her fingers traced the streak of red in his fur. "That doorway can be dangerous if misused."

Yes.

A child with such a gift would need intensive training, as well as constant supervision, until of a certain age.

"Why didn't you tell me?" It would've made a few days of heartbreak much easier if she'd know Joryn's reasoning for keeping his distance. "I suppose you didn't trust me enough." She continued to stroke his fur. Her feelings were not hurt by the revelation. Joryn had never been one to give his trust easily. The Grandmother was likely the only person on this earth he'd ever truly trusted. Until now. He had not said so, but he did trust her.

"You leapt off a cliff after me," she said softly. "What if the doorway hadn't worked properly in the air?"

A chance I had to take.

She had offered Joryn her throat, and he had jumped off a cliff on the *chance* he might save her. Could anyone doubt that they were mated?

Keelia sat up quickly, disrupting Joryn's position. "Is it possible that Maccus is not dead, as Vala and Druson said?" When she remembered how compliant his enchantment had made her, she shuddered. She didn't want to lose herself again, ever. "He can't possibly make it down the mountain as quickly as we did, but . . ." She looked into Joryn's green eyes. "But my parents don't have any idea what he's capable of, and they're directly in his path."

She shifted instantly to red wolf. Perhaps she could transform herself to another, faster animal, but now was not the time to experiment with untested abilities. The wolf was still a very large part of her, and she needed it now. She looked into Joryn's green cat eyes. *We must hurry.*

MACCUS CAME ACROSS THE THREE OF THEM WELL PAST midnight. The red wolf, the insane black and gray cat, and a blond . . . wolf? Was the Queen's magic so powerful that she could command her chosen mate to shift into the animal she called her own? He did not wish to be a wolf, but then once he had control of the Queen, she would do whatever he desired, as she would have no desires of her own other than to obey him.

The three animals seemed to be alert, and Maccus studied the situation with calculating eyes. He no longer had his soldiers to call upon for assistance. Those he'd kept close to him were dead, thanks to Joryn's fire. Those who were far away from him, fighting the demon's war, had been stripped of their powers and would find themselves weak and bewildered, soulless and dedicated to doing the demon's work, but without Maccus's direction.

He must take the Queen on his own.

Certain parts of the ritual to make her his bride must be followed, but all would not be precisely as he and the Isen Demon had planned. Keelia had destroyed the stone which had enchanted the half-transformed creatures, so he would not be in that enhanced state when he made her his bride. They could not be washed entirely in moonlight when the ceremony took place, as he would change into his feline form without his full power. No, the ceremony would have to take place when both moon and sun shone, and he maintained his human shape. How else was he to make his daughter?

But Keelia *would* wear the blood of her lover. That was required. It was necessary. Even if it were not required, he wanted to see the man who'd burned him suffer. Maccus studied the large blond wolf below, and then his eyes were drawn to the red wolf who would soon be his. At the moment, all three animals were very much on guard. He could see and sense their tension, their readiness. Three against one was not favorable odds, and Maccus had never been one to place himself in danger if it could be avoided.

The silver and gold medallion, all but ruined by the Queen and yet not entirely without power, hung from his neck. In the morning he would have full use of his magic, and he could take them at that time. Once he made the Queen his again, the others would be easy to take.

The black cat with metal at his throat settled down to watch and wait.

AFTER MUCH DISCUSSION, IT WAS DECIDED. ARIANA and Sian would march to Arthes to heal Arik and send Sibyl and Bronsyn to safety; Merin and his men would descend upon Ciro and his unholy army so that they would never reach the capital city; Sophie and her husband, Kane, would search for Liane and her lost children—the lost heirs to the throne.

Ariana wasn't sure who had the toughest job ahead of them. Merin and his soldiers were prepared to fight, and their task was, perhaps, the most straightforward. Some of them would die, but they would die nobly and with purpose. She planned to rejoin them once her task of healing Emperor Arik was completed, so that she could tend soldiers and return battered gray and dark souls to those of Ciro's Own who were captured. Healing was her most important gift in this war. It always had been.

With her newly enhanced powers, could she heal the emperor? Could she save him? He'd been so ill when she'd left him, she couldn't be certain that he was still alive. Sibyl was a talented healer. If anyone could keep him alive, it was Ariana's little sister. Facing what his son had become would be more difficult than death, she knew, but Arik's survival was necessary.

Her parents' task would, perhaps, be the most difficult. Not only did they have no idea where to search for Liane and her children, but if Ciro found out that he had elder cousins who could lay claim to the throne, none of them would be safe. In truth, no one was safe while Ciro lived.

The three parties would travel together for a few days more, and then they would part company and go their separate ways. Ariana had so hoped to have Keelia's counsel before continuing on, but she could not turn back, and she could not wait any longer in the hopes that her cousin would find her. Lyr and Duran were surely on their way to join Merin by now.

Ariana wasn't quite ready to face her brother, not after sending him away before telling him of her part in this war, and she didn't know what to tell Lyr. Was he to wield the crystal dagger as she suspected? If so, they first had to find it and she had no idea where to tell him to look.

She studied the full moon. Where was Keelia? The
Anwyn Queen had her part to play in this war, and
perhaps she was entrenched in her own battles at this
very moment.

While she could not know with any certainty, it made
sense that Keelia's part in the Prophesy of the Firstborn
was betrayal of love. Lyr was the logical bearer of the
crystal dagger, and Keelia . . . Keelia was capable of betrayal, of that Ariana was certain. Even as a child, Keelia
had always held something of herself back. She'd been
quiet and thoughtful and secretive. Not for the first time,
it occurred to Ariana that the love Keelia was destined to
betray might be the love for a cousin. Maybe Keelia
knew she was desperately needed, but chose not to join
the fight. The very idea made Ariana's heart feel heavy.

Betrayal in the name of victory. Of course, the prophesy had not said whose victory that betrayal would bring.

It was late, well past midnight, but few in camp were
able to sleep. As far as Ariana could see, beneath the
light of the moon, fires blazed, and soldiers sharpened
their swords and spoke in low tones. Merin and some of
his most trusted soldiers studied maps and battle plans.
Sophie Varden and her husband planned their own route
of travel. They knew in which direction Liane had been
traveling when she'd left Arthes, and they also knew
she'd planned to get as far away from the capital city as
possible. With that in mind, they made their own battle
plans.

Ariana paced alone, near enough to a blazing fire to be
bathed in its light, but not so close that the heat was too
overpowering. She saw Sian walking through that light,
his face stark against his long black hair and black clothing, his every move sensuous and graceful and strong.

She did love him, so much.

He had a determined look on his face as he approached her, and she wondered what was wrong. She didn't have long to wait before he informed her of the reason for that resolute expression.

"There was a preacher among the troops that joined us tonight."

"That's nice," she said. "The men will need spiritual guidance, as well as Merin's leadership."

"He can also marry us."

"We're already—"

"You call me husband, I call you wife, we are bound together, yes," Sian interrupted. "But I want it all. I want the words in front of friends and family. I want God's blessing. I want—"

"I want all that, too," she said, cutting him off. "But I also want a perfect wedding day, without the knowledge that tomorrow is uncertain."

Sian placed his hand on her shoulders gently. "Tomorrow will always be uncertain, love. Always."

She knew he was right, and still something inside her wanted to hold back. "Yes, but when we say vows, I should be wearing a pretty gown, not a sloppily altered sentinel's uniform. I should carry flowers, not a sword. I want our wedding to be perfect, Sian."

His face remained hard, but his eyes softened. The purple there danced with emotion and love. "No matter where we are or what you wear, it *will* be perfect." He waved his hand and bathed her in enchanted purple light. Suddenly her uniform appeared to be a pretty blue dress, and the sword that hung at her side looked like a bouquet of spring flowers.

But it wasn't real, and she knew it too well. All she

did was lift her hand in silent protest, and Sian instantly made the enchantment go away.

"Do you love me?" he asked, only a little frustrated.

"I do. You know I do."

"Did you mean it when you said that every time we love or laugh in spite of fear, the demon we're battling grows a little weaker?"

"Yes."

"Then why not now? While your parents are here and we're surrounded by men who love you and call you sister, why not *now*?"

Ariana had been waiting for the perfect moment to arrive, and it struck her that in spite of her fancies of flowers and silk, perhaps this was it. Her parents were here, and so were many friends. Tomorrow might be uncertain, but tonight all was well.

They gathered near the fire, Sian in dusty black and Ariana in battered green. She did not allow him to make the scene prettier for her or for others. No, she wanted reality in her wedding. Not flowers, not contrived beauty, but the reality of love and commitment. Her parents and her friends, her brothers in this war, were present. They loved her, and in the predawn hours of yet another uncertain day, she said the words that made Sian Sayre Chamblyn her husband in that one, final way.

When the final words were spoken, a shout went up. Men who had been solemn of late laughed heartily. Ariana's mother cried, but the tears she shed were tears of joy. Her father shook Sian's hand, which was an improvement over wrestling him into the dirt for boldly and truthfully answering his question and revealing the nature of his relationship with an overly protected eldest daughter.

In the midst of it all, Ariana realized that Sian had been right to remind her of the words she'd spoken when they'd been waiting for Keelia in the palace of the Anwyn Queen. The Isen Demon that infected this land fed on fear, and it trembled and weakened at the growth and declaration of true love.

17

THEY RAN MOST OF THE NIGHT, STOPPING ONLY FOR water and very short periods of rest. Joryn had never thought to follow *anyone* while embracing the body and power of a cat, but he followed the red wolf up the mountain path without a moment's hesitation.

Beneath the large and brilliant moon, through feline eyes all was gray. All but Keelia. She had burnished red fur and golden eyes. She was bright and powerful, as if he saw her with another part of himself than with eyes alone.

She was his. His Queen, his lover. His mate.

They raced up the mountain, but they weren't quick enough to reach camp before the sun rose. Joryn felt his body begin to change, and he had no choice but to stop and allow the natural progression of transformation to claim him. Muscles contracted and reformed. Fur retracted. Color bloomed all around, as his human eyes took the place of those of a cat. There were a few brief moments of minor pain, as always, and his progress up the mountain was halted.

Keelia did not stop, nor did she begin the change into her human form. She remained wolf, with a wolf's speed and agility to help her to her destination.

A man once again, Joryn had no choice but to run on two seemingly inefficient feet. Still, his years on this mountain had acclimated him to the steep and rocky trails, and he continued on without a misstep, even when the red wolf he followed disappeared around a bend. On the other side of the bend was the camp where they'd left the others.

Maccus might've attacked in the night, taking the others by surprise . . . but Joryn didn't think so. It was possible that, like Joryn, Maccus had to be in human form to call upon his magic. He would want use of that power when confronting superior numbers.

The sun was rising, which meant that Maccus was a man once more.

And Keelia was completely out of Joryn's sight.

KEELIA REALIZED THE PRECISE MOMENT WHEN THE others would change; she felt it as they did—and *not* as they did. As always, she felt the call for change but was not commanded by it. She did not shift, nor did she pause at that important moment. Thanks to her gifts, she easily maintained the body of a wolf as she rushed toward the site where she'd left her parents and Druson last night. She knew what Maccus was capable of, and there was no time to slow down, not even when Joryn fell behind.

She startled them all, leaping into the peaceful camp-site as her mother, father, and a mumbling Druson were getting dressed in simple traveling clothes, after passing the night in their animal bodies. They were all well, seem-ingly. But then, she supposed she herself had *seemed* well enough while under the wizard's spell.

Then her mother smiled, recognizing her daughter as a familiar red wolf, and Keelia knew all truly was well. That smile was not touched by dark magic, not in the least. She shifted into her human body easily and quickly, startling Druson. The Caradon was accustomed to the change taking much longer than the blink of an eye.

"Maccus lives," Keelia said abruptly. "He's still a danger to all of us."

"I told you . . ." Druson began.

Juliet's smile died. "How do you know this?" She di-rected her question to Keelia, ignoring the Grandfather. "And what happened when you fell? Keelia, I have so many questions, I don't know where to begin."

"Begin with clothing," Keelia's father said. "Juliet, you have an extra frock in your pack, don't you?"

"Yes, yes." Barely dressed herself, Juliet grabbed her pack and pulled out a short-skirted dark green shift. She tossed the traveling dress to Keelia, who quickly pulled it on. Her father had always possessed an oddly human need for modesty where his daughters were concerned.

"Where's Joryn?" Druson asked.

"He's coming." Keelia smoothed the skirt of her mother's frock. "I didn't want to wait for him to catch up, since I did not know if Maccus would be here or not." She looked squarely at her mother. "He's the one who's blocked our psychic energy."

"How do you know?"

"When I was . . . where I went," she said, not knowing how to explain any of this quickly, "I was unaffected by his spell. Some things which had been dark to me were illuminated. If we kill Maccus, the spell will be lifted and we'll be able to see again. We must see, Mother. There's a greater threat than one dark and power-hungry Caradon wizard at work, and our gifts will be needed." Keelia had begun to believe, as she'd run during the night, that this horrible threat was the very reason for her abilities. It was not a coincidence that some in this world were born with certain gifts. The test in life came when one had to choose how—or even if—to use those gifts.

She turned to watch the curve in the path. Joryn should be here by now, by her reckoning. Even on foot and naked, he should've been close behind her. She reached for him, in that way she had learned to rely upon, and for a moment she touched his mind.

Joryn?

Almost there. Are your parents and Druson well?

Yes. Hurry, we have much to . . .

Before she could finish, she felt the connection end. It was severed without warning, and she realized the precise moment that mental link vanished. Had Joryn unconsciously blocked her, as he had in the past? Or was something wrong? It was true, in the past their link had been most reliable in moments of crisis, but that didn't mean they couldn't learn to call upon it in even the most peaceful of times.

She tried not to panic. He was very close, and she hadn't heard a sound of alarm or a scuffle of stones from the path. If he'd fallen, she would've heard.

But if Maccus had been lying in wait . . .

Keelia turned and ran back the way she'd come, but

she didn't get far. The Caradon wizard walked calmly around the bend, a length of Joryn's hair grasped in his hand as he dragged the unconscious man along, the other hand closed tight, obviously clenching something. Maccus wore a long purple robe and a small leather sack which hung at his waist. That damned medallion, dented and with a cracked stone at its center, hung against his chest.

"If you want this one to live awhile longer, you'll remain very still. All of you," he said calmly. Much too calmly, considering the odds. Four to one. Five, if Joryn awoke. Keelia looked down at Joryn's face as Maccus moved closer. He wasn't dead, but the rise and fall of his chest was weak and uncertain.

Her father took a step forward. "You assume that I care about this Caradon who has dared to touch my daughter. Kill him. See if I so much as flinch when he dies."

"Father!" Keelia admonished. Joryn had leapt off a cliff to save her, and her parents had been here to witness that act. How could they be so careless with his life?

"We need him," Druson mumbled. "We still need Joryn."

"I don't need him." Ryn rushed forward, and the wizard calmly lifted his hand. He whispered a curt word in the ancient language of the wizards as he tossed a handful of sand into her father's face. Ryn dropped in his tracks, instantly and completely unconscious.

Maccus reached into the pouch that hung from his waist and grabbed another small handful of the sand. Keelia recognized it as that which she'd used to draw a map to lead Maccus's men to Joryn's hiding place, when she'd been in his command. No wonder he had gasped when she'd tossed it onto the table. The seemingly ordinary sand was a powerful weapon.

"Anyone else?" Maccus asked calmly. "What must happen here can be accomplished with all of you senseless, or even dead. I would prefer to wait until tonight, when the moon rises again, but if I must kill you all now . . ."

"Won't kill the Queen," Druson mumbled. "Need her. Need her. Better to be dead."

Maccus glanced at the rambling man, annoyance etched on his face. "Who *are* you?"

"No one," Keelia said, stepping between the wizard and the Grandfather. "Surely you can see that he's not right in the head. Ignore him. I'm the one you need to speak with. What do you want, Maccus?"

The wizard dragged Joryn farther into the camp, carelessly dropping the limp body near Ryn's. Maccus's attention was on Keelia, so he barely noticed when Juliet ran to the two unconscious men and dropped to her knees. Keelia could see the relief on her mother's face, and she knew both men were alive. For now.

"I want everything, love," Maccus answered. "Power. Fortune. Immortality. And you."

Keelia wished she'd had more time in the world inbetween, where her powers had worked as they should. The few minutes she'd been there had been filled with bursts of information, but she simply hadn't been there for very long. If she understood all that was to come, maybe she'd know how to stop Maccus.

One thing she did know: All his magic was in the things he wielded, not within himself. The sand, the medallion, the stones he had enchanted . . . stones she had destroyed. The only way she could defeat him was to make sure he was stripped of his implements.

Behind her, Druson mumbled, "Take his heart, take his head. Let them stay not together."

Maccus either did not hear the lowly spoken words, or else he had already dismissed the mumbling man as insignificant.

But Keelia knew that her mother heard. Juliet's head came up slowly, and she caught her daughter's eye before nodding once. They knew what they had to do. Could they accomplish the feat with the strongest members of their party insensible?

MACCUS KEPT A CLOSE EYE ON HIS PRISONERS. HIS mistake last night, in assuming the redhead and the blond were Keelia and Joryn, was an understandable one. Apparently the Queen and her lover had spent the night beneath the full moon elsewhere, not in the camp with her parents and the odd, muttering fool. Since Keelia's father did not care for his daughter's lover, it was understandable that the couple might make their own camp in another place.

Even in their human form, mother and daughter favored. Keelia was more petite, and her hair was silkier, but there was a resemblance. Of course, Keelia's powers were much stronger than her mother's. Only the current Queen had the ability to maintain her woman's shape when the full moon rose.

With the proper spell and the Isen Demon's assistance, it was a power Maccus could steal when the time came. When he shifted into his animal form, his magic was silent. He had tried many different spells and enchantments to fix that failing, but nothing had worked thus far. Once his child was growing in Keelia and she was under his bewitchment again, he would re-create the enchantment that had called his servants to him. Just a few nights ago he had planned to join his soldiers in that enhanced state where he would be part human and part cat, so that he would always have the power of the animal and the magic of the man. But if he could steal Keelia's power, he would not need to embrace that sometimes painful change. He could have it all.

He looked at the two who remained unconscious. Those two strong men would be the first of his servants this time. They would wear the amulets which connected them to him, and they would become creatures which Keelia called monsters, and they would worship him. The mother, too. She would be next. He liked the idea of owning the soul of a former Anwyn Queen, and he looked forward to making her his servant in all ways. How interesting it would be to have both mother and daughter at his command.

It was necessary that Keelia wear the blood of her lover when they wed, but it was not necessary that she shed all of the Caradon's blood. If Maccus had still had his soldiers, then he'd have insisted on the death of the Queen's lover, but since he was in need of new servants, a less drastic bloodletting would suffice for now.

It was Keelia's fault that he had to start building his army all over again, but he did not hate her for her strength. He admired her greatly. Soon her strength would be his.

Timing was crucial, as the Queen and her lover had

ruined his original plans. The ceremony and the consummation would have to take place just before full darkness fell. While both moon and sun hung in the sky, he would make the Queen his own.

VERY SLOWLY, JORYN BECAME AWARE OF HIS SITUATION and his surroundings. His hands and feet were bound, and he lay on the hard ground. A large, motionless body lay close to his. He opened one eye to see Keelia's father in a similar position to his own.

Early that morning, Joryn had been rushing toward Keelia as she spoke to him with her powerful mind. While listening to her, he'd come across something odd on the narrow path. The thing on the ground had looked to him like a piece of discarded metal, and since metal of any kind was hard to come by in this place, he'd stooped to study the piece.

It might've been dropped by one of Maccus's soldiers in days past. Even though he did not have Keelia's abilities, he detected the stink of bad magic. He decided not to touch the thing. When he'd stood, all he'd seen were the grains of sand coming toward him, and the fuzzy outline of Maccus's face. Everything had quickly gone dark.

Now that he was awake again, he didn't reveal his consciousness to the others. Instead he took a moment to watch, listen, and assess the situation.

Judging by the way the light fell, it was late afternoon. He'd been senseless for the entire day, when they did not have a single day, a single hour, to waste. Out of the corner of his eye, he saw that Keelia's mother, Juliet, had been bound as he had but remained conscious. Druson was out of sight, but now and then Joryn heard a mumbled word that surely came from the Grandfather.

He could not see Keelia, but he heard her calm voice.

"If I'm to be naked, then you should be naked, too," she said, her tone absurdly serene and reasonable. "It's only fair."

Joryn pulled against his bonds. He could sit up and call upon fire without the use of his hands, but unless he knew where everyone was situated, he'd have to move very quickly—before Maccus had a chance to attack with his sleeping sand again. He'd lost an entire day with its first use. He could not afford to lose this night.

With great restraint, Joryn reached for Keelia with his mind. *Naked? What's happening?*

He felt her rush of relief before he caught the word. *Wait.*

Wait for what?

Just wait.

Her voice came again. "You insist I am to be your bride, and yet there is no equality in this situation. A man and woman who are wed should be equal."

"Equality?" Maccus said with a snort of laughter. "Why should I concern myself with equality?"

Keelia's voice was serene and strong, and sent chills down Joryn's spine. "It's only right. If I am your equal, I can assist you in all your efforts." She sighed loudly. "Do you think I don't want the same things you do? Power. Fortune. Immortality. I can share my considerable power with you, and I will do so. Willingly, Maccus, I will share. But only if there is fairness and a like share of power on both sides of this marriage."

"You fought me before."

"You tried to take away my mind!" Keelia argued.

"Of course I fought you. I am a strong woman, and no one will take away my will or my identity ever again. That does not mean I'm not eager for all that you have promised me." She positively cooed. Even if he had not been able to touch her mind, Joryn would know she was lying. She was drawing Maccus in, making him relax.

"It's almost time," Maccus said, his voice sharp. "Draw the blood of your lover and paint it on your body as you wish."

"No. Not until you are as naked as I am," Keelia said stubbornly. "This marriage will be evenly balanced in every way, or there will be no marriage at all."

The wizard was obviously annoyed. "I can send you to sleep and make you my bride without your consent."

"You could," Keelia responded, seemingly unconcerned. "But if I remember correctly, you need me to draw Joryn's blood. Besides, surely you realize that our strength will be much more forceful if our connection is one of mutual consent. My power freely given will be tenfold my power taken."

For a moment, the wizard was silent.

Now? Joryn asked.

No!

"Fine." Maccus's word was followed by the rustle of clothing.

It took all of Joryn's will to remain motionless while Maccus undressed himself with the intention of making Keelia his dark bride. His body shuddered, he was so anxious to burst to her rescue, but he had to trust her to know when the time was right to fight. He who had never entirely trusted any woman or any Anwyn waited for Keelia's signal, for her word that it was time to make his move. Trying not to make a sound or move too much, he continued to wrestle against the knotted rope at his wrists.

"That, too," Keelia said when the rustle of clothing ceased. "Take it off."

"No," Maccus snapped.

"Then where is my medallion?" Keelia said stridently. "Where is my symbol of our power? It is not fair that you should have something I do not, at this time when we are supposed to be equal."

"You already sound like a shrew!"

"I sound like a woman who knows what she wants and doesn't mind commanding it," Keelia responded in a tone Joryn remembered from their early days together. "I demand that you remove that piece of jewelry so our marriage will be entirely natural and without unnecessary embellishment. We will be wed with nothing which is not of ourselves interfering. When that is done, we will make our special daughter with you and I each embracing our union without either of us having power or superiority over the other."

If you think I'm going to lie here while . . .

Keelia's response was fervent. *Get ready.*

"I cannot remove this," Maccus said, but there was a hint of reluctance in his voice.

"You would share my considerable power with a demon when it can be yours? You would willingly pass what I offer you to an entity who would gladly kill us all for even a small portion of what I possess? Really, Maccus, I did think you more ambitious than that."

For a moment all was silent, and then Keelia purred, "Better."

Now!

Joryn rolled over and up, his bonds loosening as he

leapt to his feet. Keelia jumped away from Maccus and scooped something from the ground. It was his medallion, which she had coerced him into shedding for their "wedding."

Naked, caught by surprise, and without his magic, Maccus looked stunned. "You lied," he said, turning to Keelia and sounding very much as if his feelings were hurt by her betrayal. "You told me you wanted the same things I do. You said you would join me and together we would rule the Mountains of the North and all the people upon them. You said . . ." He reached out one pale hand. "Give me my medallion."

Keelia backed away from the wizard, the symbol of his power in her hand but held as far away from her body as possible.

Juliet squirmed, trying to free herself. The large Anwyn, Keelia's father, moaned as he came slowly awake.

Druson mumbled, but he managed to rise steadily to his feet. His words became stronger and clearer, and he reached out his bound hands. A gentle glow surrounded the knotted ropes there until the twine literally came apart, dissolving into small pieces that fell to the ground, leaving his hands free.

Maccus's reaction to the threat was to reach for the nearest person. Keelia. Still clinging to his medallion, she was able to dance just out of his reach. She rushed toward the cliff's edge and drew back her hand, intending to toss the medallion over the side, but Druson's shout stopped her.

"No! We must destroy it, not throw it away where it might be found by yet another dark soul. The demon will guide one of his followers to the medallion if we allow it to survive."

Maccus turned his attention to a suddenly coherent Druson. "Who *are* you?"

Druson's eyes remained ancient, and his hair was a bit grayer than it had been the day before. No, not gray, Joryn realized, but *white*. There were still a few strands of dark hair mixed in with the white, but at this rate his hair would be like snow within days.

But for now, at least, the madness was gone. Or sleeping. "I am your Grandfather, Maccus, and I am so very disappointed in you." Druson shook his head. "With your love for magic, you might've studied hard and become a great healer or a force for harmony, but you choose instead to embrace a darkness you do not even understand."

Druson's hand shot out quickly, much too fast to be natural, and he gripped the wizard by the throat. Maccus tried to fight, but he could not. The newfound strength of the Grandfather was too much for him, and he could only choke and sputter as he fought for breath.

"I . . . I cannot be killed," Maccus protested breathlessly. "The Isen Demon will not allow it."

Druson smiled. "When your heart and your head are separated, not even the Isen Demon will be able to save you."

At this, Maccus began to fight more savagely, but Druson seemed unaffected by his struggle. "Pathetic creature," the Grandfather whispered. "Do you not know that the demon chose you because you are so very weak? You think you were chosen due to your strength, but that is not the case. You were chosen because you were easy to manipulate, easy to guide down the path to your destruction and the destruction of your people. I understand what it is to crave power that is not meant to be yours, as

I once was so foolish. We were cursed, pathetic creatures, cursed to have what we wished for thrust upon us." Druson sighed, perhaps mourning for his own fate. "You are nothing, wizard. Nothing at all."

Druson glanced past his prisoner, laying eyes on Joryn. "It is the duty of the Queen's true mate to kill this one who dared to attempt the corruption of that sacred union. Take his head, burn his heart to ashes, and when that is done, his spirit will be trapped in a dark and faraway place from which he will never depart."

Ryn appeared at Joryn's side, and he offered a long, plainly crafted dagger on the palm of his large hand. Joryn had expected some protest from Keelia's father at the hint that he and his daughter were mated, but while Ryn's face was solemn, he seemed accepting of the situation which was not of his choosing.

Joryn did not hesitate to take the dagger from Keelia's father, nor did he hesitate to do that which was required of him.

KEELIA KNEW MACCUS WAS TRULY AND COMPLETELY dead because her psychic gifts grew clearer as the night passed and the dark magic he had created faded into nothing. As they descended the mountain—three wolves and two mountain cats traveling together, a pack united like no other—she began to see all that had been hidden from her in months past.

Ariana needed her.

They were all at war, but most didn't realize it yet.

The throne of Columbyana was at risk, and while it was not her country, she realized that whoever sat on that throne would change the world not only for Colum-byanans, but for everyone. A darkness that had begun there was spreading like a toxic disease, and it would not stop spreading unless the Isen Demon and all those who served him were defeated.

More personally, Keelia realized that she and Joryn were one species, not two as she and all others on these mountains had always thought. Their children, and the children of others like them, would usher in a time of evolution, a return to the remarkable ways of the past. They'd been punished by separation enough, for what-ever long-ago sins had created the division.

They made good progress on their way down the mountain and toward Ariana, more than they would be able to make once the three nights of the full moon had passed. She could continue alone, in whatever form she chose to assume, but she did not wish or need to make the trip on her own. Besides, Ariana was traveling with an army that marched slowly, and Druson claimed to know shortcuts aplenty through these mountains.

She sensed thousands of years of knowledge locked in the Caradon's mind. Whether or not he could handle that knowledge had been uncertain for a time, but he had passed the point where permanent madness was possible. He had fought for his sanity and his power, and he would be a great ally in the months to come. Druson still had much to learn, but he would make a good Grandfather to the Caradon, and to the Anwyn.

When dawn came, Keelia transformed with the oth-ers. They would rest for a short while before moving on, but not for long. She had much news to impart to her cousin. Much news. She found she was anxious to join the battle, though she imagined she would have to fight her father and brothers, and a few of her guards, in order to do what she knew had to be done.

Joryn would not fight her, though. He would join her. He would be beside her through it all.

The five of them changed by morning light, and in their human forms again they dressed in ragged traveling clothes, clothes which had been carried in a lightweight pack Juliet had carried on her back through the night. Normally the clothing and food would be left in a safe place to which the animals would return when the night was done, but as they were traveling and could not afford to track backward, that was not possible.

No, they could not go back. From here on out, they could only move forward. It would not be easy, but they were united. Keelia's father had accepted that Joryn was his daughter's mate and therefore his King, but he did not like the development. He would accept, in time. Her mother had already accepted Joryn. Knowing that the Caradon would leap off a cliff after the woman he loved was enough to bring the Queen Mother completely to his side.

Druson was a treasure they would all protect. He had insisted all along that Keelia was Queen of the Caradon as well as the Anwyn. In that same way he was Grandfather to all people of the Mountains of the North, a keeper of magic and history like no other she had ever known. If Maccus had realized the power in his presence, he would've been in awe.

Exhausted after the night's run, Druson lay down and immediately dropped into a deep sleep. Juliet was not far behind, and Ryn reclined beside his wife and protected her with his arms as he, too, fell toward slumber.

Keelia was about to follow suit when Joryn took her hand and wordlessly led her away from their camp.

You need to sleep, she insisted.

Not just yet.

She knew he had sex on his mind, and even though she was exhausted, she didn't mind. Not at all. She needed him in all ways. It was the way of mates, she imagined, but the feeling was much stronger than she'd realized it would be. She had seen her parents' love through the years, but she had never experienced the depth and strength of that love. Not until now.

There was something else on Joryn's mind, something he was able to hide from her. She did not poke and reach for the knowledge he attempted to conceal, but willingly followed him along the narrow path to a secluded chunk of mountain where a wide fissure gave them walls on either side but also allowed the sun to shine down upon them.

In this place where they had privacy and sunlight, Joryn placed his arms around Keelia and pulled her close. She willingly melted in his arms.

He sighed and stroked her hair almost mindlessly. "I've always insisted that I did not want or need one mate for life, but you changed my mind."

"Yes, I know," she said, awash with contentment.

"I love you."

Keelia smiled. "I love you, too."

"I am yours in every way possible."

"I like the sound of that," she whispered.

Joryn moved slightly away from her, took her face in his hands, and turned his head far to the right and up. He very gently drew her face to his offered throat, where she felt the throb of his heartbeat and tasted the salty maleness of his skin. "In all ways, Keelia," he repeated, "I am yours."

She kissed his throat languidly, as he had kissed hers when she'd offered it to him. Smiling, content, and increasingly aroused, she raked her mouth and her teeth gently along the column of his strong neck.

So close, so intimately connected, she saw some of what was to be for them. Not all. Even with her powers returned to her, she could not see all that awaited her. It was best that way; it was as it should be.

But she did see love, and remarkable babies, and the peace her people had been promised in the prophesy that had been written so long ago. She was the promised Red Queen, and Joryn was her lover in all ways . . . and together they would fight for that peace, and for the union of two peoples who should be, and would be, one.

The longer she kissed his throat, the more aroused she became. Her exhaustion was erased by something much more powerful. Need. Not only the need for physical release, but the necessity for a complete connection with her mate; the man she loved. Mind, spirit, and body.

Joryn knew what she wanted, and he wanted it, too. He freed his erection and then lifted her easily. Keelia wrapped her legs around his hips and guided herself onto him. She rode him fiercely, as if she were in the heat of her fertile time and he was touching her for the first time. He was the man of her dreams, but no pristine fantasy could compare to her reality.

Reality was wonderful, and every moment was to be cherished.

When completion came to them both, sparks of flame danced on the air around them. Once again, Joryn had lost control. The flames he created were quickly restrained.

The fire died slowly and dropped to the rocky ground as their heartbeats and the flow of blood in their veins returned to something near normal.

"I can't believe you once commanded me to pleasure you and I refused," Joryn said breathlessly. "You can demand anything of me at any time. Anything."

Keelia rested her head against his shoulder. "I command that you love me forever," she whispered.

"Yes, My Magnificent Majesty. Anything else?"

"Nothing else matters."

"Nothing?"

"Nothing."

Babies, war, discord, harmony, bloodshed, happiness . . . it was all coming. But for now, nothing mattered but love.

Epilogue

FOR A LONG, TERRIFYING MOMENT, CIRO FELT AS IF he'd been drained of energy. The strength he had come to rely on, the power that had become his, flickered and then departed, and then it disappeared completely and he was *nothing* once again. He was a scared boy, an ineffectual prince, a pampered lad who was afraid of life.

And then the power came rushing back . . . but he could still remember too clearly what it had felt like to be without the strength of the demon, however temporarily.

There had been a defeat of some kind, a blow to the demon and his plans. At one time Ciro had felt as if he and the Isen Demon were invincible, that he himself was invincible. He had been convinced of that invincibility as the power of the demon filled him.

Apparently that was not the case. Somehow the demon and all those he commanded were connected, as if they shared one mind, one body, one black soul. When there was a defeat, they all felt it. When a battle was lost, the demon and all those he led were weakened. The Isen Demon, Ciro, Ciro's Own, the wizards and witches and ordinary people who waited to be called . . . even the child Diella did not yet know she carried.

The demon had expected to be stronger by this time, and Ciro felt its disappointment, and its rage. There were many reasons that the growth of dark power had not progressed as planned. In a manner the demon had not known was possible, the healer had snatched back dark souls which it had once taken. The fear that should've swept the country and fed the demon was tainted with naïve disbelief and arrogant defiance and—worst of all— hope. Every wound was felt by all those connected by the demon, and on this night Ciro and the darkness inside him were weakened.

It was also true that victory fed them all, but it was not victory that Ciro, and all the others, felt at this terrible moment.

He stood atop a small grassy rise and studied his growing army. His soldiers were being well trained, but they were not unbeatable. An army of another sort was coming. An army more prepared, more dedicated, even more willing to die for what they believed. He knew all that to be true; he felt it to his bones. Now more than ever, he felt the coming defeat.

He could not stay here.

Ciro walked calmly to his tent, where he packed a small bag, choosing a change of clothing and a healthy portion of the drug Panwyr, which he still needed on occasion. Food was not a problem; he would find nourishment along the way. There were many farmhouses and small villages in Columbyana, and while they might have been warned to keep an eye out for a brutal army of soulless soldiers, they would not be alarmed by one young and seemingly harmless traveler. Not until it was too late.

When he was ready to depart, he had one more important decision to make. Did he ride for his father's palace and the throne that should and would be his? Or should he turn back and collect his bride from the mountain palace where she was imprisoned?

Rayne is for another day.

The Isen Demon still spoke to him, though it did seem weaker on this night. Was it possible for a demon to be melancholy? It seemed so. The demon was much more subdued than Ciro could remember, but it remained a force which he did not dare to fight.

On to Arthes, then.

Ciro had no qualms about traveling unescorted. It would be much easier to make his way past any guards who might've been foolishly placed between him and his destination, and he was certainly capable of handling any resistance he met along the way. Alone he could . . .

Not alone. Take the empress. Take the child within her.

Ciro did not care for Diella, even now. She was loud and demanding and her requirements were plentiful and stridently voiced. Pregnancy would likely not agree with her. More precisely, pregnancy would not agree with those around her.

Still, the demon had insisted that Ciro allow the former empress to live, at least until the child she carried was born, and so far he had obeyed. He had done everything the demon had asked of him. Now he was to take

Diella with him on the journey to Arthes? Weeks of travel with just the two of them?

Her place is there.

Since the demon lived so much inside Ciro, he had no choice but to obey once again. If he did not, then the demon's constant voice would surely drive him mad . . . though some might insist he had already passed the point of madness.

"I TOLD YOU WE WOULD ARRIVE ON TIME," KEELIA said. She and her mother led the way as their party approached Ariana's army's camp on a bright, warm summer afternoon. They were intercepted far from the gathering of soldiers, of course, but two of her own Anwyn guards were among the soldiers posted at the perimeter, and they recognized their Queen in spite of her travel-worn state.

Druson, who was not yet completely white-haired, had been silent for days. Once he saw the traveling party safely with the army they sought, he wordlessly turned back toward the Mountains of the North. His home was there; his people needed him. He himself still had much to learn.

When presented to the army's beloved leader, Keelia hugged Ariana fiercely, and they laughed. Juliet's reunion with her sister Sophie was much the same, with a close embrace and laughter and tears. Ryn and Uncle Kane shook hands, but they were less jovial than their wives. They knew war, and they could not find even the smallest smile in the knowledge that it was upon them once again.

Keelia drew Joryn forward and introduced him to her

family as her husband. Columbyanans—humans as a whole—didn't quite grasp the concept of being mated. Any sort of ceremony to make Joryn hers would have to wait for another place and time. There was much to be done before that would happen . . . but it would happen. She could envision with great clarity the sacred ceremony that would take place in the courtyard of her own palace, in her own beloved City. They would pledge themselves to one another before her people and the priestesses, and there would be great joy. Joryn would be her King, and their children would fill the palace she had always called home.

But not until this task was completed.

When their greetings were done, they wasted little time getting to the business at hand. Ariana's husband, Sian, shared with Keelia and the others the Prophesy of the Firstborn. Keelia easily saw her part in it, a part which had already taken place. She had betrayed love, and even though she'd been under Maccus's spell at the time, that betrayal was no less real. Betrayal in the name of victory. Maccus's victory. The Isen Demon's victory.

Joryn had placed one finger on the margin of the prophesy, drawing Keelia's eye to what very well might be a sketch of her falling from the cliff and finding her wings. The others had thought it to be an ordinary bird, but to her and to Joryn the drawing had greater significance. He'd also suggested that another sort of betrayal had taken place when she'd broken Maccus's spell and renounced the false love he had planted in her heart and mind. Perhaps, he suggested, it was the betrayal—the *defeat*—of that false and unnatural love that had been prophesied.

Keelia did not waste much heart berating herself

over past choices. It was done, and all was as it should be for now.

Ariana told of her visit to the Land of the Dead and the miraculous return. According to the prophesy, that left Lyr to wield the crystal dagger. Keelia immediately grasped the importance of her cousin from Tryfyn's part in this war.

"He'll join us within days," Keelia said, confident of her prediction. "Lyr and Duran, Aunt Isadora and Uncle Lucan, and half a dozen others, they ride toward us quickly. They'll join us before this gathering divides."

Keelia reached for the knowledge of where Lyr might find the crystal dagger. She had an inkling, but could see nothing certain. Not yet. When he was closer, perhaps she would know. There was simply so much to consider that she was having a hard time concentrating on any one matter.

"You will go to Arthes to the emperor," Keelia said, and Ariana answered with a nod of her head. "Aunt Sophie and Mother will try to find Liane. I suspect Aunt Isadora will wish to join them." Which meant their husbands would also be on that journey.

"And you?" Ariana asked. "Where will you go?"

Keelia closed her eyes and tried to see where she would be needed most in the coming months. With the army or with Ariana? She thought her place would be with her cousin, but she was not yet certain.

"Will they find Liane?" Ariana asked.

"Yes." She was quite confident they would.

"Can you tell them where to look for her?"

"Not tonight, but perhaps tomorrow." Her mind was tired, and she was seeing nothing clearly at the moment. Snips and flashes, half-truths and faded pictures. There was simply so much to know . . . and still so very much undecided.

"What of the sons?" Ariana asked sharply. "The heirs to the throne? They would be just your age. Did they survive their mother's escape from Arthes? Do they live?"

Keelia looked at her cousin with calculating eyes. Ariana had not yet revealed that her own husband had a claim to the throne—a claim he did not wish to pursue. Since he had asked his wife to keep the secret, Keelia could not be angry that Ariana remained quiet about the matter.

"They live," she said confidently. "Both of them. One dark, one fair. One touched with a shadow he fights, one noble to the pit of his soul." A crystal-clear stream of knowledge burst through the jumble of what was to be and what might be, and she could not stop the sharp intake of breath that followed. For a moment, reality was lost to her, and all she saw was one clear truth.

Keelia leapt up and ran to the tent opening, so she could look out on the army that spread far and wide around them. As far as she could see, there were armed men who prepared for battle; there were campfires and tents and horses. There was the ring of blades being sharpened, and even the occasional odd trill of laughter.

"He's here," Keelia whispered.

"What?" Ariana laid a steady hand on Keelia's shoulder, and together they looked out over the army.

"Sebestyen's eldest. The next emperor of Columbyana. The man who must take Arik's place if we are to defeat the darkness." Keelia turned and looked into her cousin's eyes. "He's here."

Joryn slipped his arm about her waist, and for a moment Keelia was surrounded by and washed in the comfort of love. Her cousin on one side, her mate on the other. "I do not yet see exactly who this man is, but I will see, in time." At that moment she knew, without a doubt, that until this war was over her place would be at Ariana's side.

Ariana slipped away to tell her husband about the newest revelation, and Keelia faced Joryn. "It isn't over," she said softly. "We are still meant to fight. We are needed here."

"I suspected as much," he replied.

"You are needed as much as I am. Surely you recognized yourself in the prophesy, he who walks through fire."

"I can't see how I might show these humans the way," Joryn said skeptically. "Maybe I've already done my part by showing you the way. Maybe there is more to come. All that matters is that wherever you are called, I will be with you."

His words sent a wave of relief through Keelia's tense body. "You're going to be a wonderful King."

Joryn's eyebrows arched slightly. Had he not yet realized that he would be King? Of course he had. He would be King of the Anwyn and of the Caradon, if Druson's predictions about the days to come in the Mountains of the North were correct.

"It occurs to me that fighting a demon might be easier than bringing your people and mine together," he said.

Keelia understood Joryn's reservations, but soon enough he would know that his worries were unnecessary. "I don't think so," she whispered. "If we can defeat the demon before us, then our people will come together well. Not without problems, but still . . . very well." Keelia closed her eyes and touched Joryn's mind with her own, offering to her mate a crystal clear vision of a wonderful future.

Read an excerpt from

Prince of Swords

as the battle against the evil Ciro continues . . .

Coming from Berkley Sensation
May 2007!

RAYNE HADN'T ATTEMPTED TO ESCAPE FROM HER prison for several weeks. In months past she'd tried everything from pleading with the old man who was on constant guard to attempting to physically yank the chains that bound her from the wall. Her jailer was deaf to her pleas, and she didn't even make the mortar rattle with her physical attempts.

She was doomed. Doomed to wait here in the dank cellar of her home until Prince Ciro returned to make her his bride. Doomed to helplessness. Doomed to rely on people who despised her for food, water, implements for the occasional attempt at bathing.

Rayne hadn't even known her father's odd guest was a prince until after his departure. The servant whom Ciro had left in charge of her care referred to him as "prince" often, and when Rayne had challenged the ridiculous notion, it had been explained that Ciro was

indeed the only son of the Emperor Arik and next in line
for the throne. The man in question did not fulfill any of
Rayne's notions of what a prince should be. From a distance, he had the outward appearance of a finely bred
prince, she supposed, but his eyes were alternately dead
or heart-stoppingly wicked, and his actions were not at
all what she considered to be majestic.

Sitting on her cot, as she had all morning, Rayne
stole a glance at the guard who kept constant watch over
her. Jiri was an elderly man who had worked for her father for many years. A simple and quiet man, he'd always been pleasant enough in the past, as he'd gone
about his odd jobs on the grounds and in the house.
She'd certainly never thought of him as threatening in
any way.

The thin old man still didn't strike her as being at all
fearsome, but he was mightily afraid of Prince Ciro. Jiri
would not help her in any way, not if he thought the man
who commanded him might be displeased. When Ciro
had left this servant in charge of her care, he'd promised
to drink his blood and eat his soul if he failed. That
wasn't possible, she was sure of it, but Jiri seemed to
think that the threat was a real one.

In the early days of Rayne's imprisonment, a few of
the maids who'd worked in this house before Ciro had
incarcerated her had remained. These female servants
were always skittish, and Rayne could understand why.
They'd constantly sported bruises and small cuts on their
hands and faces, injuries they refused to speak of when
she asked. They'd brought food, and they'd helped her
with her awkward baths, but there was none of the easy
banter she remembered from the days before all had
changed. Like her, they were helpless. The frightened

girls followed orders, and were too afraid to so much as speak to the woman who'd been their mistress for many years. They didn't even dare to whisper.

Rayne's view through the one high, narrow window of the basement signaled the time that had passed. Summer was gone. She'd spent an entire season chained to the wall of her own cellar. Autumn, with its cooler winds and changing leaves, was upon them. What had become of her garden? She could not imagine that any of the coarse men above stairs would've bothered to tend it. Without watering and weeding and loving attention, her garden had likely perished long ago, the flowers wilting and the vegetables drying on the vine. Such a shame.

Being of agreeable spirit, Rayne had bided her time, taking comfort in her hours out of doors and dreaming of the day when her father would arrange a suitable marriage for her. When she had her own home, she would fill it with love and light, as her mother had tried to do here. Even if it was much smaller and plainer than this home where she'd been born and raised, she would make it agreeable.

That simple dream had begun to fade long before she'd been imprisoned. Rayne was almost twenty years old, and her father had never mentioned marriage. In the weeks before she'd been trapped here in this cellar, she'd begun to fear that her father intended for her to marry Ciro. Those two had spent much time together, locked in her father's study. Her father was a talented wizard who had always openly mourned the fact that his daughter, his only child, possessed no magic. Perhaps Ciro was a wizard as well as a prince, and when her father and the man who called her "beloved" were alone, they honed and practiced their magic.

The wizard Fynnian, who grieved because his daughter had no magical gifts, might've been planning to demand that she produce gifted grandchildren who would follow in his footsteps.

Rayne wanted no magic in her life. She wanted a simple marriage with an ordinary man, but that was likely a foolish desire. Her father would never allow her to marry anyone ordinary or simple.

Since the age of fifteen, she'd more than once thought of running away, but when faced with reality she'd always been too afraid to confront what might await her beyond the walls of this home. In all her life she'd never been forced to fend for herself, and her father had always painted a bleak picture of what existed beyond these walls. She'd been spoiled horribly. Did her father realize that making her dependent upon him and his servants would keep her tied to him? Or was she simply weak of character? Her skittish nature had never before seemed to her to be egregious, but now, trapped as she was, she wished she'd been braver. She wished a thousand times that she'd followed her instincts and taken her chances in facing whatever awaited beyond the walls of this house.

Rayne looked again at haggard, elderly Jiri. Though he had worked in this household for many years, he was now Ciro's servant in a way she could not explain. She remembered the last time she'd seen Ciro, and she wished with all her heart that she'd run away from this place when she'd had the opportunity, that she'd taken a chance at discovering what lay beyond these walls.

As if her father would've allowed that to happen.

Ciro, who was young and handsome, well dressed and well spoken, had no life in his eyes. At first glance he was every young girl's dream, with long fair hair and lovely blue eyes, but when one looked into those eyes and saw only darkness, that dream became a nightmare. She could not think of anything else but those dead eyes when she remembered him and his last words to her, words that had followed a cold kiss and a terrifying grab at her breasts.

"We will be married," he'd said with confidence. *"There will be a priest of my choosing in attendance, and we will have a few witnesses as our guests. And if you do not happily agree in front of them all to be my wife, I will kill them one at a time until you do. I'll start with your father, if he lives that long."*

Her father had left this house with Prince Ciro at summer's outset, and she could not help but wonder if he had survived. There was no goodness in the man who claimed to love her. There was nothing even remotely human in the eyes of the man who called her "beloved." Rayne could very well imagine Ciro taking her father's life without a moment's regret. Perhaps if she and her father had been closer, she'd know somehow if he lived or not. More than eight years past her mother's death, there were times when Rayne was sure she felt her mother's spirit near her. She did not think she would sense her father's spirit in the same way, if indeed he were dead. A daughter should know, shouldn't she?

The sounds from above changed. A distant shout spoke of fear, but it was not of the type she had heard in the past. Rayne glanced up, even though all she could see was a plain wooden ceiling reinforced in many places with sturdy rafters. As she watched, the ceiling shook slightly and dust drifted down.

Metal met metal, clanging even though the conflict

was far away. Sword fight! This was unlike the brief skirmishes she had heard from above in months past, when those men fought among themselves. This was more intense, and it spread and continued long after a burst of temper would've ended. She was not the only one who realized that something had changed. Jiri drew a short sword of his own, but he did not run up the stairs to join the battle. Instead he placed himself before Rayne and adopted a defensive pose, ready to take on any who tried to rescue her.

Rescue. This was the first moment she'd dared to think of such a possibility. The house her father had built long before her birth was isolated and high in the mountains, no one knew that she was being held prisoner, and Jiri had told her that the men above were fearsome fighters sworn to do as their prince commanded. Even if anyone did attempt to rescue her, it was unlikely that they would succeed.

Did she dare to hope?

"Jiri, there is no reason for you to stand guard as you do." Rayne spoke in a calm voice, even though her heart pounded hard and she had not known *calm* in many months. "If the men above are defeated, then you do not stand a chance of winning against the intruders. You are a gardener and a carpenter, not a swordsman. If someone you do not recognize comes down those stairs, step aside. Surrender."

"I cannot," he said evenly. "You are to remain pure for Prince Ciro. No man is to come near his beloved before he returns to collect you."

Pure? Ciro himself was anything but pure, so why did Jiri seem so adamant that he was to protect that attribute in his intended? "I'm sure he would not want you to sacrifice your life. There are other women in the world, and I can be easily replaced."

The old man turned to look at her, and she saw the depths of fear in his eyes. "No, it must be you. The prince told me so, you see, before he left. You are pure of soul and heart and body, and you must remain so until he gives you a child on your wedding night. Why do you think the men above have not come down here in all this time? Why do you think Prince Ciro has allowed me to keep my soul thus far? He does not trust his Own to guard you. He's afraid of what they might do to you in a moment of rage or lust."

Rayne shuddered. She hugged herself with trembling arms, and the chains which bound her to the stone wall clanked gently. "What has Ciro promised you in return for this betrayal? What does my sacrifice gain for you?"

"Everything," Jiri whispered. "When you are wed to the prince, my wife and child will be returned to me, whole and alive after all these years in the Land of the Dead. There will be eternal life for all of us, and we will live together in a place so beautiful it would take your breath away were you allowed to see it."

"You know what kind of man he is," Rayne whispered.

"Yes."

"And yet you would sacrifice me for a promise that is impossible. The dead do not come back! There is no eternal life on this earth!"

"Ciro said . . ."

"He lied!" Rayne insisted. "Do you really believe that a man who threatens you as your prince did would reward you in such a way?" She yanked at her chains in frustration. "Release me, and while the others are fighting, we can escape."

"I can't," Jiri said. "Ciro will know. He knows everything, and there is no hiding from those eyes. If I fail, if I run, he won't just make me pay, he'll take out his anger on the souls of my wife and child. I cannot allow that. I failed them before, when I let them die. I can't allow that to happen again."

Jiri was lost in his illusion that his long-dead family would be returned, that they could be threatened by whatever Ciro had become, when in fact the dead were the only ones safe from such a monster.

The sounds from above gradually faded, as the fight waned. Who had won? Did it matter? Even if the invaders defeated Ciro's men, would they be any better? Would their victory mean her rescue, or would she simply exchange one jailer for another?

The door at the top of the stairs opened, and solid footsteps pounded on the stairs. Rayne did not know what fate awaited her, but she was about to find out. Her mouth went dry. Her heart beat in an odd rhythm, as if it might stop functioning at any moment. After all she'd been through, it was unexpected that she could still experience such fear, but there was great fear in the unknown.

A bald and sturdy middle-aged man was the first to step foot in the basement where Rayne was kept prisoner. He held a long-bladed sword stained with blood, and wore loose pants, scuffed boots, and a purple vest which revealed a hairy chest and muscled arms. He'd been cut on one arm but ignored the bloody wound. The man was sweaty and breathing hard as he quickly surveyed the cellar and lifted his sword to challenge Jiri.

"Step aside, you old geezer." His oddly accented voice

was rough and too deep. "I don't want to harm you but I will if I must."

"I will protect the prince's beloved with my life," Jiri said, his voice and his sword shaking.

The armed and bloody man sighed. "You can keep the girl. We have no interest in her. We want the crystal dagger, that is all."

So much for rescue. "Please, sir," Rayne began, wondering if the rough-looking man had a heart beneath that broad, hairy chest.

"Silence, wench," the swordsman said without taking his eyes from Jiri.

"I am not a . . ." Rayne began haughtily, and then they were joined by yet another of the intruders.

This one was not middle-aged or bald. He was, in fact, so handsome he took her breath away. His dark hair was cut very short, and while he had muscles they were not quite as oddly bulging as those of his companion. He was dressed in a similar fashion, in boots and dark pants and a purple vest over a well-formed but hairless chest. It must be some sort of uniform, but she was not familiar with the markings on his vest. The handsome man with narrowed eyes that seemed to see everything was much younger than the gruff bald fellow, and yet it was immediately evident that this new arrival was the man in charge. "Wench," Rayne finished in a whisper.

The bald man nodded toward Rayne. "I have found Prince Ciro's *beloved*," he said, his tone dry and disrespectful.

"She is promised to the prince; she is his betrothed," Jiri insisted. "Leave her be."

The younger man responded with a slight lifting of his eyebrows, and then he, too, readied his sword.

Jiri realized that he couldn't defeat the two men before him. For a moment, Rayne thought he would surrender, but she'd underestimated his devotion to—or his fear of—Prince Ciro.

"No one else shall have her," Jiri whispered.

The intruders were prepared to fight. They were not prepared for Jiri to turn the sword he wielded on the woman he had sworn to protect. All Rayne saw was the sharp blade of Jiri's sword moving closer to her throat so quickly she couldn't even find the time to scream.